Charles Be

With best wishes and
kind regards from the
author —

Barry Hartley

OF LOVE AND SLAVERY

A Novel

OF LOVE AND SLAVERY

A Novel

B.M. Hartley

The Book Guild Ltd
Sussex, England

The Book Guild Ltd
25 High Street,
Lewes, Sussex

First published 1996
© B.M. Hartley 1996
Set in Baskerville
Typesetting by Adhands, Bracknell
Printed in Great Britain by
Anthony Rowe Ltd.
Chippenham, Wiltshire.

A catalogue record for this book is
available from the British Library

ISBN 1 85776 062 X

I
dedicate this novel
to
Sunit
and to
his whole family

CONTENTS

INTRODUCTION

It would have been impossible to have written what you are about to read without my having experienced so many things. Glorious and inglorious they have been, at times. The exquisite suffering that is love has always governed my soul and guided my heart, however faltering may have been my steps. Hating myself at times, I have never hated anyone. I would like to tell you in advance, how grateful I am to all the people whom I have met in my life, whether or not I have liked them. I suppose that you may say that I have pestered people with my love. Perhaps that is true, but I shall never give up or shed the responsibility of the duty demanded of a vulnerable person. What God has made you, you cannot unmake. Foolish is the man who pretends to be his own master.

There is no escape from what you are; you are enslaved in advance, even of birth. Do not forget that slavery is for ever noble. Tolerance and love are the forms that it will ever take. They are a privileged burden.

1

Two Wives

Sunday was as usual. Or so they thought. They left behind the big farmhouse and the part of the day they preferred to forget, exchanging it briefly for the small party they both enjoyed. They did not know then that any Sunday could have its surprises.

Down through the glades they came. Teddy Osmond and his daughter came through the glinting leaf shadows of the late December hillside down to the village in the dell. They had left the farmhouse directly behind them, their cares too. This occasion was looked forward to by both of them each week as an oasis of peace, if only just for three-quarters of an hour. Both knew its relief, but neither spoke of it. The weather that morning was frosty, but now blessed and adorned with golden sunshine. The informal paths gave them a grip of the gravel bound by a frozen night. Their leaves rustled and moved with their loving tread; they both liked scuffing them as they walked. Silently, Teddy reminded himself of the carefree days of his boyhood. A mutual confidence set the step of the two at the same pace and in the same direction, with the same will. For all its sameness, this Sunday walk – if only there and back to see how far it was – proved to them what warm hearts they really had and that human respect was never dead. As it happened, each was in thrall to a bitter captivity from which there appeared to be no easy or immediate escape. This might have been thrown off neatly but nastily, but Teddy had hesitated until too late. He wondered quietly whether fate would favour them; Teddy expected not.

Little children take likes and dislikes with a surprising and spontaneous immediacy. They seem to know very quickly whom they can trust; to them they show their simple love in a charming way. It was thus with Penelope towards Teddy. Foley, her father, took scarcely any notice of her at home, or anywhere else for that matter. It was Teddy who took her to pick flowers in the garden, who sat her on his knee in the kitchen and told her nursery rhymes. Later, his stories would be about big, bad bears, which would make her eyes open wide, and about lovable rabbits and kittens, which would make her laugh or smile. It was Teddy who gave her a kiss every now and then. Penelope came to love him and held his hand when they went on their walks.

Sometimes Teddy thought that she must know that she was his daughter and the thought warmed him in advance of the day when she would have to be told everything. At times, this worried him, for he did not know when or exactly how he would do it. As it happened it would be easier than he could have imagined. That was a long way in the future. Meanwhile, he realised that she could not possibly have any idea of her true parentage, although those few moments of romantic self-deception thrilled his honest heart.

Meanwhile, Teddy Osmond and his daughter Penelope walked towards their village local, The Three Trees. There she would drink a ginger beer and he a large gin and tonic. They would meet a few people whom they had always met and a few whom they had never seen before and would probably never see again. Both liked the twin challenge of sustaining their well-knownness and to impress it upon those whom they had never met. They seemed to enjoy the uncertainties of life and not being sure that they would always be liked.

As Teddy and Penelope trod the last of the downward slope, the winter sun did not forget to remind them that they wore their winter tweeds. Perhaps that was one of the messages of winter, thought Teddy; a reminder of earthliness. So at least he hoped, because even that slight warmth held the hope and promise of spring. As if to make more firm this hope, he gripped all the more tightly his daughter's small hand and wrist, swinging her arm lovingly as he did so.

There was not much time now in which he might have to do what there might be to do. He was forty-two and his daughter five. His enforced subservience to his brother Foley seemed endlessly and boundlessly to enclose his life, as cliffs without issue do a lonely beach.

The comely barmaid, whom Teddy rather fancied, in a remote kind of way, loved children and sat Penelope down near the fire whilst her father talked with the locals. Always when they arrived, the Sunday morning was in full swing. It was a friendly place.

The shock came just over forty-five minutes later. It was 1954, and near Christmas.

*

Charles Foley Osmond, at the age of twenty-seven a fairly rich man, was becoming richer. Born in 1873, the youngest son of a wealthy family, he was given the choice at twenty-one of joining and making his way in the family firm, with the promise of eventual financial reward and an easy life, or of the gift of rather a large lump sum, not enough off which to live, but sufficient to strike out on his own if he cared to. He chose the latter path.

Charles sank the whole of his advanced inheritance into a large and, at that time, unprofitable farm, set in the rolling Wiltshire downs. He gambled his all in its broad but impoverished acres.

When he bought it, its equipment lay dozing and rusting in all seasons and there was little stock. Upon the slight eminence that looked over the land stood the great

13

mediaeval farmhouse, altered, twisted and extended since its foundation in 1430. The labourers' cottages were in a deplorable condition, their occupants depressed and uncaring. A few of the farm dwellings were uninhabited. Within the dungy farmyard stood a small, neglected Saxon church and a huge, Elizabethan barn, E-shaped, where in better days the cakes and ale had been served to happier workers. All about were ryegrass and weeds, much of the thatch had gone off the great barn, the house was in a shocking state of disrepair and the farm had been, in places, left fallow for years.

But Charles Foley Osmond, stout, tough and stocky, was a man not to be deterred. In 1894 he had, at the derision of his family, purchased a white elephant. Seven years later, after a little further grudging help from his father, he had reached the uplands of success. All Wiltshire smiled upon his wheat and his cattle, as he smiled upon his labourers and their children.

These seven years, however, had not been without their problems. He was determined upon marriage, but this he could not have contemplated until he had put his beloved farm in order. Once he had done this, he cast around.

Although his troubles were not over, he still owed his father for the extra help that he had given him; but he felt confident enough in what he had behind him to look for a wife. His aims were mixed, however. If he could marry a little more money in the shape of a beautiful, loving wife, he could repay his now pressing father and satisfy his own considerable and natural needs. It is unfortunate that one can rarely kill two birds with one stone.

Every so often, Charles rode over to his nearest neighbour, Thomas Sheldrake, owner of a smaller but better-established farm. They discussed matters of farming moment and events of the day. Although Sheldrake was much older than Charles, they got along well together and he and his wife appreciated his visits. They gave him much welcome advice about farm management. He was often their guest at dinner, when he met their only daughter, Gwendoline, to whom, Charles supposed, the Sheldrakes would leave their farm. The idea of trying to win her appealed to him therefore on two counts: her money and her looks.

Gwendoline Sheldrake was a tall, slender girl, two years younger than himself. She had long tapering fingers, graceful arms and attractive shoulders. Her breasts were not large but looked firm and shapely. Her face was oval, set with almond eyes of a brown, nearing jet. Her black hair was long and sensual. He could imagine it on the pillow, then falling over his body while her sensual lips lingered over his body. Charles was an experienced lover and he prided himself upon the fulfilment of his predictions. In short, he was certain that Gwendoline's sexuality would spare nothing. He wondered casually why no one had swept her away before. Such was his impetuousness that he cast further thoughts to the four winds and shut any questions from his mind.

Gwendoline was going to be his, and the sooner the better. With his new authority over his own domain, he had already become unused to anyone questioning his quick decisions. He was beginning not even to allow himself to do so.

Accordingly, he went to courtship with a will. Nearly every evening he rode out to the neighbouring farm, where he was allowed by Thomas Sheldrake to walk his daughter up and down the main avenue. Under the lime trees, they held hands; she with a little uncertainty at first, he with more positive ardour. Conversation came fairly easily and, if her tastes were a little more refined than his, Charles managed to show enough interest to prolong these walks as he wanted.

In fact, he would have liked to have raced off into the woods, torn off her clothes and satisfied his ever more burning desire for her, but that, he sensed, would have frightened, offput or even outraged her. Besides, it would have ruined his chances with her father and he had not to forget his other aim.

With this in mind, he went to Thomas one July evening, asking permission to seek her hand. The elder man was delighted. So much so that he offered Charles a third of the farm neighbouring his own as a gift upon marriage. He said that his own properties were proving too large for him to administer, adding that all that he had would be for him and Gwendoline upon his death. By way of assurance, Thomas said that he would arrange everything with his lawyer in Shaftesbury within a few weeks.

Gwendoline, although she looked slightly bewildered, accepted Charles's proposal and in January, 1901, they were married.

It was a cold day.

*

It was a cold night, too.

They drove straight back to the farm, as Charles had decided that they should stay there for a week. He had cancelled all his own work so that he would be able to give his whole attention to his new wife. She was to spend the week, he told her, getting to know him, his requirements and his house. She accepted this demurely, but her black eyes registered a bewilderment tinged with indignation. She had few cogent thoughts about the matter; at least, none that she released. In her inexperience, she concealed an undefined disappointment by what she hoped were convincing smiles.

The house staff came to greet her in the hall. They would have done this outside, but the weather was too cold and wet. Dinner was served early in a small dining room, after which they would be alone until they decided to get up the next morning.

They talked of nothing in particular, gazing into each other's eyes, seeking they knew not exactly what. Charles thought of bedding her soundly and well into the night. Gwendoline did not know what to think or to expect, or what she ought to do. A cold uncertainty gripped her. The candles began to gutter in the rural draughts. The fire,

16

although still hot, grew low between the iron firedogs.

The bedroom was vast, with its huge furniture standing upon uneven floors. Heavy black beams strode under the rugs, up the walls and across the ceiling. The wood creaked in the frost that contracted it and the lattices rattled in the icy wind. Another fire was still just alight in the small hearth.

Charles undressed with easy confidence until he stood virile and naked in front of her. The bed was open, inviting. Gwendoline fumbled with her ribbons, buttons and stays until she, too, was naked. Her body was perfect; her outlines, highlighted by the dying fire, showed sensuously against the white wall behind the bed, her breasts proudly smooth and ripe. Her nipples were medallions of passion.

For no reason, thought Charles suddenly, she looked ashamed in an uninterested sort of way.

'Come in with me, Gwendoline, I want you. Come on, my love,' he whispered thickly.

He drew her sallow body with its long stomach and exciting perfume towards him. He buried his face in the hair under her arms, strongly musky yet fragrant, between her breasts and in the nest of her open, slender legs. By now he felt that his longing, stored all day and for some time before, would soon be at the point of release. He forced himself, but unguided, deeply inside her and, gripping her in the small of the back, feeling her spine, raced for the wave-break of passion and the sleepy beaches on the other side of the tide.

Afterwards, as he lay back, he realised that only his own ardour and brute sensuality had brought them to the shore. She had, he saw, remained calm and perfectly remote throughout. Her faint grip on his hand after a dubious response made him know that there would not be another time that night. He had also discovered that Gwendoline was not a virgin.

*

The ensuing years until 1910 were not happy ones, either for

17

Gwendoline or Charles. Although the farm prospered, enlarged now by the dowry portion and the farm of Thomas Sheldrake – it made over a thousand acres in all – the house became the safe haven of bitter resentment interrupted by only the occasional and widely-spaced joy. Any rejoicing was always very private to Charles Osmond; it was limited to him alone.

The first and greatest of his delights was the birth of his eldest son, Charles Foley Osmond, named exactly after himself, in October, 1901. The birth was difficult, leading to frequent discomforts and illnesses afterwards, which Gwendoline subsequently used to deprive her husband of what he craved; a perpetual sexual intimacy, which he respected with ever more delicacy, a regular solace from all his toils and, above all, for the large family that he so much wanted.

When he and Gwendoline rode on horseback together round the estate, as custom and duty demanded, she always had the glad eye for a farm labourer in the fields or in a byre. Charles knew in his hurt heart that she must have been with one of them before, but he never dared enquire; nor later had he the interest to do so. Somewhere, he knew, in a swarthy, dark loin lay the key to her discontent with him as much as to the reason for her dead father's enthusiasm for their marriage. It was now that he realised that this could never have been anything but a stale sham from the start. Sometimes Charles cried in his fields. His wealth could not cover the bareness of his soul, the deprivation of his heart.

In the meantime, there were three miscarriages, followed by a final, full birth which killed Gwendoline. The child, another male, was stillborn.

Charles was rather more relieved than sorry. He was certainly sorry about his dead son and mourned him genuinely, even if the baby had not by then had any time in which to gain identity or consciousness. One could not rail against nature, he wisely reasoned. His release was a substantial relief, in some respects. She had, after all, never been a proper farmer's wife, nor indeed a real wife at all.

She had never given herself willingly in any way. She finally begrudged him his final forays into the arms of attractive farm girls; the only ones that could assuage his desires and whom he treated with a beautiful gentleness. Everyone knew but nobody minded. He did not do these things until he finally realised that all joy with his wife was out of the question. What pleasure or delight could there be in mere duty? In the end, her resentment and coldness turned to complete indifference, which inflamed and infuriated him even more. He was already, in a subconscious way, looking beyond her grave ...

Within this not very welcoming family bosom there grew up Foley, as he came to be called, Charles's only son. Until recently.

From the age of six or seven Foley was a tall, spindly lad. As his mother appeared to dislike everyone except herself, including all children and especially her own son, the boy was brought up largely by Anne Force, a woman from the village. Her name fitted her nature, but she could be compassionate where compassion was needed and she was devoted to little Foley.

They walked in the now cared-for gardens, watched the birds and the animals and played a kind of croquet on one of the lawns. But Foley's eyes were remote. He could coldly cast off any affection if he felt that there were better or more advantageous claims upon his time. This attitude stayed with him for nearly the rest of his life.

It disappointed Anne Force, but she never gave him up. A sort of interrupted affection, more, perhaps, on Anne's behalf that would continue long after either of them expected.

*

After the death of Gwendoline, Charles sent Foley away to a private school. It was high time that he went, although Anne

Force had taught him to read and write in a rudimentary sort of way. No one mourned his departure except Anne, as he was precocious and priggish, cold and remote like his mother. Anne Force swept a couple of tears aside at the child's departure whilst Charles was disappointed in a vague kind of way. He was sorry that his son seemed so self-contained that he did not appear interested in communicating with anyone especially.

Although he was as busy as ever with his farm and with the growing interests of his business affairs, Charles had eyes on a far horizon. Happiness might come unexpectedly, he hoped. His hopes were not to be frustrated. He was a conscientious, right-thinking man, for all his wounded love. He liked to feel that his soul was clear of reproach, within the bounds of forgivable human frailty. To this end and in duty, he thought that it behoved him to have someone to look after Foley. The boy needed the care of an educated woman. Besides, the Christmas holidays were not far away.

His lawyer, George Mowden, had become his friend. He had seen George for advice and consultation ever since he had owned the farm. You either make a firm friend or a mortal enemy of your lawyer. Their relationship had blossomed into mutual respect and confidence. George was now a man of just over sixty. He took a fatherly interest in Charles and his family. He trusted Charles in everything except where women were concerned. Even there, he had great sympathy for the forceful, direct farmer whose kind honesty was obvious and in the middle of his true heart.

'George,' said Charles one day, after they had finished their usual business, 'I need someone to look after young Foley. I know that you have five daughters, two of whom are as yet unmarried. I want you to lend me one of them!'

George laughed. Tears of mirth came to his eyes.

'You are not, of course, serious, Charles. How on earth could I trust one of my two remaining girls to a dreadful old womaniser like you?'

'It is quite simple, George,' replied Charles Osmond. 'You know that I have never broken my word to you yet. Neither will I ever. I have never let you down and our friendship and respect are far too valuable to be ruined by misbehaviour. I will look after her, as my own daughter, whichever of the two girls that you send me.'

'One of them will come then,' said George Mowden, 'but I shall not tell you which!'

The plain one, Elizabeth arrived in November 1910.

'I knew he didn't really trust me,' said Charles to himself, with a wry but kindly amused smile.

*

Elizabeth Mowden was certainly plain. She tended to the plump side, but she had round, clear blue eyes, honest ones, and a straight nose. She had a comely figure, not elegant, but beckoning. She had a sense of humour and a good brain. Her hair, a delicate brown, was always, and despite her best efforts, a little untidy, which lent her a homely air.

She summed people up quickly, at the same time not letting them know it, giving them enough confidence to betray themselves. The men on the farm and the servants soon came to like her because she was neither aloof nor arrogant. She took good care of Foley, whom she never really got to know in the least degree, despite the fact that she never tried to assume the demands of his real mother's affection. Probably had she done so it would not have made much difference. He was cold and remote in all aspects. He never gave and did not appear to mind if he did not receive. Worse than hate is the sentiment that does not mind either way. Towards Elizabeth, Foley was annoyingly obedient and economically frigid.

After the first school holidays, Elizabeth went home to her father in Devizes. When she went upstairs, she found an envelope on the dressing-table of her bedroom. Inside there was enclosed a cheque with the following letter:

Dear Miss Mowden,
I would like to thank you for all the kindnesses that

you have shown my son. Not less for those to my
household. I hope that you will not be insulted in
accepting this small amount of money, a sum that I
know that I must owe you.
If you are not otherwise engaged, please would you
come back and do the same for Foley next March?
Yours truly,
Charles Osmond

Blunt, but not exactly impetuous, Elizabeth also made decisions quickly. Immediately after having received the cheque and the letter, she got into the trap, without telling her father, and drove straight to the farm. She had to wait in the drawing room until Charles had returned from wherever his horse had had to take him. She flushed slightly and privately as she wondered what exactly she thought she was doing. But she appeared to be doing it all the same. She concealed her intentions even to herself.

Charles, upon his return, was informed at once of Elizabeth's arrival. The butler had an unaccountably glad smile. Unhurriedly, Charles made his way to the drawing room.

'Hello, Miss Mowden,' he said evenly, 'this is a surprise.'

'Yes, it is,' replied Elizabeth, speaking abruptly and turning from the window overlooking the south lawn.

For once, Charles did not know what to say next. Elizabeth came to his rescue.

'I have come to return this to you,' she announced flatly, standing awkwardly and twisting her fingers.

'What is it?' asked Charles.

'Well, you can open an envelope, can't you?'

Her words were far more graceless than she had intended. Her straight gaze met that of Charles. Temporarily, they were both wordless, but something must have passed between them in the way that unspoken things do.

Elizabeth spoke again.

'What I mean is that I will come back to you all here, that is to say to look after Foley. I mean, at any time that you want. Money does not come into it. After all, I have to do something with my life, you see. I love people and I need them and it is so lovely here. I mean … '

There was a pause after her words tailed into silence.

'You see, if I were pretty, or anything like that, someone would do things for me – look after my life, I mean … '

Her words, uttered in honest, groping sincerity, seemed to lose themselves in muffled insignificance among the carpets. Her eyes were lowered to them.

She stopped speaking in the face of no apparently forthcoming response, suddenly realising that she had perhaps gone too far. She had said more than she ought, but she had meant it just the same. Blood rushed to her plain and distressed face.

She left the room impulsively and by the wrong door, rushed down a wrong passage and emerged into the wrong yard. She stood awkwardly in the sunshine as Charles stood happily astounded in the big drawing room. Meanwhile, a stable boy walked Elizabeth round to the front of the house where she had left her trap. He helped her up and she drove home with a feeling inside her she was not sure whether she should have had or not.

Somewhat at a loss to identify his own thoughts, newborn and without his foreknowledge, Charles Osmond wondered whether future happiness had just announced itself.

*

Unexpectedly, the snows of winter, light though they were in the south, disappeared in early January. Neither were they to return until the same month of the next year. The cold, and that inner one to which Charles had become accustomed, began its melting departure from his heart at the beginning of February. He could not wait for March, nor could his loins either.

He decided to accelerate March's arrival by a visit to Elizabeth's father in the latter days of February. He told himself that he had some business to do in connection with the farm. He had, but it was not nearly as pressing as his own. His acres filled his pocket but they did not do likewise to his heart. He felt curiously numbed by his prosperous loneliness; everything seemed to contribute to his isolation. He now never saw any of his own family. Its members were a world and a good many miles away from him; he had voluntarily and effectively, like a lone pioneer, cut himself off from his people. He did not envy their lives. His father was dead and he did not know the children of his brothers. In a word, he was a lonely man of thirty-eight years.

He hunted once a week, it was true. He had his own pheasant covers and his partridges were thick in his straight hedgerows. His hunting and shooting friends invited him to convivial dinners, which he reciprocated, but he still felt that his life was all but empty. Although he could have had the entrée to several London clubs, which his family and his riches would have easily ensured, their false and expensive gaiety did not appeal to him. A direct man, his lungs were too fresh with the wholesome smells and scents of his farmlands for him to appreciate the vapid, social task in costly, tawdry surroundings. Effete people held nothing for him. The farm was now magnificent, the house old, friendly and spacious; all his servants and farm workers respected him, loved him and did not, unaccountably, resent their age-old thralldom. His fairness towards them all obliterated what could have been any shame or self-contempt.

Yet Charles was not truly happy, not yet completely fulfilled. There was an experience in his life, as in that of many, that he saw with sadness that he had somehow missed.

His distant and not particularly pleasant little son, now nearly eleven, afforded him neither pleasure nor comfortable companionship.

The fact that Charles could never remember his age within a year or so reflected his final lack of love for his dead wife. He now had equally little affection for her weedy offspring with his cold, supercilious eyes and his fussy little ways. He would have wanted to hug a loving son. As it was, only his own tender conscience prevented him from finding Foley contemptible. He did not then know it, but he had underestimated him.

Foley was, even at his early age, brilliantly successful at school. He regularly invited his aristocratic, pretentious friends to stay at the big farm, where he had never laid a hand to work and where his companions laughed at the feudal devotion of his father's servants and labourers. They disdained the humble but important pleasures of the country. Foley's attitude offended and hurt his father, whose good people were amused, if in a sad sort of way.

Meanwhile, the farmlads enjoyed the sweat of the harvest, the summer field-dust and the cider that slaked their thirst after the long, friendly toil. They loved too the earthy humour of their fathers and mothers, the simple food and their nightly, quiet rest, crowded as they were under the beams of their cottages, ensuring their energies for the next, hot, threshing summer's day. Charles shared all that.

As the binder cut nearer and nearer to the middle of the field, (one of the many), they enjoyed pulling their rabbit supper out of the holes into which they had bolted. Stretching their neck deftly so as to cause the minimum of distress to their necessary victims, they would line them up just off the middle of the field for the farmer to allot them in quality, and quantity, according to the standing and seniority of each labourer. The fattest and the longest went to the foreman, the smallest and the youngest to the little lads who came in from the cottages, not necessarily owned by the big farm. Charles stood out from the middle of each field, shooting the bolder ones who had unsuccessfully tried their escape.

Foley and his high-nosed friends looked on with sweatless disgust, returned to the shade of a drawing room somewhere in the house and played cards. This disappointed Charles, although he was somehow proud of Foley's academic achievements. Unfortunately, Foley was too.

Charles knew that Foley would never take the farm and that, if he did, he would ruin it by indolence and disinterest. So, instead, he took a decision, one quiet evening; a decision for his farm and for himself. The decision worked, but the sequel thereto could never have been foreseen.

He saddled his horse promptly. He was a man of firm clear intention. He rode the twelve crisp, clear, wintery miles to Devizes, mostly over his own land.

*

The horse's hooves clattered and echoed down the main street of the town. Charles turned abruptly, as abruptly as he had made his decision, up a side road where he quickly came to his destination; George Mowden's quiet, mellow seventeenth century town-house. It stood silent, as if at rest, except for the yellow glow of its windows; you could have said like cats' eyes, amber, watchful but homely, gazing from an inner knowledge of warmth out into the cold which they did not have to suffer.

Behind the conventionally railinged, slightly pretentious facade, lay the spacious, calm, well-worn family home of a cultivated provincial lawyer. Behind that again were its walled garden, billiard-table lawns, bordered hugely with old English common flowers, over which presided elderly walls almost supported, it seemed, by prolific pears, apples and plums. They were too old for you to have told their name. It was in this garden that Charles had first seen Caroline, in the days of his miserable existence with the now-dead Gwendoline; he had not even noticed little Elizabeth for whom his soul and body were now both purely and kindly burning. That was to come later.

George, his friend at all times and in all circumstances, was as ever at home. Amongst his solid eighteenth century furniture, his sober family portraits of lawyers long before him and his books, strewn, piled and wedged everywhere, George was playing chess against himself in his library.

26

At Charles's ring, Emilia, ancient, fat and waddly, opened the door to a man she liked. She was a wonderful old servant.

'You are late, and that's a fact, sir,' she croaked peremptorily. 'But I know that the master will be glad to see you, though Heaven knows why at this time. All the family's abed, sir, and Mr George is playing himself at that chess again.'

'I hope that I shall not disturb him,' offered Charles uncertainly.

'Oh dear me, no sir, not at all. I even daresay he might be glad of a little company for a while.'

'Is that a fact?' asked Charles, with more the emphasis of a statement than of a question.

Without answering, old Emilia hobbled bandylegged in front of him, having first shut out the winter draught as well as the stars.

Elizabeth was no glittering star, Charles was aware, but he thought, and passionately, of her inner glow which, like a deep fire, would burn on and on into the warm mornings of the future. Her light seemed to be beckoning and constant, seen and yet unseen. He loved her as he had never loved another before, with an extraordinary tenderness of heart and the will to make her happy, cherished above all others and unbelievably wanted.

George arose heavily from his chess table, seeming not sorry to do so. Portly, but alert, he lumbered carefully towards a sideboard to pour his Young Friend, as he called him affectionately, a rather large tumbler of whisky. They had not yet spoken, other than with the smile of their eyes, one pair old, the other young. An understanding, trusting and friendly, yet inquisitive, shot mutually through their gaze.

Offering the heavy crystal tumbler to Charles, George Mowden said:

'Yes!'

It was an affirmative not an interrogative. It was a statement, not a question.

27

'"Yes" and how do you mean, George?' asked Charles, more suddenly and emotionally affected than he would have ordinarily liked to have shown himself.

'Well,' answered his old mentor slowly, 'you have no problem with that small land dispute of yours. I have settled it all. Wait until you come in next time.'

Here the old man paused.

'Now, tell me about how the farm is this week. And about those new tenants' cottages. I hope that you have not got in that awful fellow Wheelwright to put them up for you. He's a rogue, and if I were to tell you one or two things, which of course, I can't ...'

And so it went on. Charles's heart sank.

His courage, so high on horseback over the frosty countryside, evaporated for no good reason that he could explain. Subconsciously, he was a nervous man, trying to put on an honest, confident front. If his marriage with Elizabeth, his sweet and only Elizabeth, should be as dismal an affair as his so-called marriage with the cold, hard Gwendoline, whatever then?

How could he ever face old George Mowden if he ruined the life of his last daughter?

He was therefore nervy and on edge. His answers to whom he hoped might be his next father-in-law were short and uninterestingly disjointed. Awkwardly, he played with his elegant cigar-case, offered one of its contents to George, who he knew did not smoke. He spent a space looking vacantly at the fire.

'And how are the barns, Charles?' asked George for the second time.

'The barns. Oh, yes. Well, the new thatching will soon be finished, I expect.'

There the conversation, if such it could have been termed, ended and Charles rose to go.

'I must be off now,' he said, unnecessarily enough. 'I only just dropped by.'

He had the uncomfortable feeling that his wily, friendly old lawyer had been playing him about. As their talk had dried up, he noticed a disconcerting although good-humoured senior mockery in the old man's blue eyes. They were the honest eyes of his Elizabeth, too.

'By the bye,' said George quietly and just as Charles was leaving, 'the answer to the question which you really came to ask me is "yes"'.

Charles stood bewildered as a boy.

To fill the gap which he had deliberately created, George Mowden said: 'You and Elizabeth will be completely happy so long as you behave yourself as a proper man. I know that you will and you shall be as my son.'

With sudden emotion, the two men spoke a small world of understanding and an unsaid promise one to the other with their eyes. They spent a long handshake under the stars of the present and the future. With a double promise in his heart, Charles rode dangerously home.

*

Charles Foley Osmond took Elizabeth Mowden to be his lawful wedded wife in June, 1911.

'Lawful!', he thought to himself, with genuinely delighted amusement, thinking of her father. He, bless the old man, had never done, or even thought of doing, anything unlawful in his life.

'Lawful!' he thought again. Gwendoline had been lawful, but only that. The wretched woman had not given an ounce of her heart or herself to him throughout the whole of their marriage. So often had he been dying for the pleasure of her beautiful body, long, slim and sallow, without any hope of response. Cold passivity, on her side at least, had been the best that he had ever obtained; the mere and basic needs of a sensual man. It was like going to bed with a prostitute. His immediate needs were satisfied, at greatly interspaced periods, but that was all. All he did not have to do was pay for it. He felt degraded, unsure, unsafe. A man, he reflected, had to be pretty hot and greatly in need to be able to make love to such an icy block. Perversely and with a certain relish, he decided that, even while she was still living, he would make her end hot. He had her cremated.

This was unlike the fate of her stillborn child, Samuel, who had been buried proudly and with deep sorrow in a small grave in the Saxon churchyard which was part of the farm. It was in an area of the late Roman village that had eventually died in the Black Death. Charles still walked about its crumbling walls. A murdered village, murdered by God, he thought. His own way of murdering Gwendoline, who was not to have the privilege of lying anywhere near Samuel, the vicarious pleasure of her husband whose soul she had crucified, was to have her well and truly burned. Samuel, as he would have called his second son, and did so in his own heart, would never be part of his mother; upon that he was determined. He was buried with love and reverence in the little Saxon churchyard, where the autumn leaves came down to keep his heart warm. The heart of Samuel lived forever within him.

The stout old farm had suffered a good many winters of discontent but, as had its present owner, had come through somehow. Charles felt a partnership of an indissoluble nature with the great old house and its timeless lands. He wanted an equally timeless wife too; he knew he must have found her in the sweet Elizabeth Mowden. All now seemed set for an uninterrupted summer. His hopes were certainly to be realised or, at least, some of them.

He thanked God that Gwendoline would lie nowhere near him. In fact, she would not be lying anywhere at all. She would be carried away on the winds as far as they could take her from him, his farm and the people whom he so much loved. He had prayed in his little church by her coffin, shiny and new through the moonlit windows, that he would be for ever delivered from the sterile bondage of even the most fleeting thought of her presence. His prayers did not even need the hearing of them to be answered. He was never to think of her again. She had been an insult to his kind manhood and would therefore, he felt, be an insult to the earth, to which he felt so great a duty.

He deliberately contravened the wishes expressed in her will. She had wanted to be buried and remembered in the Saxon churchyard. She had said her hypocritical prayers there, and those to a God, thought Charles, who would never very much have enjoyed her company. Her ashes would certainly neither stale nor stain his land with their bitter, arid memory.

However, for appearances' sake, he had had her enclosed in a small, wooden casket. This he took from the crematorium in his trap. Balancing it on his knees, he wondered quite what to do with it. Stopping to relieve himself against his carriage wheel, as the saying goes, he had a sudden, uncharacteristically vengeful idea. He smashed the box, as his heart had been smashed, over a roadside drain, tipped her ashes down it and threw the shattered remains of the casket over a hedge. Returning to the trap, he pissed away the spillings.

Having refused the presence of any of his household at the final ceremony, and Foley was too young to go anyway, Charles drove himself home with a kind of demoniac relish in part of his mind; but in another part he experienced a sort of longing sadness for his own happiness as much as for the opportunity to make others happy with him. In short, he wanted desperately to share his life with another woman, all his wonderful feelings for her.

A few months later he did.

When he had returned to the farm, he celebrated the end of Gwendoline in a couple of glasses of cheap Madeira, chosen deliberately in an act of calculated disrespect. But he never would allow his soul to harden; if you are born with compassion, it never leaves you. Or does it?

Today, his real marriage day, was special. He had a special feeling all over and all through him. Not just in his mind, not just in his heart, not even just in his loins, but in his melting soul.

Recently, he had sometimes wondered whether he had

one of those. If you have a true one, it never withers, no matter how cold and dry the wind of disappointment.

Elizabeth afforded him gladly the highest, deepest pleasure such as he had, unaccountably, never before found in any woman. Their need met in complete satisfaction; hers for what she had not known but had only yearned vaguely for; his for what he had long known in part but which had never satisfied him as more than a primeval necessity. No one could have told how shallowly buried was his cruelty.

His home was their bed; their bed her home.

Everyone in the house, except for Foley, became happy again. Elizabeth busied herself quietly and delightedly about the great place, came to know it and love it, caring for all its people, especially for Charles. Old Anne Force – she was not really old but was one of those women who look ancient from the age of eighteen – somewhat resented the new mistress at first, but she either forgot her feelings or put them behind her. Perhaps she resented initially the fact that Elizabeth took over the family care of Foley, whilst she naturally looked after his clothes, packing them in his trunks upon his return to school and unpacking them afterwards.

Foley became ever more remote, developing carefully, it seemed, a look that might easily have been mistaken as reflecting alternately stupidity or lofty disdain. In fact, this is how he concealed his chilly shrewdness. Elizabeth did her duty by him, feeling neither guilt nor regret that she did only that. Foley had now developed asthma, for which she felt sympathy although it was a very mild condition. Keeping him indoors on windy, cold days was the only treatment that he needed.

Every day, when Charles returned from his rides about the farm, he looked forward more and more to his wife's bright eyes and lovely kind face. He loved her fine, warm kiss and the promising feel of her honest body. They both made especial efforts to please each other in all ways. They could do so without speech.

In May 1912, the couple were both delighted that Doctor Gray was in no doubt that Elizabeth was with child. Their gratitude one to another was boundless. Edward Foley Mowden Osmond greeted the world noisily in December. The doctor, too, was very happy about it, but he recognised that a rather difficult birth had strained the mother a little too much. She was to rest as much as possible for the next month or two but be sure to feed the baby at her breasts. He felt that all would be well.

Unfortunately, Elizabeth did not recover properly. The results would be saddening for both Charles and for herself.

Meanwhile, all was bright and fine in the house and Edward was everyone's favourite.

2

Departures

The story of the Osmonds from the time of Charles's blissfully happy marriage, that is until the dividing time, may be quickly told. There was no stirring event, but the quiet flowing of a peaceful family life. It was a calm new world, developing all the time within itself. There was nothing to report to anyone else that would have appeared of any striking import. Nothing of any surprise or interest other than to the family. They all thought that they had a touch of greatness but, because they did not advertise this almost subconscious feeling, perhaps they held to themselves a certain private grandeur.

Charles, with the years, grew a little greyer and a little stouter. He was still handsome, although port, roast beef and contentment did not quite cancel the calories that his work burnt away. In 1915, he had a rather painful fall from his horse. By 1925, he was suffering arthritis of his left hip. Finding it painful to ride, he drove for some time in an uncomfortable trap, which bounced unevenly over the hard summer ruts. So, suddenly as he made all his decisions, he made up his mind to put it away, replacing it with an immense Daimler sedanca motor car in 1930. He never liked it, missing the wind in his hair on horseback; and did not like much more Herbert Wilken his chauffeur, who had seemed to arrive with the package. His wife Hester helped fat Ellen, the cook, to make butter and bake bread in the kitchens.

Elizabeth had developed a slight heart condition and, as a result, was told by doctor Gray – a weekly visitor at the farm – that it would be extremely inadvisable to have further children. Charles was too devoted and considerate to show his disappointment and therefore to ask her for a successor to Edward. They still indulged their love safely and with delight, still undressing one another tenderly, still on the same Persian rug in front of the fire in the great bedroom; they had done the same since the first night of their beautiful marriage. Whatever they chose to do in bed, they melted swiftly into one personality, each adapting to the wishes of each other in mutual trust and complete love. They felt that this union would remain sure for always. It did.

The farm ran itself, or so it might have appeared to the outsider as much as to their always informal dinner guests. In fact, Charles still worked extremely hard to ensure his fortune and his continued prosperity. However, his tranquil family happiness seemed to make his burden light. In short, he did not particularly feel his middle age except, perhaps, on those penetratingly cold, damp days when the pain made itself more than usually felt in his hip. At those times he would drink a little more. On occasions, the hard spirits would tend to fray his normally even temper.

Foley went to his stark public school in September, 1914, when life was all the greyer for the whole nation, not just for himself, under the drear clouds of war. Foley, however, was a survivor. He had a cold, unattractive nature which rendered him more dispassionately single-minded than some. The food was, as ever it had been, practically inedible, but Foley managed to have better and more interesting sustenance purveyed to him. This was entirely thanks to the money that he was able to earn through doing the classical proses of his less gifted schoolmates, whom he despised without letting them know it. Later, he was to know the meaning of that nearly untranslatable French adjective *serviable*.

His personality was apparently neuter enough to avoid him the atrocious bullying meted out to the unpopular. This escape seemed to add a certain compulsion to his evidently negative character. Whilst looking as grey and uninteresting as the dull walls of the buildings, he learnt how to be academically and financially successful without being noticed. As it was with King Henry VII, his cap was his counsel. Other than in human terms, this attitude to life would serve him well in the future, even though it would endear him to nearly no one. Although he could not then have known it, his final dissolution was to be due to his deliberate disregard for any human or humanitarian sentiment. But this was far off in the future.

At home and away from home, his life was even, progressing along its lonely, quiet way, so far as his father and stepmother knew. They wondered at times about his aloofness and chilly personality.

Edward was proving to be quite different. He was open, engaging, jolly and cheerful. All his friends, of whom there were legion, called him 'Teddy'; Foley did not, if he called him anything at all.

Foley left school just after the end of the First Great War. He was thankful for both terminations. He had rejected the idea of university, although he could well have distinguished himself in several fields. He was now an accomplished classical scholar and he had entered recently, in his abstract kind of way, the realms of mathematics. Foreign modern languages held no appeal for him, although he had a modest competence in French. He liked, not unsurprisingly, the acid humour and the sometimes twisted, cruel absurdities of the later nineteenth and early twentieth century writers.

He had decided that he would never become a farmer. What then? he asked himself. A profession? No. That would have been too stable, unmerciful and drab. There would not have been enough to have challenged his selfish mind.

He wanted money, earned with financial swordmanship,

far from that gained by the well-worn paths of the doctor, the farmer, the lawyer. He had that deceptive quality – as he saw, when, in his cold way, he voluntarily evaluated himself in character and potential – which would allow him to deceive and dupe to his own lonely advantage any victim, without, at the same time, causing the slightest suspicion or offence. They would not be victims in their own eyes if their loss were pleasurable to them. He thought that he would be able to make it so. He did not now see that there might be a stronger hand than his own that guided fate.

He decided that he had a gift. However, in order to bring this into effect, he had to ensure another gift, one at that of a rather more concrete, mundane nature. Money was his key.

His father's arthritis might be a problem. On those days when it troubled him more than ordinarily, he could be intransigent, even intractable. In these cases, it might spell ungenerousness to Foley. He knew equally that any impatience and intolerance on his part might fatally endanger his plans. He well knew that his father loved him not but that he, his father, was ever a man with a sense of duty. He would always do his sacred devoir even if it crucified him.

Duty was therefore the key. He would, he decided, have to play upon that sentiment as hard as he could for his own advantage. He would not have to be too particular as to whether, in his own mind, duty came first to his father or to himself. An expert dissembler and self-dissembler, he had already decided in which direction his loyalties would sway him. He looked distantly even upon himself, but without disgust, which was surprising.

*

Once Foley had left school, his father began to wonder, without particularly airing his doubting thoughts, what course his elder son would take in life. Clearly, this would not lead him along the furrows of the field. He recognised now his son's different abilities, through his easy, quick appraisal and solution of a problem (an ability in part inherited from himself); his economical, laconic but never offensive remarks, unless you read into them; his urbane, neatly-turned conversation at the dinner table. He left anyone who met him the impression of restraint and self-contained, self-sufficient capability. He was neither approved nor disapproved of, neither liked nor disliked, neither recognised nor totally ignored. The French would have dubbed him *personnalité neutre*, which would have been exactly right.

'I have another son' thought Charles to himself, almost subconsciously. 'He will have the farm and cherish it as I do. It will be he who will gild my furrows with corn, who will have a loving wife and a band of children.' It was therefore with little surprise and with no misgivings that Charles greeted Foley's polite, if firm announcement that he would rather not join his father in the continuing venture of Hetherick Farm.

At the discreet knock on his study door one evening in December, while he was smoking his after-dinner cigar and verifying his recent accounts, to the wheezy strains of some heavy German music on his phonograph, Charles answered, 'Come in!'

On seeing his tall, slim elder son standing in the doorway, dressed as always with a certain elegant dismality, he motioned him to a chair behind his at the bureau. Turning his own to face him across the untidy countryman's lair, he said quietly: 'Sit down, will you Foley?'

'Thank you, Father.'

Charles looked at the thin face with its neutral colouring, out from which gazed those hooded, grey eyes which, it seemed, claimed nothing nor gave anything either. Impassively he began, without hesitation or preamble.

'Father, without wishing to disturb you, let alone upset you, I have recently come to a conclusion or two. Not without forethought, of course.'

There was quite a pause before the elder man replied, anticipating correctly what the other had come to see him about. Still Charles did not know precisely what to expect. Foley never wished for anyone to know exactly about anything that he kept in the cold storage of his mind. A polite, well-considered surprise, Foley had often found, normally achieved better results than precipitate or over-emotional revelations.

'I gave you a little time for thought on purpose,' resumed his Father.

'Thank you,' and here Foley smiled thinly in simulated gratitude. The small mouth soon drew down at its corners to a pointed but slightly receding chin.

'The fact is, father,' he continued smoothly, 'I feel that I should be no asset to you in the running of this great farm.'

His father just managed to avoid nodding his vigorous, relieved and enthusiastic assent, contriving instead an interrogative expression of slight interest. He allowed his son to continue without interruption.

'I have been, am now and shall always be grateful beyond bounds for all that you have done for me, despite our marked difference of temperament. You have never made me do anything here that I would have found distasteful and yet,' he went on slyly, 'I did not give too bad an account of myself at school. Thanks to the education you gave me and, in a small part, to the advantage which I took of it, I think I may safely say that I am now equipped to make my own way in another sphere.'

The rehearsed speech, Foley felt, was going well. There was another pause. He had aroused just enough interest, he thought. He knew instinctively how to be self-deprecating.

'What do you intend then, Foley?'

'To enter commerce, business if you like. You see, Father,' he added perhaps a little too ingratiatingly, 'I would not wish by any means to spoil by my incompetence, and ignorance too, this wonderful estate that you have built up over so many fruitful years. And you have Teddy to think of. He is far more like you than I am.'

Yes, Charles said to himself, he had known all this for some time. He was therefore relieved rather than disappointed. Especially as there was Teddy. He took care not to mention him in his reply because Foley knew, as did everybody else, that the younger son was the apple of his Father's eye, the spoilt one. This had not made him jealous; he merely regarded the situation with faint contempt.

'I was going to give you,' replied Charles carefully, 'the choice that my own father gave me. But I see that you have, perhaps more sensibly than I, made this already. Naturally, I will still make you the offer. It is to join me, or to take a lump sum and make your own way. The farm, on my death, will be divided between you and Edward (he always called him Edward on formal occasions) and you will both look after Mother if she lives on after me. If Edward could buy you out or wished to, then that is between you both to arrange.'

Once more, Charles turned his chair towards his bureau and wrote an extremely large cheque: 'Here you are, Foley, here's twenty thousand.'

Foley's face showed, if it showed any emotion at all, rather more relief than gratitude. Before he had had time to frame his next sentence, his father spoke: 'Well, what are you going to do with it? Not that you are in any way bound to answer this question. But I would caution you, as my father did: you may henceforth expect no further financial help from me unless it is a business arrangement. I wish you good luck.'

'Thank you, father. That is perfectly understood. You have been more than generous. As a matter of fact, a friend of mine and I plan to start a wine business in London. I shall look after and expand the retail side in the city while he is to do the buying and shipping from France, based in Bordeaux.'

His father looked surprised.

'But twenty thousand is surely not enough for that scale of venture?'

'For a start it will be, father. The whole concern will not belong entirely to us, initially. The money will be my stake in a large concern, already established but now poorly run in

40

England. The more I make, the more widely I shall expand the business this side of the Channel, and this out of my own pocket. I hope that by ploughing back as much as possible I shall eventually succeed in cutting myself into at least a half-share.'

For once in his life, Charles caught himself admiring his distant, calculating son. How like him in some ways and alas! how like his dead mother. Charles smiled as convincingly as he could.

'Goodnight, my boy and, again, good luck!'

'Thank you again, father,' said Foley, smiling in a pinched sort of way. It was to himself only. He walked neatly upstairs.

*

The trouble was that Teddy was spoilt, especially by his father. Without doubt, Teddy was his darling and his favourite. This for two obvious reasons: the delight that his fair Elizabeth had always given him and the sad fact that this would be their first and only child. Charles knew that he spoilt Teddy, but this was understandable, he told himself. It would not be long before he knew how foolish, either.

This adoring treatment did not, curiously, ruin his son's disposition. He could have become, like many children, petulant, bad-tempered, deceitful and generally odious. Instead, he was even-tempered, easy-going, jolly, affectionate and always of a sunny disposition. The problem would be that he grew up over-generous to himself. He was lazy and self-indulgent. The shocks that were to come to him, albeit sometimes unfairly, in later life, he was going to find himself ill-equipped for.

Life continued to smile upon him now, sometimes unexpectedly; in unforeseen ways which only served to increase the enjoyment of his existence. Always outgoing, uninhibited and immediate, he delighted from an early age all who met him. He was certainly an engaging person. Life, he had decided, was definitely good to live.

Teddy passed easily, if not with great academic distinction, through carelessly, happy schooldays, having proceeded smoothly to the same public school as his brother. Here, by his warm and adaptable personality, he helped to dispel for himself and for his many friends some of the starkness that was supposed to be an ennobling virtue.

Despite his casualness he never failed an examination, nor distinguished himself in one either. This did not unduly worry his father. He was happy in the certainty that Teddy would be his successor. So, if he murdered a few latin poets, what did it matter?

Disaster, however, was not far off.

In most respects Teddy resembled his father. True, Charles at his age had been a little more spare of figure. Teddy was equally broad and strong but rather more fleshy. Nonetheless, he was a good-looking fellow with clean features, a good carriage and masses of curly brown hair. He had soft blue eyes and sensuous lips. For the moment, he considered these attributes enough to get him along in life.

Once a boy in his House at school had reached a certain age, sixteen or so, he was accorded not only a small study downstairs but a cubicle upstairs, barren and cold but certainly private. There was a bed with a thin, uncomfortable mattress, beside which lay a threadbare mat on the wooden floor, which could be used as an extra blanket during the thickly foggy, glacial winter nights. There was a decrepit chair and their were some hooks for clothes hangers screwed into the wooden partition wall. A dilapidated chest of drawers completed the furnishings. Whatever else, however mean the furnishing, this was an oasis of luxurious privacy after the rowdy dormitories. Teddy was granted the tenancy of one of these at the end of a boarded passage. It was known affectionately as The Prison, on account of a sort of barred but openable door outside the window. This gave him a view of the night-time treetops, gables and the sky. It also opened on to something else; an entirely new experience.

Teddy's cubicle window gave immediately on to a small, flat, leaded roof, to the left of which two little gables sloped inwards to a little gutter for the rain. At the end of the short stretch of roof there was a rickety wooden fire escape ladder down which, evidently, no one could have trodden for years since many rungs were missing and the rest green and rotten. Between the two gables on his left a small dormer window peeped out into the night.

Often before going to sleep, Teddy would kneel on his chair, having thrown up the lower half of his small sash window to gaze out into the dark, imagining the freedom that would be his in the outside world after just one more year at school. He was now nearly seventeen. He could barely wait.

Often at his window, he would wonder what life would hold for him. Yet he was pretty certain. Beyond his cubicle there lay a rich land where he would be able to do fairly much as he liked, with enough money to cover almost any eventuality. His security was inviolable and, he felt, for ever. Such can be the delusions, comforting as they are, of the inexperienced.

Over to the left of the flat lead between the tiled roofs, still giving their warmth to the night after the summer-day sun, Teddy saw the dormer window. Often he watched it until its yellow light went out at about one o'clock in the morning. Occasionally there would, through a gap in the curtains, be the fleeting glimpse of a blue velvet dressing-gown. More than that there would sometimes be a tanned face, crowned by dark eyebrows and jet hair in tantalising disarray, crossing the room to draw the curtains, to open or close the sash window. It was Mary, the attractive country maid; far away, it seemed, from where she should have been in the West.

All the older boys with an eye had noticed her, but Teddy was the nearest of them all to her attic bedroom. He felt a stirring for the unknown, as yet untasted, without at the same time knowing quite what to do about his approach. A certain insistence pestered him agreeably now, as was only natural. He did not find it hard to wrestle against what every adult seemed to consider wrong; he put up no fight at all. He had already decided to end his ignorance and make it right.

So it was, then. He had not occupied his cubicle, The Prison, for more than a few weeks when he made his 'escape'. One night, not being able to sleep, he got up and looked out of his lower window. It was, he decided, too hot and close to attempt the adventure of sleep just for a while. It was around midnight. The stars were shining with a soft brightness, the moon was crescent. Mary's light was burning still. He felt a warm, unexplored yearning as he gazed at her window. He trembled a little.

Suddenly, the curtains were pulled aside. There she was, in just her plain slip, opening the lower sash, just as he had done. She too could probably not sleep. They caught each other's eyes for an instant and smiled through the semi-dark. Teddy felt a sudden exhilaration, mixed with guilt, timidity and daring all at once. His heart raced and his pulse beat hard. The thick blood of youth pumped strongly through him. He knew then that the 'forbidden' must take place.

So they looked at each other for long moments, the maid and the wealthy, good-looking schoolboy who hoped soon to be a boy no more. On an impulse he stood upon his chair, preparing to edge himself out of the small opening. Conventionality, just as suddenly, made him get down again to don his dressing-gown to conceal briefly the signs of his interest. But when he mounted the chair again, Mary was no longer at the window and the light had been turned out. The curtains were drawn, too. She must, he said to himself with a certain disgust, have thought he had lost heart. With an annoyance born of disappointment, disappointment for what he had only dreamed of, he returned to bed. Eventually, sleep claimed him. He felt ashamed that he had not shared the indefinable wonder.

All next day, a gnawing secret, the key to which he did not possess because he had mislaid it, gripped his vitals and sapped his energies. He had to find it again and open the secret of life as he now knew that it was. Dark secrets, although his personality was basically open, would always hold a fascination for him. As do many of us when young, he often associated excitement and exaltation with the darkness.

The next night, Mary's curtains remained obstinately drawn closed, although her light was on until after midnight. Had he obviously offended her, put her off him for ever, perhaps?

The night after that, on the other hand, the air close after another perfect day's hot sunshine, made her visible once again. This time our hero was ready, not knowing quite what to do or expect next. Something drew their gaze towards each other and this time there was no hesitation. Inquisitive rashness completely overcame his timidity and he stepped bravely and lightly on to the leads. He came speechless to an expectant halt against her window.

'Hello you!' she said softly in her country tones. 'Nice to see you again up yere. What's you doin', then?' she asked archly with an inviting smile.

'I just came to say "Hello",' he answered in an uncertain voice. 'It's lovely to see you, that's all.'

'You too, Mr Osmond.'

And with that she put out her little brown hand, whilst climbing out to join him. She went on holding his hand and then put the other on his shoulder.

'My, yer a good looker,' she exclaimed softly. 'I likes a good strong youngun like you.'

They went on whispering about nothing in particular, each secretly and really knowing that it was not very important. Mary pressed herself against him, undoing his gown and her own. She pushed him easily back against the sloping tiles and kissed him hard and openly on the mouth. All within both of them responded quickly, breathtakingly.

'Where's yer old pride an' glory, then?' she asked. The question was quite unnecessary because she was pressing herself flat against him. Her rough, dark hands gripped him and his ecstacy knew no bounds; at the same time she guided his to her. 'Is this what it's like?' he asked her in a husky voice, knowing perfectly well that it was not the whole story.

'It's not quite all, my dear, but it'll do for a start. It'll do for the first time. See yer morrer night, same time, an' I'll teach yer a bit more. You just 'op orf ter bed now!'

'I shan't forget, Mary,' said Teddy, who could not wait for the full revelation, although the first instalment had been wonderful for him.

Two faces saw and recognised one another through the thick, warm night, but this evening was colder than the one before.

'Doan yer get flustered, Mr Osmond, my dear. Just step up over the sill and in. Be quiet, mind.'

Quiet he was. Out, over his own sill and over Mary's in no time. And there before him was his girl; his little, brown Mary, as he thought of her. She stood boldly naked and yet without shame. Her window was invisible to any other than his own – that of The Prison from which he had so magnificently escaped! He threw off his pyjamas at once. They enlaced each other excitingly, kissing all over their body. Mary had folded back the bedclothes and in no time they were on the clean, stretched sheet. In their mutual exploration they both took delight, he in her musky scent and firm young body, she in his muscular body and his evident manhood.

'There you are my lad,' she whispered sweetly, 'take my gift.' So he did.

'Stay there, Teddy. Doan' leave me for a spell.'

There indeed he did stay, as she taught him some more; then they made splendid, longlasting love again.

*

The new-found, happy life of Edward Osmond continued until just after the middle of July. Almost every night, he tiptoed late across the leads to find the generous charms of Mary; a lovely, simple girl, or so he thought her. She seemed always willing, except when nature forbad; at those times they would sit chatting about country life, cuddling up very close and not leave each other until the small hours of the morning. Everything seemed perfect. They learnt about one another in the most pleasurable way. Teddy was boundlessly grateful for her tender, delectable instruction.

It happened to be cricket, his other love, that undid them both; in some respects he more than she. One night he told her that he could not be with her on the next. His match was to be played two counties away; the game was to last over two days and he would therefore have to stay the night at the other school. It was, he told Mary, one of the best and most important matches of the year but, not understanding, she looked disappointed. It was then that a sudden idea flickered through his mind. He told her that she was to look on her bed after the day's drudgery; something would await her. She smiled.

'Yer naughty boy, Teddy. But I ain't goin' ter try an' guess!'

That next morning, Teddy, whose father gave him a more than plentiful allowance, went down to the town and bought a Victorian shilling made into a silver brooch, framed and clasped on to a silver bar with a long pin behind it. He could hardly believe what he was doing. He felt manly and kind, both of which he was. Obligatory Christmas and birthday presents had so far in his life been the only claims upon his pocket, although never made upon a reluctant purse. Now he was spending something because he really wanted to, because he had been given something almost unrepayable. It marked the beginning of his first encounter with the ways of the world outside trust and innocence.

When he returned to his House, the team was outside it and on the point of departure. He was late, but he hastened to his study where he wrapped up the brooch in a short, intimate letter. He quickly laid the untidy little package on Mary's counterpane, packed his essentials and was just in time not to miss the excursion.

'There,' he whispered to himself contentedly, 'that'll be a nice surprise!' This indeed is exactly what it was going to be, although not quite in the way which he had expected.

The match went well in the sheltered, tree-bordered English cricket field. It was even exciting. Teddy, unfortunately, did not distinguish himself quite as he usually did. His mind was on a girl, a bed and a brooch rather than on the vagaries of wicket, bat and ball. However, the journey home the next day was accomplished pleasantly enough, with a stop or two for refreshment and a couple of sneaky beers.

By the time that Teddy arrived at the House, most of it was in darkness. Nothing, normally, was provided to eat, so he went straight upstairs. After a quick wash and a glass of water, he was in his cubicle. He felt tired, but went to his window and looked leftwards. There was no light and yet the curtains were parted on a dark room. He could not see into the interior. Sliding out of his window, he went softly to Mary's and looked hard. As his eyes became accustomed to the blackness, he saw that her bed was empty. More than that, it had not been unmade and there were no clothes draped over any of the furniture. There was not even a shoe on the floor.

He felt uneasy but went to bed where he lay awake. The usual fatigue after two long days of physical exercise eventually overtook him and he was about to fall asleep when he noticed a small white envelope on his chest of drawers. He had not observed this when at first he entered. He accordingly went to the lavatory down the corridor, switched on the light and opened the letter. It was addressed to him in the small, precise, pinched handwriting of his Housemaster:

> Dear Osmond,
>   I would like to see you at noon.
>   F.D. Worseley

'Good God!' he said to himself aloud. Anxiety robbed him of any real sleep, but he managed to doze intermittently until the sun came through his window.

Frederick Delacroix Worseley was a small, grey, twisted little man with rheumaticky hands and cold black eyes. He had a weak, dented-looking face that never announced forgiveness, let alone understanding. One would have thought that his only strength lay in his authority. He wore shabby brown suits which matched his tatty shoes of the same colour. He had pointed, decayed, brownish teeth, no doubt through having smoked cheap cheroots for years, mostly in secret and once his wife had retired to bed for the night.

Mrs Worseley was a short, dowdy woman of indeterminate age and unbalanced proportions. All that one would have noticed of her, if one noticed anything at all, were her dull, prim clothes, burnt-out eyes and an immense nose. Her face was colourless and flabby. She never wore jewellery, apart from a thin wedding ring. With her over-developed sense of propriety and inquisitiveness, she was known, not without justice, as "The Nose".

The Nose, it appeared, had been busy. As with many of those who have little to do, the insignificances of life occupied her entire, unflagging and unwanted attention. She managed to lend an air of Christian duty to her unspecified responsibilities. Her duty was, in fact, solely to her insatiable curiosity in regard to what did not concern her. Her husband, who looked for all the world like some dusty, forgotten curio in the corner of a junk shop, claimed none of her attention other than when she caught him smoking a cheroot. They both looked as though they had been born into the world, stale already.

The unlovely, sour odour of yesterday's smoke penetrated the cracks of the loose brown door which led from the hall outside Mr Worseley's study. Teddy knocked upon the tacky paintwork. The indeterminate, stained and faded colours of the study shot even the dingy Housemaster into a certain, if indistinct, relief.

'Good morning, sir,' said Teddy in a breezy tone, but

without confidence. He tried to look as if there were nothing untoward to expect.

Worseley did not answer, or not immediately, He extinguished, imperfectly, a rather early-burning cheroot in a caked brass ashtray.

'Osmond,' he began without preamble, 'you may take this trinket and do with it what you will.'

The lad felt his heart displace itself, as it seems to do in an ancient aeroplane or maladjusted lift. He could think of no reply. The point of the pin on the brooch dug into his sweaty hand.

'And there is this,' continued Worseley proffering the note in Teddy's handwriting. 'Read it aloud to me so that you and I may the better be reminded of your witless and revolting incontinence, you dirty young libertine.'

The speaker was enjoying himself. His eyes glinted darkly and his stained lips puckered into a pinched, supercilious smile.

It was aloud therefore that Teddy, with a sense of ridiculousness and outraged privacy, read the following note:

'My darling little dark Mary,' he began. And then asked 'Is this really necessary, sir?'

'Continue, Osmond, as you have been instructed.'

'I cannot be with you tonight because of my silly cricket match. I shall be missing our lovely time together and our warmness with me inside you. I cannot wait for your sweet lips, your soft body and the sweet-tasting fruits of our love. I love you, dark, sweet girl. Your loving lover, Teddy. P.S. don't prick yourself with the pin – wait for me!'

The embarrassed reading was over. He was scarlet to the roots of his hair. He stood awkwardly, his mind a total blank.

'And now give me back the letter, if such it may be called,' ordered the sharp, thin voice. A nasty, rather dirty smile, twisted the arid lips.

'Your father will receive this obscene missive, together with a suitable letter from myself.'

He paused. Teddy said nothing. The man was relishing the moment.

'You may be assured,' he resumed, 'that my wife looks after the welfare of the servants. She goes so far as to inspect their bedrooms in the interests of cleanliness and good order, while they are at work. It was she, poor lady, who discovered this infamous epistle. I need hardly tell you that she recognised all its impure and disgusting connotations at once.'

He placed the letter on the one that he was in the course of writing to his father. The sour silence divided the two.

'You are to assemble your possessions forthwith and be ready to take the midday train to Waterloo. Thence you may have yourself conveyed where you will, but I suggest that you had better make your peace, uncertain though it may be, with your father. The maid,' he added unnecessarily enough, 'has been dismissed. She has already taken her departure. I did not enquire either about her intentions or her destination.'

*

Especially with his cumbersome luggage, the journey to Hetherick Farm, with its numerous railway changes before Devizes, passed as heavily as the baggage. At last the little town hove into view. Teddy had not even considered how he would reach the farm, but Worseley must have telephoned his father, for there on the platform was Wilken, the chauffeur, waiting for him.

'There is the trap outside, Mr Edward,' he said.

He did not need to ask why it was not the Daimler, which he liked so much.

'It's home then, Sir?' asked Wilken unnecessarily.

'I suppose so, Wilken. Yes, I suppose that it is. Thank you for having waited for me.'

'That's nothing at all, Sir, just nothing.'

Unlike his father, he quite liked Wilken. He asked no questions and did his duties quietly, without fuss or obsequiousness. They drove silently home, save for the clatter of the hoofs and the grating of the wheels over the rough country roads and lanes. It was a beautiful night. Thus Teddy rode with his luggage, his brooch and, in his heavy heart, his Mary. He felt unutterably depressed.

'I'm afraid all at the farm are abed, Sir,' apologised Wilken, as they made the last few yards of the drive up to the house. 'But the master said to see him before you went up above. He said as he'd be waiting for you.'

'Thank you, Wilken,' said Teddy, with a dry mouth and a not very comfortable anticipation.

The trap drew to a halt on the moonlit gravel sweep, unromantic enough under the circumstances. Both of the men pulled out the baggage and humped it into the old stone hall. 'I reckon that bides 'ere until tomorrow,' observed Wilken.

'I think so too, Wilken. Thank you again. I am so sorry to have been so late.'

'That's no matter, Sir. And goodnight master Edward,' he added kindly. He waited until the driver's heavy, booted tread had done echoing along the passages and until he heard the last door close behind him. All fell silent then. It was rather gloomy inside.

Charles's son stood for a while longer, getting briefly adjusted to the familiar surroundings and adjusting himself in his own mind to the unfamiliar circumstances in which he fancied he might now find himself. His suddenly gained manhood seemed to desert him now and he felt crushed to admit that, in his father's eyes, he would probably be no more than a silly schoolboy. A sacked one at that.

It was past eleven o'clock. He knew that his father normally liked to be in bed at least half an hour earlier than this. It would not improve his temper to be kept out of it much longer. He hastened his step towards the study.

The door was open. His father was standing in front of the empty fireplace. Before his son could greet him, this stocky, greying, rather lame man took two steps across the carpet. He stood squarely before his son.

'I have received an unfortunate telephone call,' he

announced gruffly. His words sank into the fishing pictures, guns, rods and stuffed animals on the walls. Teddy felt as inanimate as any of these; like one of the game-birds encased in their glass sanctuaries.

'Yes, father, I suppose that you have.'

His father never swore, even if he felt like it, which made his upbraidings all the more uncomfortable for their retained reasonableness and disciplined calm. This was almost the first reproof that Teddy had ever had; almost the last, too.

Despite the summer air, the silence was chilly. Charles outstared his son, who felt enfeebled in his present insignificant rôle. The romantic *seigneur* had deserted him. He felt paltrily at a loss.

'So, finally, you have succeeded in making a mess of everything. A mess I can only be ashamed of. What, I am asking myself, is what will become of you?' he asked rhetorically.

'I wonder indeed,' he said after a pause. Charles expected no answer either to his statements or his questions. It was almost a soliloquy.

'When the post arrives tomorrow, it will bring me the letter that Mr Worseley promised. Then I will learn the full truth. You may take yourself to bed, Edward. We will talk of the matter further when I summon you. I am now fifty-seven. You and Foley are my only sons, my only progeny, indeed. I hope that there is not worse to learn of you. Of you, Edward in whom I did put my trust.'

The son made to speak, but his father was evidently much upset. He motioned him silently from his presence. After a choked word of good-night, he walked up the great, wide staircase to bed. He did not disturb his mother who, by now, would have been sweetly sleeping for an hour or more. He eventually found the sleep of shame and his eyes welled with tears as he did so.

Frederick Worseley did not equivocate. Enclosed with his own was Teddy's letter to Mary, written in love and simple longing on the eve of the cricket match. How pathetic the game and the adventure seemed to him now! Although he was perhaps too critical of himself, for he had a genuine, honest heart.

Alone in his study, Charles opened the letter. He recognised the precise, crimped writing and from whence the letter had come. It was the one that, among all his correspondence, he had chosen to open last:

> *Shelley's*
> *Leybourne Drive*
> *Penshurst*
> *Kent*
>
> *Sunday*
>
> *Dear Mr Osmond,*
> *It is my painful duty to enclose with this letter a disgraceful missive written by your son, who dishonours your name.*
> *As has the servant concerned been dismissed, so your son also. Your son has not, unfortunately, completed his public examinations, but immorality has no excuse and the welfare of others around him must be fully considered. He has damaged and contaminated sufficiently already, one must suppose, the fine, upright reputation of this House.*
> *Yours truly,*
> *F.D. Worseley*
> *P.S. Your fees no doubt will be forthcoming at the usual date.*
> *F.D.W.*

'I will give you, Edward, two months in which to think what to do with your life. That is, for the present, all that I have to say,' began Charles.

'May I not join you on the farm, father?'

'You have distressed your mother to such an extent that I am not at the moment able to say. Anyhow, who are you to ask me any favours?'

Charles turned his back and looked out of a window on to the quiet, pastel-shaded rose-garden. A world of worthless, wordless regrets welled up inside him; a grim foreboding invaded him.

'I wonder whether there will be another letter from somewhere?' enquired Charles of no one in particular.

Just six weeks before Teddy's decision was supposed to be made, a second volcano erupted. The decision was then and there made for him. A further letter arrived, albeit couched in a rather different style.

> *218 Terrace Gardens*
> *Brighton*

> *Dear Mr Osmond*
>   *I am no scoler as yer may see from my riting. But I must contak yer orl the same. Yore son did me rong and he will have ter pay for it. I am now three month gorn and am going ter keep the child. I must ave sumthink ter live orf of. I am livin with my arnty and she as nuthin ter speke of. So yore check fer mony would be wellcom. I knows you ain't bad orf so I will acsep five thousan. Then me and the child is caterd for. You can aford it so stump up quik or ile spill the beens. I got another arnty ner Devizes. Fact is yer doan want a harf gipsy relashon in the famly de yer? I could easy come over and live with yore Teddy, mind.*
>   *I know I will ear from yer soon.*
>   *Mary Devrel*

Where would it all end? wondered Charles in quiet anger in the cool of a harvest morning. It ended soon enough, however. He rang his bell. Anne Force came in, bent-backed now, grim and nearly dotty too. Charles thought her a ghastly old woman and none too clean either.

'Please fetch me master Edward at once.'

'I doan know as 'e's in the 'ouse, Sir,' she croaked.

'Well, wherever he is, find him.' Charles was not usually peremptory with his servants, but now he was beside himself.

'Very good, Sir!' she rasped and stumped unevenly out of the room, her dirty heels emerging with every scraping step from the backs of her rung-over shoes.

'God!' exclaimed the Master. He did not know whether he was railing against, or praying to, God.

Soon he heard Edward. He came along the flagged passage with a step rather less sprightly than usual. When those whom you really love, upon whom you have perhaps doted excessively, offend you, your anger nearly exceeds its bounds and is tinged with regret and self-criticism all the more bitter because you do not want to blame yourself. Charles had worked himself into a fine fury in the short space of half an hour. Never could he remember having been quite so sadly angry. Although it was barely ten o'clock in the morning, he caught himself pouring a rather larger than ordinarily large whisky. Offence flushed his face. As the footsteps halted outside the bounds of his lair, he turned away to take an unhealthy gulp. Edward stood mute. He knew that it would be 'Edward' this time.

Charles paused to regain a little breath, and more of the composure that he knew at once would now desert him.

'Come in here, just you come in here now, you stupid little bastard, and shut the door behind your idiotic arse! Sit on it or stand as you please!'

Teddy had never heard his beloved father speak in this way before. He stood rooted to the worn carpet, breathing hard and going paler by the second. His eyes stared wandering round the familiar room. He thought ineffectively that the friendly old furniture might help him and recognise him from happier days. But all the oak pieces seemed to turn their back, keeping a disinterested silence. Friendless, he stared blankly ahead.

'Here I am, Father, you wanted to see me.'

'Yes and what?' exclaimed the tough old landowner. 'Yes and what, I may say! You sprawling, lounging, Godabandoned idiot! You've done it now. You've ripped it good and proper. Look at what you have done to me and then you may hear what you have done to yourself. Read this bugger just for a bloody start!'

The father's tough hand was trembling with rage, his face purple, as he shoved the illiterate letter of demand directly under his son's nose.

'Just take a good read of that, you selfish bloody ignoramus. My gentle Christ, if I were younger, I'd take a crop to your bloody carcass, whip you from Hell to breakfast-time and tear your little balls off!'

Not even when a careless labourer had ruined, by stupid inattention, a valuable piece of farm machinery, had Teddy heard his father speak in such a way. Under sheets of uncontrollable rage, all his doting love seemed to disappear. But he never thought, even then, that this was more than a forgivable passing moment of undue choler. He was to learn better; far better and far worse.

He took the piece of lined paper offered him, hardly knew what he was reading, and slowly reached the end of the letter, which he handed back.

'Well, the little bitch! Of all the ghastly things to do!' he gasped without colour or conviction in his weakish voice.

' "Little bitch", you say', Charles blustered, "Of all the things to do", you say. You're wet behind the ears. All she is is a nymphomaniac peasant with a shrewd eye to the main chance. Don't you see, you bloody little fool, that she actually wanted you, yes, wanted you to get her pregnant? Which is exactly what you gave yourself the privilege of doing. Now she's made, isn't she? Now she's got enough money out of seducing you to retire from servitude. All thanks to you, you bloody little bugger. And who's paying, glorious son of mine? I sodding well am and not bloody glad of it.' He paused for breath after this tirade.

'But,' and here Charles's voice became extraordinarily calm, almost with undertones of revenge in it, 'you will be paying later, my lad. You will not be joining me in the farm. It will finally never be yours. I was going to offer you, as my father did to me, a choice. I offered the same to Foley and he took it. I was going to offer you twenty thousand pounds or a partnership. As matters stand now, I will give you ten thousand. You will have no inheritance. You have therefore forfeited ten thousand pounds for your whore and your entire share in the farm. I don't care where you go or what you do. You can clear out of this house and off this land before tomorrow noon.'

'But Father, listen to ...'

'Bugger off out of my life and stew in your own expensive filth!'

A coarse and unforgiving farewell.

Edward, as he henceforth thought of himself, was to see his father only twice again in his life. Both occasions provided bitter, strange encounters, as futile as they were unproductive and without love.

He bade his mother farewell. He was only to see her once more. He was speechless with tears and unable to say anything at all coherent. He tried with a supreme, unfluent effort all he knew to console her and promise better. Her convulsive, shoulder-shaking grief allowed her no comprehension at all. At last he left. His heart was as full of grief as it was empty of hope. It appeared that he was to begin life for a second time.

3

Two Brothers

Teddy had always been the complete optimist. Expecting things to go his way, he was delighted when they did and desperately despondent when they did not. As with all true optimists, however bleak the prospect, he was usually quick to recover with enough courage to meet the next disaster. When this occurred, he would feel almost completely at a loss before what he considered must have been a total miscarriage of justice and a misjudgement of himself. Life was unfair at these times, if not incomprehensible.

Foley was the reverse. A cynical pessimist, he expected the darkest and worst but afforded himself only the slight pleasure of a wry smile when things turned out well. This attitude helped him to remain tenacious in his already successful business undertakings. It did not seem to worry him that he did not attract friends; they could prove unwanted and expensive social appendages. He found such connections tiresomely unrewarding; at times necessary for commercial interests, when he would humour them without conscience. By 1930, he was well on his way to becoming a rich man. At the time when Teddy hit London, Foley was twenty-nine and prospering whilst his brother was a green eighteen.

Foley had bought himself a smart flat in Kensington, which he had had furnished economically and with no taste.

He gave small dinner parties now and again to influential customers and to a few selected friends, provided that the latter were influential too. The Bordeaux-London liaison had gone unbelievably well. A cautiously ambitious reappraisal of the company's London business had led Foley into a succession of swift, well-considered decisions. He had increased the outlets – and its profits – threefold in four years. Now, after just over a decade in the business, he had opened a dozen discreet, tasteful, old-fashioned wine shops for wholesale and retail trade in several of the wealthier and more select quarters of the capital. From his apparently small stake in the affairs of Boucher Fragolard Osmond et Cie, he was doing well. In order to make his share of the profits redeem his working partnership, he had been willing to live frugally off cheese, rolls and soup. His suits were the cheapest he could wear with decorum and he never took out women. He knew his clientèle; after all, he should have done because it was he who had chosen it. Dignified butlers who bought for the cellars of their town-house employers were frequent customers and Mr Osmond's personal advice was sought in camera. Department stores and restaurants had begun to consult him on a grander scale, referring to him as 'our importer'. His reliability had won him a reputation. None of his customers – or "clients" as he spoke of them publicly – ever invited this grey, efficient phantom to their houses or clubs. This suited him well; he had nothing to repay. Within a few years and thanks to a great deal of hard work and straight talking, he had insinuated himself into a powerful position. It was true that he had issued some very gentlemanly threats to the upper échelons that he might sell his share; leave the company and sell beer in the East End unless his expertise were valued more highly. Soon he had won himself a half-share in the company, partly due, it must be said, to the demise of Monsieur Boucher whose name remained upon the labels, of course. Foley was made.

Justifiably complacent and therefore in no haste, he turned his somewhat clinical attention towards finding a wife, in the same businesslike fashion as that in which he would have gone about promoting a little-known wine with a hitherto unacceptable label. 'If Mr Osmond says so, you buy it', was a frequent refrain among the fashionable (and pseudo-fashionable) rich. However, it proved that 'just because Osmond says so' did not seem to be enough to find him a wife, much less to endear him to a potential one. Womankind, he discovered (slightly to his discomfiture) was not so susceptible to mercantile dealing.

Although his brother did not know it, Foley had been apprised of his sudden fall from grace. Charles had written to Foley and, in a letter of violent reaction to his favourite son's 'unaccountable conduct of himself', enjoined him neither to cushion his existence nor to be in any way weak with him.

'Let the little devil sink or swim by his own efforts, or by the lack of them!' he wrote vindictively. He need not have worried. Foley had never known, nor ever would know, the finer feelings of compassion.

Predictably, even understandably, Foley had no intention of doing anything for his brother. The latter, although he knew where Foley lived, knew also he would not care which side of any surface of the earth he occupied. For once he was right; his rich brother did not give a moment's thought for him, let alone give him anything concrete in the shape of advice or help. The elder knew that the younger would eventually contact him and for that event he was quite prepared to wait in an uninterested kind of way. There would be nothing forthcoming at the end of any contact in any case, since the rich brother had always resented the more lavishly-accorded affection that the now poor one had received. More than this, he could not see any good reason for helping anyone who could not possibly be of any material use to him. A wayward brother of an indolent if charming nature, soon with an illegitimate child to adorn his fame, would, after all, hardly increase his sales of the best Bordeaux, let alone enhance his relations with the discerning rich. Had Foley analysed his feelings, he would have been ashamed of them.

He found his own particular unsuccess in the snubbing glances of women. At their hands – if ever he got as far as those – he knew a humiliation that he could not admit. This is why he became cold towards them and remained without knowledge of their nature. He viewed them with what he considered a deserved contempt. He did not care for people who baulked him in any field.

It was not long after Teddy came to London that Foley met Joan Hubertson at a party. Although he could not have known it – and who knows anything but the most foreseeable about the future? – his meeting with this small, auburn-headed creature of no particular social standing but, as he thought, of considerable physical attraction, would influence a good deal of his life at different stages.

Foley had had various and coldish passing affairs of no great depth or reward. No woman looking at him could decide whether or not he was a dedicated virgin, perhaps set on a path of deliberate and perpetual abstinence in favour of his bank balance or whether, inside him, there were the poor, trapped spirits of Legion, struggling for an inhibited and none-too-easy release. In rare moments of introspection, he was sometimes given to wonder about these matters himself. But he soon pulled himself out of these short abstractions in favour of concentration on more profitable things. If he dressed himself up with any enthusiasm or pleasant anticipation, it was for a fashionable and, he hoped, profitable wine-tasting.

But Joan Hubertson was different. Foley learnt fairly swiftly that although Joan showed herself not averse to the lusts of the flesh, higher upon her list of priorities featured the companionship of wealth and its attendant prospect of a comfortable, cosseted life. So money, it appeared, guided them both, but it guided them alternately one step towards, one step away, one from the other. The question would be in which way the final step would be taken.

*

Foley met Joan at a small party given in the flat below his own in Kensington. Hitherto, he had hardly glimpsed its occupants. Her father, a disused empire-building major from the Indian Army, had just retired. His querulous, demanding wife had a voice like a nutmeg grater and a taste for London life. She was possessed of a face and a manner of speech, neither of which belonged to her. At times of stress or after a rather too heavy intake of sherry, the latter slipped, giving place to a rather irritating home counties vowel or two. She was small and thought that she was beautiful for ever, but years'-long inattention to the ravages of colonial climates upon her complexion had rendered her face like a russet apple, dusted lightly with bakers' flour. The emaciated remnant of once beautiful hands carried the now contracted rings that she had forced her malleable husband to buy her. Even though possessed of a small private income, he had never easily been able to afford his wife. Now she made increasingly frequent inroads into his dwindling capital by throwing inadequately-funded parties for her attractive daughter. Upon these rather faded occasions, there was never enough of anything, when empty glasses became hot in the hand before they were half-filled again with cocktails which tasted like hair-oil. Nevertheless, through this unlikely and largely unsuccessful expedient, she set out to catch someone rich for her daughter Joan, who would be just as interested in getting rid of her future husband's capital as her mother had been beforehand with her father.

Accordingly, one night, James Hubertson opened the door to Foley. The major's white moustache, bristly but neatly trimmed, seemed freshly gummed to his weak, red face. He looked perpetually stunned, if not overcome, by the sledgehammer of life. A pith helmet would have topped him off, thought his visitor. A pair of watery, blue eyes twinkled a tired welcome.

'Do come in, Mr Osmond and, if I may say so, it is indeed agreeable to see you.'

63

Foley uttered imparticularities and entered without grace.

'Come in,' repeated the major from behind him, 'and join our little gathering. You will find that everything is in full swing, as they say!'

The full swing was evidently not much to shout about. A few dessicated ladies of a certain age were steeping their parched lips in the usual, greasy cocktails of low alcoholic content. Scattered, superannuated bachelors of unlikely countenance, primped up for the occasion, adorned the walls and some of the furniture. Vulgar cravat pins and spurious signet rings did not entirely persuade one of the elevated status of the guests.

Foley mingled, as he was perpetually and annoyingly enjoined to do, with the crowd, small in number as it was. He was spoken to about the political scene, the weather, the price of writing paper and the modern prevalence of bad manners. His interlocutors did not know that he cared about nothing so much as his own pocket. Any other considerations might be important, although they would always remain secondary.

Occasionally however, a brave sexual thought rose to the level at which he, with his slight perception, could recognise it. He noticed Joan had drunk four too many of her father's Indian cocktails. The distant Raj seemed to beckon faintly. They fell into a halting conversation about trivialities, during which she drew increasingly close to his uninviting person.

It was at this point that he noticed that her armpits' fragrance was somewhat unlovely, to him at least, but she nevertheless breathed a sexual desire born, as it must have been, of higher things. Ambition and money could go to bed with anyone, she thought. She knew that Foley was well on his way to real wealth and if his physical charms did not interest her greatly at outer sight, she yet thought that she could learn to love him for his needs and his money. He did not beckon her but, to their mutual surprise, they discovered that they were not exactly averse to one another.

Foley, normally cold, became intrigued by the situation. It smacked of a business challenge. He knew that he ought to get married in order to enhance his image of solidarity and reliability in the false, high commercial circles in which he moved. Thoughts and dreams scattered themselves and spread through his mind in a lightning space, so that worlds were encompassed in moments. This, he supposed clinically, was what was happening and what was supposed to happen. In a none-too-savoury instant, he knew in his calculating mind that he would be able to command her body whenever and if ever he wanted it. She would prostitute herself willingly for her social and financial aspirations. For a short moment, he wanted her. He promptly made an appointment, between further banal exchanges, for the next evening. This was to be a dinner at a famous London Indian restaurant. A good, hot dinner might do something for us, he persuaded himself.

In this way, he played her along. After a drink at a rather stuffy hotel, they bored themselves mutually over an excellent Madras. It was possible that they realised that they were two unattractive people with a common need, not so much physically as in the soul. A sort of inhuman depravity compelled them one towards the other and a relationship devoid of loving or forgiving opened between them. Lust has an ugly face when unaccompanied by self-respect; a virtue for which neither gave a rap at that time.

Foley drove Joan home after their first so-called encounter, promising himself that he would make her the hungrier for him in that he had not taken her to his flat the first time. All the same, their dinner-time absence was more prolonged than her father would have liked, but his scruples were easily overcome before the prospect of an alluring financial arrangement in the event of all being brought to fruition. Not bodily yet, he hoped. Foley was entering the world of impoverished morality, knowing without caring. Teddy's kind, simple and loving heart would have been disgusted.

With intentions guided strictly by his own immediate requirements, Foley invited Joan to dinner a couple of nights later. With hypocritical decorum, he called in the early evening at the major's flat, drove her out to a drink instead of inviting her to his own apartments and took her afterwards to a modest restaurant where he regaled her with a modest meal, a modest wine, a watery coffee and no liqueur, all at a modest price.

'We shall have a liqueur at home.' he stated flatly. Neither felt the need nor the desire to talk. Each knew that the other had his and her own duty respectively.

'How nice of you, Foley.' Joan was just beginning to feel the desire more than the duty.

She could hardly swallow her cognac quickly enough before beckoning him to the bedroom, where she started to undress with untimely haste. She was evidently not a stranger to this routine, probably in the interests of her father's straitened circumstances. Foley, fastidious as always, found this performance disgraceful and distasteful but, knowing that his money was the only attribute that could draw anyone towards him, he put up with the displays of this common little woman. After all, he told himself, she had all to lose and he nothing much to gain. He might as well take a grim advantage. She was about to become victim to cold, licensed rape.

Afterwards, she could not quite make up her mind whether their lovemaking had been a disappointment or something of a new experience. She decided, after contemplation, that it had been like going to bed with a frog. On his side, it was neither more nor less than a kind of sadistic relief. But that was only after their first time. The dismal little dinners gradually became more frequent, eventually to assume the pattern of regularity. Proportionately, their passions became more outlandishly private, both taking a certain depraved pleasure in them. After a few weeks, Joan came to like her partner's selfish brutality. He murdered her breasts and made her gloriously sore. Teddy would have been revolted to the pit of his gentle heart. Joan came to enjoy making his ingratitude rise to her further demands. Money and sex mingled into a half-world, cloudy in its reciprocal gratifications, entirely without love.

They both grew to love the evil of anti-love. It was a dangerous and potent reversal of natural procedures which, for a time, drew them close in the vicarious pleasure of being lower than animals. They both had grasped what they thought to be life in a spirit of mean selfishness. It was this that eventually sterilised their poor lives.

The couple now went out to an early dinner once a week. The wine was free because it was purveyed by Boucher Fragolard Osmond et Cie, which was why their range of establishments never varied. It was enough, regardless of the quality of the meal, to commend itself to Foley. An unlate meal ensured an unlate return to his flat which ensured a small, clinical orgy, an early return of Joan to the flat below and a prompt attendance at work the following morning. She thought that her parents did not suspect her forays into a sexual relationship of which they did not suppose that she would have approved. In fact, had she but known it, they would have approved her relationship with an Egyptian donkey as long as it had a bank balance of adequate proportions to absolve them of their responsibilities towards her. They even hoped that some of the affluence of a well-contracted marriage might devolve upon them by some lucky, pimpish proxy. Their respectability thus became obscene. This aspect of their noblesse oblige had not escaped Foley's notice either.

As for him, he could ditch her at any time, without prejudice, regret much less. There were, after all, plenty of pitiful little girls who were the victims of grasping respectability posing as *aristocratie déchue*. Cavorting was fun, especially upon a bed of share certificates.

Foley was thinking of disencumbering himself of Joan when something presented itself from a completely unexpected quarter. Foley had changed his mind. Unknown to him, Joan also was already tiring of his regulated, irregular behaviour, his clockwork meanness and his calculated expenditure of love. She felt like a parcel done up for the post-box, like that of the weekly, sickly chocolates that she was doomed to receive at every cheap theatre performance to which she was commanded regularly. The chocolates were neatly packed, opened, swallowed and sickly dismissed, eventually to be consigned to the sewerage system of Kensington. No word of permanent relationship, let alone of marriage, had ever passed her lover's lips. It had not crossed his mind either. His life, her life, she thought, promised no more hope of delight or of the unexpected than the predictable clack of a metronome.

Eventually, after six months of even dismality, interspersed with sexual activities which she did not find elevating, she determined to be rid of him. It was true that, in a perverse and almost perverted way, she had enjoyed his bed and his body. For that she could have settled had she not demanded a good deal more. As it was, marriage had not been mentioned, neither therefore had money. She realised sadly and with some annoyance that she had, once again, advanced no further forward than a dubious spinsterhood. She had come away with the worst of a bad bargain.

It was just as she was casting around again – and her mother's mediocre cocktails hardly attracted all the world, with or without his wife – that something happened fortuitously to end her plaintive recriminations. She had not yet learnt that stars do not descend to demand; neither did she realise that some were made of tinsel. As she always would, she disregarded real substances in favour of the dazzlement of unreality. Her petty world was doomed to the ravages of a perpetual tarnish until much later.

Suddenly one night, Foley proposed to her. She accepted. Open-eyed she had embraced hell. Her father and mother were delighted. Joan's was not a truly mercenary soul; it would one day be relieved; but not before it had crossed a desert.

Meanwhile, Teddy had not much to encumber his life or his person. Certainly, very little luggage. A suitcase and two trunks, together with the clothes in which he stood on Devizes railway station that September day, comprised the totality of his material possessions. His mind was a complete blank. He had no idea what he would do. The end of his present journey would have to suffice for the time being, he thought, and then something would turn up.

'Waterloo station is your destination' an unidentified voice seemed perpetually to be saying in his ear, 'Waterloo station is your destination'. As the train clicked over the hot, summer rails, this silly refrain ticked evenly in his head. He could not rid himself of it. People with a perpetual fear of heights cannot rid themselves of the desperate dream of falling from their tenuous grip of a loose shrub at the top of a sheer cliff or of falling over the balcony of a tenth floor flat. Teddy was, in the same way, afraid of the future and of the void in his mind which induced this ridiculous and inane jingle.

As he roasted in the close atmosphere of his second class compartment, he adjusted the waistcoat of his only suit and eased his jacket under his armpits. They were sweating. He felt his wallet in his inside pocket under his left arm to assure himself that he still had enough with which to pay for something. It contained two five pound notes, now no longer crisp in the stuffy heat. The ten thousand pound cheque was already in his bank in London. Despite the realisation that immediate starvation did not threaten, he was becoming less and less debonair and self-assured as the iron miles increased the distance between him and his prosperous, calm, country family. He felt vulnerable, dejected and remote. The optimist in him nearly drowned in a flood of repressed tears; that kind is always the most painful; they sting you behind the eyes. No matter what the optimism nor the outward bravery, nothing can hide the pure sentiment of sadness.

Force majeure, as the French say, overcame his passing debility. Ten thousand pounds would open ten thousand opportunities, he thought ambitiously. He would be able (he told himself), to stand back for a moment and consider the prospects that life was sure to offer him. Had he taken the same posture to look at himself, perhaps that would have given him a better chance. He did not, as it happened, look very much further than the end of his funds. The fact that even limited good fortune is a privilege had no impact upon him.

Waterloo was hot and crowded with people. An anonymity which he had not encountered before on the farm or in the peaceful enclaves of his school House, in which places he had led all his life, invaded and enveloped him completely.

'No one knows me here', he said to himself unnecessarily. Porters passed him by in favour of first class passengers, nameless crowds thronged intently towards their own goals. They too were nameless and unknown. He felt that everyone, except himself, was going to some appointed place. This was not an inaccurate judgement.

Behind the train and beyond the dirty Victorian glass canopy, the bright, hot rails shone in the dying sun. The heat rays arose from their callous, inevitable metal in the sulphurous late-afternoon heat. Teddy thought of them, as he gazed backwards, leading to the farm rather than the other way to a new life which held he knew not what. He was not really a hewer of wood or drawer of water, but there was no wood here, no water either, merely the alien cries of strange people in a smoky wilderness. He felt that his own loneliness was mirrored in that of the begging children and the tired prostitutes. But he assuaged his own desperation in the thoughts of a comfortable existence not far off and for the time being. Tomorrow would take care of itself, he thought erroneously.

On the empty, hot and dusty platform, he waited indecisively for a porter. Eventually one arrived. It was the end of a hot day for him too.

'A taxi then, Sir?' The wizened, wiry little man had a powerful moustache which looked as if it could have benefited from a good soak of beer.

'Thank you, but I think that you may need a trolley for my baggage.'

'There's not many 'ere, Sir. I'll carry the two big cases and you take the small one.'

Teddy felt even more insignificant and lost than ever as the porter took off at a brisk pace for the barrier. It was hardly an elegant beginning; the new master of his new life trotting behind an impatient porter.

'Where yer orf ter, then?' asked the porter, without any great deference.

'Hammersmith, I think,' said Teddy unconfidently.

Once he was installed in the noisy and badly driven taxi, which smelt of late-afternoon Havanas at the best, the cabby asked him where 'hexackly' he wanted to go?

'I would like to find a small hotel. Nothing too expensive, you understand. I am just starting off in London, you see,' he added by way of explanation.

'I'll just drive orf a bit, then,' returned the cabby, dropping the 'Sir' conspicuously.

'This is abaht your 'ammer, I fink. Clean but nice, as they say. Fourteen and a tanner.'

Teddy paid and gave a small tip. He had been conveyed without great ceremony to the Hotel Torquay which was situated in an airless and dusty side street. He carried his own baggage, in two relays, to the grimy circular swing door. The hall was built and decorated like an Egyptian public lavatory and smelt as stale as a collapsing empire. Years of introdden cigar ash made the carpets look even more well-worn than they were, and lent the air – and not much of that circulated here – an odour of second-hand *richesse*, for the day only. A couple of dusty aspidistras and a punctured sofa led the way to a sombre mahogany counter at the end of an otherwise empty hallway. No one was behind the counter. Teddy rang an ivory button set in a verdigrised bell-push. A blowsy woman in bedroom slippers answered his second application.

'Good evening,' offered Teddy in a dispirited voice.

Mrs Tooley did not answer at once. Drabness seemed to deprive her of words. Her flabby, unencased breasts drooped hopelessly misclad over the counter. She regarded her new customer without any great interest.

'Yes, dear? Just one night or longer and are you alone, then?'

As she had done herself, her voice had evidently retired long ago. She had gone hopelessly to seed and was too weary of life to worry about it.

'One week at least,' Teddy assured her.

'Just on yer own are yer? All the time?'

'Just on my own,' answered Teddy, feeling very much so.

'Well then, dear, you best take number eighteen. Quid a night that is. Pay in advance. Just hand over the green ones and sign on the dotted.'

'Green ones?' asked Teddy.

'Yes, dear. Quids, pound notes, greenbacks, white ones if yer like.'

Her small puffy eyes opened wide when he handed over two white fivers. The film of the morning's gin seemed to disappear as if by enchantment. The gleam of her pupils fairly started out against the blotchy rouge of her shrivelled cheeks.

'Shall I keep the rest, Sir, in case you wants a possible extension of your stay?' she asked eagerly.

'You may as well. heaven knows what I shall be doing or where I shall be going,' he muttered, betraying quietly his deep and sudden uncertainty.

The landlady understood him completely and assumed an air of sympathetic complicity. She had received failed gentlemen before but had never hesitated to kick them out once the money ran short.

'If there's anything else you should be wantin', Sir, any kind of company fer instance, I can personally arrange anything to suit.'

'Thank you, Mrs Tooley, but I think that I shall be fine on my own for the time being.'

Despite everything, he all at once thought of Mary.

A few faded photographs and a couple of nicotined prints led up the linoleumed stairs to the first floor, after which there was nothing further to hide the yellow plaster than the stained, torn wallpaper which hardly did that either. The nearer that he approached the reaches of Room Eighteen, the further he felt from home. He even regretted the hot, late September smell of the railway, which he had so recently left and which was slightly closer to home. Even Waterloo station would have seemed home to him now. He installed himself in his tiny bedroom in the Hotel Torquay. The ozonic air of that resort was more than a sniff and a railway ticket from here! On the spot, even before he pulled back the bedclothes, Teddy had resolved upon something better. This conviction was strengthened by the stained counterpane, the moth-eaten blankets and the coarse, yellow-white sheets.

Teddy decided to leave and rent a flat as soon as his week at Mrs Tooley's had expired. But what would he do?

With no particular end in mind, he walked round the corner to the nearest pub. It was shabby, rowdy and jocular. He ordered himself a pint of bitter which he started to drink at a beer-washed table. His smart clothes were noticed by the people sitting near and next to him. He fell in with some fish traders who told him that fish was certainly the thing. They asked him what he was doing looking like a country gent in London. He told them his story. They were immediately sympathetic. After a good few more beers, not at his own expense, he had signed a large cheque to the credit of a downtown chain of fish shops with the promised expectation of a quick fortune. His problems had been solved in however undistinguished a manner. His share would ensure that all he would have to do was to stroll around in his suit and bowler to see that all was being conducted as it should be. A sound if inelegant start, he thought to himself.

After six months, he had received hardly any revenue. His quite pleasant flat cost him more than he could afford. He wondered why the good people of Whitechapel bought none of the lobster or oysters that he had commanded to be displayed in every shop. he had no head for business and was easily duped. The sum of money that his father had given him was rapidly dwindling, whilst his flat was always noisy with friends regaled generously with expensive drinks and trays of delicacies. He never seemed to recognise fair weather friends, of whom he had plenty while his money lasted.

By October 1931, Edward Osmond, son of a very rich farmer and brother to a rich entrepreneur was in dire financial straits.

4

Marriage and Return

Joan and Foley were married in 1931. They accepted one another placidly. It was an icy, February day, augur perhaps of the icy relationship that they would enjoy. The small London church was hardly packed. Charles Osmond presented himself, Major Hubertson and his wife, a few friends and Monsieur Fragolard, adorned with a carnation buttonhole. Teddy arrived in rather shabby style, but gave his brother two silver napkin rings and his wife some beckoning glances. These she appeared to receive willingly. Clearly, she was not enjoying the proceedings. He then knew, as they both knew in that electric second, that both were capable of the sort of love of which Foley would always be totally ignorant. His cold body was and would ever be an invitation to a depraved kind of gloom, the door to dread, fear and dissatisfaction.

The reception was hardly a joyous affair. Major Hubertson could not afford it, so Foley got a rather staid restaurant to do it. There was plenty of uninteresting buffet food to eat and the champagne was very moderate.

After some dreary speeches, one of which Teddy was not invited to make, people circulated cautiously as if they were treading upon the ice of a new era. They were. It was during this unfestive invitation that Joan came up to Teddy, who was standing alone by an ugly Victorian fireplace.

'Hello, you're Foley's brother, aren't you?'

'Yes,' replied Teddy, 'I am.'

Teddy, who had already started to become a little maudlin, told her spontaneously about his unspectacular life to date. She listened with sympathy, telling him that her own had not been altogether a bowl of cherries.

'Then I hope it will be now,' said Teddy unhopefully.

'Yes,' muttered Joan, looking sad and rather remote.

It was then that they looked into each other's eyes and struck a spontaneous friendship, although they could not have known it in those little seconds. At the same time, they both seemed to feel sorry for they did not quite know what.

'It has been so nice to have seen you,' said Joan, 'and we will certainly not lose touch.'

'I hope not,' replied Teddy, sincerity in his deep blue eyes.

Teddy pitied Joan and perhaps she pitied him too. One day later she did. Teddy thought how miserable and small she looked on her wedding day. Her lovely breasts looked lifeless, sunk and unsearched-for. As it happened, Joan was soon to know the sour taste of a kind of demanding frigidity, the love of a living corpse, the experience of being a mere piece of machinery, designed only as a device for unfeeling gratification. She would thenceforward always long for the spontaneous warmness of Teddy, which she had guessed even in that brief encounter. A foolish man he was in many ways, but he was imbued with real kindness.

Teddy thought of Mary whenever he looked at another woman. He supposed that this was some kind of fidelity. It was, in a way. His heart screamed its poor hope for his lover and for his son, for whom, one day, his pride would know no bounds.

By the age of nineteen, Teddy was bankrupt. The fish business had collapsed, partly due to his ineptitude and partly due to the rapaciousness of his partners. He had only enough off which to live for a fortnight. He thought that he would have to appeal to his family. He did so first to his Father.

He had to write two letters because the first was unanswered. He begged him to help him, with the promise of repayment. He said that he would look for other outlets and advantages and that this time things would go better. He admitted that he had certainly made mistakes but that he never meant anyone any harm. Would it be possible for him to come back to the farm? Could he be forgiven? Could his loving heart and soul rest in peace? He would, he declared, work for nothing other than love. He received this letter:

> *Hetherick Farm*
> *Sunday*
>
> *Edward,*
> *You have been excluded from this family. This was an exclusion that I will not waive. You may come to my funeral if you wish.*
> *Charles Osmond*

Teddy was devastated by this letter. He could not believe that love could have been so suddenly withered and perished to nothing. His heart felt emptied of all the lovely things with which it had once been filled. All he wanted was for somebody to hold his hand in his time of need. He wanted, unselfishly, to be given a present from God, in the same way as he had given his love to Mary. There were, however, two more bullets that he was yet to receive.

He decided to write to Foley. This heralded the first one.

> *Whitechapel*
> *Tuesday*
>
> *My dear Foley,*
> *Having had some rather bad luck recently in regard to my business venture, I have to admit to you that I am nearly penniless. I do not wish to ask you for money, but would you be prepared to employ me in your business? I am willing to learn about wine and I am good at establishing personal relationships which might enhance trading connections.*
> *I look forward to hearing from you as soon as you can manage.*
> *Your brother,*
> *Edward*

The reply was not long in coming. It was obviously typed by some secretary and only cursorily signed as a matter of routine by Foley.

Kensington
Thursday

Dear Edward,
Although your admirable ability in regard to personal relationships is well known, the answer to your enquiry is No and always will be.
Catch a safe ship.
Yours,
Foley

The next bullet was both a deep pain and a magnificent delight. Teddy, being a very sensitive man, did not know which emotion to savour most or first. He was incredibly moved and equally distressed by the letter that he next received.

218 Terrace Gardens
Brighton
April 3rd 1931

Dear Teddy,
I thort yer would like to know that you now have a son. I have called his name John. Thanks to the ten thousan yer farther gave me we will be alrite. Doan bother ter see me if yer doan wont ter but yer may like ter see yer boy. Probably yer doan believe me but I love yer arfter all. You go yer own way an I'll go mine. Does little John tare yer eart strings? Come an see us. I'm sorry but I ad to do wot I done.
Same kisses as wen yer wos a boy,
Mary Devrel

Teddy wept in his miserable bedroom. He wept until his eyes nearly fell out. He wept for his first love and for his second. No, they came first equal. He must see Mary and

John. They were part of his body, mind and soul. They were the stuff of which he was made. God had made all three of them into a unity which was indissoluble. He felt a man and a fool at the same time. He decided to go at once to Brighton. He bought Mary a little gold ring for her wedding finger, in guilty but proud disgrace.

*

Before his visit to Mary, Teddy went to see Joan. He was desperate for money. He was desperate for love also. He knew that she could probably provide neither; a sympathetic ear would do. He loved her and he loved Mary also. He just loved people, everybody. He could not imagine how everything had gone so wrong for him. Loving two women at the same time, without trying to be unfaithful to either, is always a heart-rending process. It holds delights, but they are never simple or without pain.

Teddy arranged with Joan to visit her when he knew that Foley would be away in France. After having descended from his taxi, he rang at the elegant front door of the house in Kensington. A maid opened it into a broad hall, high, hung with expensive pictures of varying tastes and encumbered with numerous pieces of antique furniture. Like its owner, the house smelt stale and felt cold. He was ushered to an upstairs drawing room.

Joan fell without ceremony into his willing arms. Teddy drew her towards him and they each felt the warmth of the other's breast. They kissed at once. They wept silently at the same time, too. Joan's dear face looked prematurely ravaged, her clothes expensively dowdy. In a word, she looked and felt alone. There was no conversation between the two for several silent moments, during which they savoured that forbidden welcome that is so sweet. They ran their fingers through each other's hair, smelling the musk of promise.

'How lovely to see you, Teddy!' exclaimed Joan with a once more youthful smile, her mouth open and lush. 'Don't you think we ought to be more careful? Your body leads to bed, as it must have done before.'

'It has, Joan and I am in a hell of a mess. I wanted to see you for yourself, quite apart from asking a favour which I know you may not be able to grant. I expect that you have got completely the wrong idea!'

'Wrong ideas are just what I need!' replied Joan.

'Well, let's have a few of those in a moment,' suggested Teddy endearingly.

'What's it to be, Teddy? Scotch and soda?'

'I cannot think of anything more contributory to the depressed mind and personality. Pour double the amount which is decent, love!' Joan did exactly that.

'Now,' said Joan, 'sit down far enough away from me so that we do not distract ourselves before … ' And here she cut herself off from what they both knew might happen.

'The fact is, Joan, that I am desperate. My business venture has failed and I am down to my last five hundred pounds. I am living in wretched conditions, but I can put up with that. I have asked both my father and Foley if they could help me, but I have received from each cold and unkind letters. I have just been told by Mary that I have an illegitimate son in Brighton. Father has provided for them and cut me off from my inheritance as a result. There appears nothing to be hoped for in any quarter. I am going to see my son John and his mother Mary tomorrow. Afterwards, it is my intention to enter the Army. Could you lend me any money for a few months and could your father write to help me obtain a commission?'

Joan thought for a moment or two. She was crying with self-pity and compassion at once.

'I cannot give you any money, Teddy,' she replied, 'although I would like to. I am kept on a very short rein and with no allowance. Foley is mean in every respect. I have to account for every farthing that I spend in the house and I am hardly allowed outside it either. That is why your lovely visit is like a breath of fresh air to me. However, I will ask my father to write to the Indian Army Office. Find love in

India!'

'Thank you for your promise about your father's good offices,' replied Teddy dimly, 'but please see him soon.'

'This I certainly will, but you have to pay me in advance, you know!'

Teddy knew. That payment would be sweet.

'What is your marriage with Foley like?' he asked after a pause.

'Suffice it to say that I made a desperately bad mistake.' Joan twisted her fingers, now adorned with heavy, expensive and unlovely rings. Her eyes shone with tears.

'I made the mistake,' she continued, 'in order to help my parents. Foley keeps them and he keeps me in a cage. I hate and fear him. I do not want to bear his children, but I know that I will have to. On the other hand, I will love them as you must love your John. Go and see him and thank God. At least, you have a heart of love, whereas I have wrecked mine for all the wrong reasons.'

A silence fell in the elegant, sterile drawing room.

'Is it so terrible, then?' asked Teddy.

'Desperately bad my love. I am his chattel. He is a brute in bed and his body revolts me. The very sight of him naked turns my stomach. He has the thin hair and the hollow chest of someone satanic.'

Joan's voice spelt hate and loathing. Teddy could see the revulsion in her poor eyes. He took her in his arms and said: 'Let's make each other happy!'

They did exactly that for a blissful afternoon. Their bodies melted into a tender union, which they knew had to be broken before half-past four. They said good-bye full of promises.

Just a few minutes later, Teddy stepped into a wet early evening and Joan into another interval of servitude. She was comforted and happy until Foley's return. Unlike Teddy, she felt no guilt. This emotion swept through him and made him shudder. Without exactly having intended to, he had betrayed his Mary. Always, when he went to bed with a woman, it was a gift of love. Perhaps he could be forgiven because of a kind of innocent purity and gentleness. He promised that, unless it were in India (man is a man and cannot help it) he would never do this again. But he could not know the future.

*

He had come to see Mary and John. His first step was downwards from a train that had stopped on a platform in Brighton. He carried a small bag, filled hastily with what he might need for a couple of nights. The nights over the lead roof, he would remember for ever and a day. Especially the night that had made his son. His love spilled over in advance in a huge effusion of powerless, devoted, hungry pity. All shame had gone now. It was pride, longing and hope for his darlings that drove his intention to help them. Intentions may be grand, but they are not always enough; he was soon to discover this, to his lifetime regret and pride.

Teddy arrived by taxi at 218 Terrace Gardens at shortly after six in the evening. A tall, hard-looking woman opened the door to his ring at the semi-detached, Edwardian terraced house. It bore the name Wastwater. This was depressing enough, in all conscience, but the lady wore hair-curlers and bedroom slippers. She had a face like a bladder of lard. Obviously, she was no blood relation to his lovely Mary. She was her father's daughter without mistake, her dark, lovely complexion she must have owed to his gypsy blood.

Teddy was shown into a small sitting room. It was clean, sparsely furnished and totally without taste. It smelt and looked unused. The cushions upon which he eventually sat were hard.

He waited for Mary in an extraordinary state of wrenching love and expectation. He waited for John, too. His love and his son he could hardly wait to see. A thousand thoughts went through his mind. How could he help them both, deprived as he was of any finance and a failure in business with nothing much to which to look forward? The trouble with Teddy was that he had only love to give. He was waiting to give that now. He would have given life itself, unquestioningly, for anyone he loved.

In came Mary, with little, dark-haired John in her arms.

'Sorry about keepin' yer waitin',' she said, 'I 'ad ter feed 'im.'

Her lovely breasts were swollen with sweet milk and the scent of infant feed reached his nostrils. Mary looked lovely and mature. He reached out his arms for the baby and tenderly took him. He had the brown complexion and the deep black-blue eyes of his mother. Teddy covered his face with kisses and held his strong but tiny hands. He cried for joy and pity. He felt helpless for his deed, grateful at the same time for the inexpressible privilege of fatherhood.

'Mary,' he said, 'I came to see you and John. Thank you for everything. I want to make it right by you and I will. It will take a bit of time, but it will be right.'

'Doan yer worry, Edward. Yer dad's seen us clear an' we's going ter make out. I knewed that 'e told yer that I did it fer the money I'd get. I did it fer yer love, my old boy. When you've made it, come back agin an' I'll be 'appy. If yer wants ter be posh an' marry high, I'll understand.'

Her eyes lowered and grew moist.

'I never want anyone but you and John,' said Teddy, without thinking much of the future. 'I have got to go into the army for a while and I shall be in India. I don't know where or when yet, but I will write. I will send you all the money I can.'

'Yer 'ave no need ter do that, Edward. We are fixed fine, the boy and me.'

'But I want to see to his education and his upbringing, Mary.'

'How can yer do that on peanuts, Edward?'

'I'll find a way, Mary.'

'Doan be talking like that, Edward. I knows yer. I loves yer, but you're all wind and piss.' This was a misjudgement.

Edward gave back John to Mary. he felt full of love and

shame. She took him upstairs and put him to sleep, after a long kiss from his father. Then she came down again into the clinical reception room.

'Come up and make love again, Edward, as we used to. I'm safe now. I can't wait for yer, lover.'

They went upstairs. Their love was long and lingering and their feeling just the same, if not more enhanced than before. They made it with the sad desperation of those who do not know when next they will join. They made many promises that they did not know whether they would be able to keep. What they did keep was the heart of each other, shared in the life of John.

The father left the mother and the son in a cheerless afternoon; warmth and coldness seemed to accompany one another, making an inexplicable, unaccountable mixture of sensation. John, Mary, Joan, father and Foley. They all left his brain in a ferment upon his lonely pillow that night. He cried for all of them, praying for them and for their pity. He was a miserable young man, even if he had grit. Where would all his love go? He did not quite know where his destination was.

*

In 1932, Teddy was twenty and without hope. He hung on for another few weeks in his lodgings, just managing to survive and keep himself clean. He kept on hoping for a letter from Joan's father, the Major. They had come to like one another; probably because they were both disappointed men, they recognised and understood the vulnerabilities of life. People in troubles of one sort or another usually try the exercise of mutual help.

The result of this for Teddy was a commission in the Indian Army which he was granted in the autumn. With what little money and luggage he had, he landed at Bombay bedecked with the humble insignia of a junior subaltern. He was naturally an unmilitary man and felt uncomfortable not only in the humid heat but in any kind of uniform. He felt, quite suddenly, doomed to failure and to a life devoid of challenge or interest. He was, after all, far away from home and from the objects of his love. Although personally courageous, he was no soldier.

The tale of the ensuing eight years is told briefly. This time represented a blank, boring space in his life, sprinkled here and there with a party and a passing affair or two. He did not care greatly for his fellow officers who appeared to him vacant-minded, officious and snobbish by turns. He was stationed in Bangalore, where he was assigned mainly to administration duties, endless parades and tiresome exercises. He met few people outside the army other than the bishop and his family, the latter only because his lordship was a distant relative of his father. They were dull and puritanical people to whom he could impart no information about his previous life. Just to have told somebody of his heartaches would have been of enormous comfort and help; he would so much have loved to have poured out his devotion for Mary and John, to have told them that he loved Joan too. As it was, he had to keep everything to himself, trying not to become introverted the while. He could not write to Joan because of Foley, but he wrote simple letters of love to Mary and his son John.

He had many letters from Mary, in her halting, dialect English. He was to keep them all for the rest of his life. People in the mess wondered about the illiterate handwriting on the frequent envelopes that were put out for him. He used to tell them, with shame in his wounded heart, that they contained news from his father's maid. He said that his father was too ill to write himself and had to dictate everything. He knew that no one believed him. There were suspicious, inane, cruel smiles on the unkind faces of the enquirers. They would have had nothing but contempt for his simple devotion to his sweet lover and his wonderful son. He was right.

One lunchtime in the bar off the mess, as he was treating himself to a rare cocktail before his curry made of tough lamb, he succeeded in dropping his open wallet where he kept his chits for drinks. The wallet was bulging with photographs of Mary and John which she sent regularly and had managed to have had taken with a cheap camera for which he had sent her the money. He could not afford, for the time being, to come home to England, so he thought that letters and photographs would be the best way of keeping in touch. Sheaves of snaps fell all about him on to the floor where he was standing. A couple of young officers helped him to pick them up. While doing so, they looked at them inquisitively.

'You're a dark horse!' one of them exclaimed. 'You never told us about a girl at home!'

'She looks pretty ripe!' said the other coarsely. 'I bet she's a good go! Looks a bit below Indian Army status, though! Some say the rough ones are the best!' He laughed disgustingly and Teddy felt sick at this distant defilement.

'Who's the brat, then? Made a bit of a slip-up, did you? No wonder you didn't let on, old chap!'

Teddy thought that his heart would burst. His fists instinctively clenched, but that was in pain more than in anger. He was not a fighting man. Suddenly, his pride swelled in his breast and he said simply:

'They are my wife and my son. They matter more than my life to me. Please do not ever again talk like that of them.'

There was a silence for a minute before one of the men, the more obnoxious of the two, said:

'No one knew that you were married. Neither did the colonel. Obviously you are not then, Osmond. You've got a doxy and a bastard. This wouldn't go down with much stamp in the regiment!'

They turned away from him and talked loudly about a polo match. Teddy went lunchless to his quarters and cried. He put up some of his wonderful photographs against the mirror on the chest of drawers in his bedroom. As he was gazing at them, there was a discreet knock on his door.

'Come in!' he said quietly.

'Am I disturbing you, Sir?' asked Briggs, his batman.

'Er, not in the least, Briggs. What do you want?'

'Nothing much, Sir. It's just that I thought you looked a bit kind of out of sorts when you walked up here. Is there anything I can do, Sir?'

He was a kind man, much older than Teddy, who inspired the young man's trust. Teddy knew that Briggs had a large family at home. He sent almost all his pay to them, only keeping the bare minimum for himself and hardly anything for an occasional luxury. Teddy was sitting on his bed and Briggs followed his gaze to the photographs. His wallet was still open and bulging with many more in front of them.

'What a lovely lady, Sir' he began haltingly. 'And the nipper's just the dead spit of you both.'

He stopped, realising that he might have jumped to an uncomfortable conclusion. He looked awkward and embarrassed.

'Sorry, Sir. I think I said too much. I beg your pardon, Sir.'

'You have no need to beg my pardon at all, Briggs. You were kind to act as you did. I appreciate it more than I can possibly tell you. After all, you know more about life than I do. The lady at whom you are looking is the mother of my lovely son, John. We are not married, but I am going to wed her as soon as I can afford it. As it is, I send her all the money I can afford every month. John is two and I am twenty. I have no doubt that that must tell you the story! I have been cut off from the family because of it, completely disgraced and disregarded by both my father and my wealthy brother. There, now you know!'

There was a pause. Briggs gave his big, open smile.

'At least you're a man, Sir! Unlike some of those pompous drips that litter the bar in the officers' mess! Beg pardon, sir, I think I've gone too far. But you know what I mean. You're a real kind gentleman. I know that you respect me and I respect you for that as well.'

Teddy told him about the dropped pictures in the mess that morning.

'Now it'll be all over the Regiment, Briggs.'

'Don't worry about that, Sir. It'll be all among the men

what a fine, kind man you are. They'll all support you. Rely on Briggs! If you ever want volunteers for anything, they'll come up trumps. They don't care too much for some of the others, I can tell you. Now then, you cheer yourself up and go out smiling with pride, chest out and shoulders back, Sir!'

'You have been terribly kind to me, Briggs. I cannot thank you enough. And get a photo of yourself and family and I will send it to Mary.'

'That's a pleasure and honour, Sir. I'll find one tomorrow and leave it on your chest of drawers. Meantime, chin up, as they say. And I hope you have no more of that awful ragging from the lesser mortals. Love is worth suffering anything for, you ask my missus!'

Teddy felt a good deal better after that. Most of the other officers ignored him, but Colonel Lane seemed suddenly, unaccountably, friendly and considerate. He wondered whether the charitable Briggs, with all his wily old soldier's craft, had had a word in his ear ...

*

Whilst Teddy's career advanced slowly and boringly, filled with administration duties, to which his kind colonel thought him best fitted, life for the rest of the family unfolded traditionally in England. Joan loved Foley no better and no more than ever she really had done, but she did her duty.

Fiona Jane Osmond was born in 1933. She was a strong baby and grew into an intelligent, lovely, simple person. She came to inherit the best qualities of her mother and none of the cold, worst of her father. She was looked after in cushioned splendour by her mother and the nanny that she did not want but who was forced upon her for social reasons. She got along well with her because it would not have been worth her while to do other.

Every now and then, Teddy sent Joan a letter. These were loving and affectionate, always full of tender solicitude for her and Fiona. He never mentioned Foley's name, neither did he send him any kind of regards. He did not revile his name, neither that of his father, but he would never keep them in his heart again. They had left his breast for good and flown the nest of what could have been an infinite love. People who have no true love cannot give it. Foley gave this to no one, not even, probably, to himself. His soul was a barren tract of sterility and spiritual debilitation.

Foley delegated more and more of his work to his over-stretched, highly-trained subordinates. He paid them well to crucify their health for his benefit. They seemed willing to do this. They did not receive luxury allowances on their trips to France, Spain and Germany in their search for the best wines at the best prices, but their expenses were scarcely ever questioned. As long as the results were right, so was their performance. Each of his senior employees was taken upon the condition that he would have to surrender his job after an unfavourable appraisement of his first year within the firm. Such were the remunerations that this hardly ever happened.

In 1934, the couple moved into an elegant house in Eaton Square. They employed numerous servants, whom Foley treated formally, coldly, but with justice. His chauffeur, George Grant, drove alternately the Rolls Royce Silver Cloud, and the eight-cylinder Daimler which Foley had bought from his father. As he became wealthier, he worked less, moved less and took less exercise. Despite his doctors' advice about taking up golf or walking, he persisted in an inactive physical life, thus sowing the seeds of fairly early frailty and decrepitude. He became pasty-faced, thin, uglier by the day and bad-tempered, in a dull sort of way. Dullness seemed more than ever to be his trademark. To Joan, it seemed that her husband was the sole shareholder in dreariness and gloom, which he appeared to communicate to everyone.

She realised early that Fiona would be his only progeny. After her birth and at the age of only thirty-two, he had almost renounced the joyless sexual forays that he used to perpetrate. The dismal event took place about once a month. Joan longed for the immediate, kind and sensual warmth of Teddy. But he was lonely and far away, pining for love but unable to give it to any object of his true affection. The girls whom he met at the senior officers' parties were, it seemed to him, but sorry damsels, paraded to gain the uninteresting attentions of wealthy young subalterns. The whole procedure made his warm, honest heart sick. On his return to quarters, he thought of his three loves, Mary, Joan and, with especial tenderness, John. The trouble was that he could not think of a way out, of how to find just a twinkle of light at the end of what must have promised to be an endless, sightless tunnel. He did not then know, and would not for some time to come, that Mahatma Ghandi would provide him with the visa to normality. Or quasi-normality.

After crowded train journeys, he made his way towards leave, sometimes in Delhi, sometimes, Bombay, sometimes Calcutta. He had learnt to speak Hindi tolerably well and he got on with the Indian people, a fact which did not go unnoticed amongst his stuffy and ignorant young colleagues. He had made friends with Indian families of discernment and education. After all, he told himself, they were writing poetry and executing fine architecture and paintings when the English were rushing about daubed in woad and hurling stones at each other! Teddy became a truly international man who willingly and generously gave his respectful heart to any nation. The regiment did not like his liberal attitude; all except the colonel and his batman, both of them gentlemen, in their different ways.

In 1934, on a hot July evening, he went to dinner, the guest of an Indian merchant in Delhi. He had met the family the previous year, when he had taken a fortnight's leave there. He and his wife and two daughters were staying at the same hotel, which they could afford to have bought, but which he could hardly manage to stay in! They fell into easy and delightful conversation. The elder daughter was of about Teddy's age, he estimated, and dazzlingly beautiful. Women can be attractive without being beautiful; it happened that Maheerah was both. She, her sister and her mother wore the most stunning saris, sewn with blue, gold and mauve embroidery upon different grounds. Their discreet but beautiful jewellery showed their fine faces, ears and hands to enchanting effect.

After a magnificent dinner, they all strolled into the garden to take the cool of the evening and to breathe the freshness always given off by fountains. In an eastern house – or hotel for that matter – it is part of consideration and politeness to go your separate ways with different members of a family. It is considered boring and ill-mannered to sit glued interminably eyeball-to-eyeball to one another. It was on account of this pleasant custom that Teddy and Maheerah met. It was plain, even from a short distance, that they got on well together and, through their immediate nature, found themselves attracted. Teddy's mind was in a whirl. Even more so when he tentatively held her delicate, slim hand. The beautiful scent of her maidenhood assailed his nostrils and invaded his body. Her comely lines beckoned him more than he would have cared to admit. Then, the distance between him and Mary seemed to shorten in no space. He thought of love and was recalled by faith and their time together. This was sacred to him. He had his heart rent in two.

Maheerah's father had watched them walking in the gardens. He was a benevolent, kind man. He beckoned Teddy to his seat and asked him to sit down beside him, whilst his daughters went inside to see their mother.

'I respect you entirely, young man,' began Dev with some hesitation, 'but you must not see my daughter again. She is promised, you see, to another. The marriage is arranged. I know that she is beautiful and you find her so. That is natural. You must understand another thing. I do not want her to marry out of my nation. I think that that is a very important consideration. By all means come to dinner here again, but do not become too fond of her or make her too fond of you. It will break your hearts. I like you far too much to think of that happening.'

'I understand all that you have said, Sir,' replied Teddy, with genuine respect. 'It is better that I do not see you all again. There is something that I have not told you, which will make you all the firmer in your fine intentions for your daughter. I am not exactly the perfect man that you seem to think. I at once loved your daughter, but I could not, in all honesty, ruin your lives.'

There was a suspenseful pause. Each man seemed to be waiting for the other to speak. Eventually, it was the elder man. He put a hand on Teddy's arm.

'You may tell me anything,' he said kindly.

Teddy then told him about Mary and John. The Indian gentleman's eyes filled with compassionate tears. He showed no disdain or contempt.

'I would have liked you as my son and the husband of my daughter, but that is impossible, my son. You must see that. Besides which, you have your duty to do. One day India will be free and so will you. Go back to your Mary and your son. I know that you mean them nothing but well. You are the sort of gentleman – and I mean a gentle man – of whom we see few. You may, as an especial privilege, kiss my daughter, her sister and my wife on the forehead before you go. I shall shake your hand. Just a minute,' said Dev, 'I have left something in the house.'

He quickly returned to see him to the gates, alone. He shook his hand warmly and Teddy felt something pressed into it. It was a gold coin of some antiquity.

'Good-bye, Edward,' he said. 'I will think of you and pray for you, Mary and John before Vishnu.'

'I will pray for you all, Sir,' replied Teddy.

When he got back to his station, he found Briggs's promised photograph of his lovely homely wife and their six children placed on the chest of drawers. There was a small envelope next to it. The letter that it contained read:

Dear Mr Osmond,
Dreadfully hot day here. Hope you had a nice spot
of leave. Delhi can be a bit cosy! Brought you this letter

which arrived two days ago. I think it's got a photo in it. You've got to show it to me, if you forgive the impertinence. Another piece of impertinence, if you can excuse it from an older man. Don't be ashamed of nothing. Just be proud. I'll help all I can and I'll bloody well come to your wedding, soldier! I've done the uniform. Hope there are no scorch marks. See you tomorrow. I never tells on a mate. That's private, though. Privilege to know you.
    Jimmy Briggs

His letter was lovely and full of thanks and expectation. The photograph inside his letter was of a strong handsome woman and a fine young son. Teddy said his prayers harder than ever that night.

*

Teddy had two women to consider, and a son. He loved women; he loved his son equally but in a different way, naturally. For Joan there appeared to be no escape but if he could manage it, there would be one for John and Mary. Upon the latter thought he concentrated. From then onwards he thought seriously of no other woman although, as a man will, he entertained a few. They were beautiful and kind, but, while he was making love, he always thought of Mary and John; he felt dirty and culpable afterwards, not out of any disrespect for his women, but because he felt that he had betrayed the heart that he had given and which had been given to him. He felt a disgust that he should not have experienced for his physical needs. He was generous to his mistresses and treated them with every respect.

His Subedar knew about his life and he never betrayed his master. It was not a master-servant relationship. They always spoke Hindi and therefore they exchanged confidences which were not vouchsafed normally between the two nationalities. For Teddy, there were no barriers.

His Subedar was a very fine-looking man. He was the essence of tact. He also had a great respect for his young master, whose years and experience were naturally less than his own. He felt a fatherly love for him. He was determined that, one day, he would display this affection because he realised that the young man was troubled and in a state of dismality. He knew, above all, that Teddy loved the Indian people, with all their dignity and culture. He also knew that he loved Indian women and above all, that he treated them with the respect that some others did not. He admired that. He was the perfect gentleman towards Teddy, who, perhaps, did not deserve all the regard that he got from him. It took the Subedar some months to come to a decision. He felt that he had to talk to his master. He was looking more and more depressed, enervated and emaciated. It was a question of how and when.

One evening, when Teddy was alone after a particularly depressing and boring day, he thought he would pour himself a whisky. He felt a presence in the lounge.

'Could I pour that for you, Sir?' asked the Subedar from behind him, uninvited.

'Oh, there's no need for that, Rajiv. You need not be here, I have my servants,' replied Teddy, who was surprised at this unannounced presence.

'You have called me by my name, Sir. I did not expect that.'

'There are so many things that are unexpected that I, myself, hardly know what to expect any more. Thank you for the whisky.'

Rajiv remained, unaccountably, in the room. His presence was strong and powerful. Teddy felt the warmth of another soul. He did not quite know how this was possible. He turned from his chair to see a kind of beseaching face. It was not servile, the eyes were kind and direct, but with a benign dignity.

'May I speak with you, Sir?' he asked.

'I would love you to,' replied Teddy in Hindi, 'come and sit with me.'

'That would be an honour for me indeed, Sir. There is something that I have to say. It is boldness, perhaps, but it is my duty.'

'There is no honour in sitting with me, other than that of one human being sitting with another. That is a mutual right and privilege. Don't feel honoured, just welcomed. Sit, my friend!'

The dignified Subedar sat. It was the first time that he had ever been invited to sit with a colonial in his drawing room. Rajiv had a magnificent beard, a delightful wife, eight children and four grand-children. He was devoted to them all. Teddy had met them. They knew that he loved them on sight. They could not, at first, believe that an Indian Army officer would sit on their prided rugs with them. He felt honoured beyond belief and shared their prayers. The Subedar knew that. He respected it also. Teddy embraced them all, dressed in the Indian clothes that he thought it was respectful to wear. He knew that it was also his duty. It was his pleasure too.

'I have come to tell you something, Osmond Sahib, which I have wanted to do for a long time. Will you let me speak? You are not among the others. You are different and dignified. I would like to ask you to hear the thoughts of an Indian. Will you listen to me? I care, you see.'

'Please speak,' replied Teddy. 'I shall be honoured and grateful. We are all equal in the world. You must know how I think. I am not too highly thought of for it, either! I have earnt the contempt of many.'

'That is why we all respect you, Sir. But we are sorry for you, too. We know that you are unhappy, both with the British Raj and at home. I have, you see, seen your wonderful photographs. I wish that you had told me about them. It would have made me so glad. They must be of your wife and of your son, but you never told us.'

Here there was a pause, full of awe, heat, gnats, calm and mutual gratitude.

'That I could not do,' answered Teddy. 'I am not married to my lovely girl and my son is illegitimate. They are the loves of my life and I cannot see them until I can rid myself of this ridiculous life in your splendid country. I have no money and I have been turned away from my family. I have a rich father and brother, but neither of them wants me, my lovely Mary nor my sweet son. I have therefore got to serve here until I can return to England and support them, which I do now, as it happens. It hurts my soul. Was it all my fault or not? To be looked down upon is a deprivation.'

'Love is never wasted, my son,' said the Subedar. 'Do not ever think that any of it has been. You just send me some photos when you return home next time.'

'I do not know when the next time will be, Rajiv, because I have to send almost everything to my love and my son every month.'

'You can do without those people in the mess, can't you, Sir? They hate you because you are loving and kind to everyone. Briggs told me about the photographs falling on the floor. All your men know about that. They are with you all the way, Sir. I'm now going to get you a nice Madras which you can eat quietly in here and in peace.'

With that, he went.

A very short while afterwards, he returned. Apart from the splendid curry and all its accompaniments, there was a little packet in his hand. His great, gentle fingers pressed it into Teddy's palm.

When he had opened it, he discovered two wonderful, perfumed silk handkerchiefs and a small note, which read:

> Dear Mr Osmond,
>   These little things are for your wife, Sir. It is always a privilege to serve you and I wish you well, especially your son. He'll be a fine man, just like you. Go on steadily and I will help you. Do not be offended.
>   Rajiv Singh

Teddy was not offended. He wept tears of enormous gratitude and reverence into his pillow. He prayed for Mary and John until he could think of nothing else to pray for. He loved them as much as that.

He loved his Subedar and his servants. He loved all the world. He had made up his mind for his son. He could never betray John and Mary.

*

There were many and regular letters between Teddy and Mary. Each one, either end, tore both their hearts. There were also exchanges of letters between Teddy and his father and Foley. The latter were frequently unanswered from the English end, but, when they were, they offered no hope. His distance from Mary seemed longer and further than ever. His distance from his son hurt his heart in a way that nobody but his batman, Briggs, and his Subedar ever realised. His life in the regiment was dreary and unrespected. He was only given the most uninteresting and banal of assignments. He stopped his affairs with the Indian women whom he loved because he realised, ashamedly, that he could not love them as he did his wife and son. He resolved to take a trip to England as soon as he could manage it. This was not to be until 1937, when John would be six years old. Not only was he saving to send Mary money but he also felt the sublime obligation to do the best for his son. The absence of class and creed prejudice were admired and respected by him; after all, his best friends were Hindus. What mattered to him most was the education that he had to give John.

In July, 1937, he had a long leave accorded to him. He had hardly taken any in the five years since he had been in the Indian Army. The colonel had called him into his office.

'Teddy,' he began, 'I think that you need to go home for a bit. You must have a few things to do there. I know a little more about you than perhaps you might have suspected. I'm a stiff, old military man and will never change my colours, but I know something about your life, from what sources I may not disclose. It is enough to say that I admire your faith and courage and want to support them both. Take the leave

97

with my blessing. Give my love to Mary and John.'

His last sentence temporarily stunned the twenty-five-year-old subaltern. Even more the next piece of news.

'When you return, you will be Captain Osmond. That will help you somewhat, I expect.'

The future captain hardly knew what to say. He stood with his hands dangling by his side and looking very unmilitary. He was blushing and the tears were starting, pricking his eyelids which were trying to keep them back. The colonel arose from behind his desk and came across to the standing young officer. He put his hand on the young man's shoulder.

'I know that you are not a natural soldier, Teddy,' he said, 'but you are a hell of a good man. Sit down and I will tell you something.'

Teddy sat in a stained, studded leather chair, while Colonel Lane, distinguished and fatherly, poured them both a generous glass of whisky. They sat silent for a while. Then the colonel spoke.

'You might think that I am a success,' said the elder, kindly man, 'but, in human terms, I am the reverse. I made the biggest and saddest mistake of my life, many years ago, and I have paid for it ever since. I happen to have done exactly the same as yourself. I turned my back upon it. I lost my wife, as she should have been, my son and my happiness. She married a worthier man than I. He took my son, he took my wife and he took my only solaces in life. I do not know where they are or what has become of them all. You must not make the same mistake. That is why I am giving you a long leave. Go and make it right, arrange everything and come back again for as long as you wish. The Indian Army, as you may know, cannot last for too much longer.'

The two men looked at one another, between sips of a sympathetic drink.

They achieved, in a few frank moments, an incomparable respect one for the other.

'You must be, if you would not mind, John's godfather, Sir,' said Teddy.

'That would be a special honour, Edward. I shall wear my

dress uniform and sword complete! Now, bugger off, you old pal!'

They shook hands rather emotionally and both turned away from the other as quickly as they could. Teddy told Briggs and Rajiv Singh the good news. They both smiled at each other in rewarded complicity. Briggs packed him off to Bombay a week later.

*

Liverpool was hardly like Bangalore but even the stench of its smoky fog smelt sweet. It was five years since Teddy had stepped on to English soil. He had alerted Mary in Brighton that he would be arriving on a certain date in July. He was not looking forward to meeting her aunt, but he could not wait to see his son and her whom he already regarded as his wife. It had been a long time and he wondered, on the long, smoky train journey, if things would be the lovely same as they had been and would always remain for him. He felt tired and anxious, longing and affectionate. His love was bursting the valves of his kind heart. He went to the bar on the train and ordered two whiskies in succession, large ones, and silently toasted Colonel Lane.

At just after midnight, he knocked on the door of Number 218. There were no lights on in the house. After a while he knocked again. His heart was filled with apprehension and was beginning to sink. Then he heard footsteps on the stairs after a dim light had appeared at the head of them. A small face looked through the letter-box and the door was opened. Teddy knew that it was John.

'It's your father come home!' he exclaimed, picking the lad up in his arms and swinging him round the narrow hall. 'It's your dad! I couldn't wait to come home to you both. I'm sorry I haven't been here for so long but I've been working for you. I've been praying and thinking for you every day!'

John was now tall and well-built for a lad of six. He looked much older. He was dark, like his mother, and would be handsome as both of his parents were. Teddy was proud at once.

As both father and son were rather bewildered at their sudden encounter, there was a silence.

'Where's mother?' asked Teddy, suddenly concerned after the first, moving encounter with his son.

'She's up above and not very well,' he answered. 'She couldn't get down the stairs, so she sent me. She wants you to go up at once.'

Still carrying John, he went up immediately to the small bedroom which they both shared. There was a dim bedside lamp lit against his arrival. Mary turned with difficulty in her bed to face her lover.

'Come here, Edward,' she said. 'How smart yer looks in all that fine uniform! I'm sorry I didn't come to the door, but I'm not well. Me guts 'urts terrible. Doctor's comin' 'morrer.'

She paused for breath and Teddy could sense illness and the sickly scent of someone in bodily trouble. Mary's eyes were full of pain, pleading and without the lustre that he had known so well. He was flattened, crushed and filled with guilt, all at the same time.

He immediately sat on her bed, leant towards her and took her in his tenderest embrace. The message of each other's eyes was, for a while, wordless. John came to join them both and his father knew then and instinctively that his son loved him. They knew that they would all love each other for ever. They did not, however, know how short one of the relationships would be.

'What's the matter, Mary?'

'I doan rightly know, my Edward,' she replied slowly, 'but I'm cryin' with pain for three days now. I think they're going ter cut me morrer.'

She paused for breath. Although sick, she still looked as lovely as Teddy's boyhood lover.

'What are the signs, Mary?' he asked gently.

'Everythin', just everythin', everythin's gorn wrong. I can't 'ardly move mornin's. Little John's bin so good and helped me to do everythin'. Jus' like 'is father, 'e's a real young man!'

Teddy was devastated. He was too shocked to cry. He told Mary that he would be back when he had found something to eat for the boy, after which he would bath her and cuddle her to help the pain. Mary dropped into sleep and John and Teddy went down to the kitchen. Teddy arranged scrambled eggs, toast and cold tomatoes. They had a glass of not-very-fresh milk; but they both enjoyed being together. Teddy thought that Mary must have told John a good deal about him, but it was too late to talk now – and perhaps John was too young. I fact, he was far more mature than his years would have given anyone to suppose.

Teddy kissed his son good-night and slipped into bed with Mary. She was writhing in pain. He put his body close and his tender arms around her. She sweated profusely. He was desperately proud to try to help her agony. He bathed his two loves together in the morning, after which they awaited the doctor.

*

At eight-thirty the next morning, the doctor arrived. He spoke to Teddy downstairs and out of the hearing both of the son and the mother. The doctor was a compassionate-looking man in his sixties. He was obviously worried and distressed himself. He knew that he could not help his patient, equally, that his last duty was to send her for an exploratory operation to the infirmary. This would only confirm his own dismal prognosis.

'Your wife is very unwell, Captain Osmond. I am sure that she has cancer of the stomach and probably elsewhere. The onset of this has been very sudden. She may be dead in a month. You would do well to make dispositions for your son. Mary has told me all your story. You are both a lucky and an unlucky man.'

All of this came out in a quick torrent of words. The

doctor wanted to make his intelligence brief and kind at the same time. He was not one for hedging and giving false hopes. Teddy appreciated his frankness and blunt sincerity. Even more so when the doctor said:

'You may not know that Mary's aunt died recently. Such was your anticipation and excitement when you got home, you probably did not even enquire about her. She was not a very pleasant woman, but Mary had to put up with her for your sake and for that of your son. She did so admirably. She has left the house to Mary in her lifetime and then to her family. So Mary and the boy will have somewhere in which to live. But what if Mary dies soon, as I have told you she must?'

'I have simply no idea, doctor. I only arrived from India yesterday. I shall have to address myself to the problem immediately. This will be a little easier since I shall soon be made up to Captain.'

'I think that you will find your way safely, Captain Osmond. I also think that I can help you while you sort things out. My family has all grown up. My daughter and two sons are married. My wife and I have a large and far too expensive house which we have no intention, foolishly enough, of leaving! How could we desert our roses and delphiniums?'

'What is it that you are saying to me, Doctor Seymour?'

'Can't you see, my lad?' said he, putting a fatherly hand on his shoulder. 'We'll look after John for as long as it takes you to get everything straight. The charge is that you come to see us as often as you can!'

A long handshake ended the interview. Then Teddy said suddenly: 'I've kept it from everyone. I can afford it now. I came back to marry Mary, you see.'

The doctor could not think of what to say. Perhaps that was because no words were sayable ... It was too late, too lovely and too tragic.

5

Nine Years

Teddy stayed in Mary's house, whilst John was in that of his trusted Doctor Seymour. He went to the hospital the day after his love was admitted to consult with the surgeon. He was a charming man, luckily. He said that he was going to operate in an exploratory way on the next day. He told Teddy that he would contact him and that her blood tests were very unpromising. He went back to the dismal home in which his beloved had lived with so much devotion and courage, opened a bottle of whisky but could not drink a drop of it. Instead, he drank glasses of water, ate no food and went to bed, not without prayer. Since he had been in India, he had learnt the respect that educated Hindus felt that they had to pay to Vishnu, father of the Gods. He prayed the same and did not feel outside respect. He wondered if his Subedar was doing the same. In fact, he was. It was no blame to anyone that their prayers were, in one way unanswered. Mary was nearer to death than anyone would have expected.

Teddy went the next day to the soot-grimed hospital. It was seven o'clock in the evening. The sister on the ward did not really wish to admit him, as her patient was not fully conscious. As she was a kind woman, she did. The disinfectant smell of the ward hardly reminded him of her lovely musk, of the scent of her bed and the warmth of his growing son. On the eighteenth bed on the right, there she lay. She was a yellow pale. She was motionless. A nurse accompanied Teddy. Her eyes spoke kindness.

'Try not to disturb her too much,' she said, 'but it's grand that you have come to see her. She must matter to you a great deal.'

'Much more than you could ever know,' he replied quietly, 'she is the mother of my son.'

'Treat her slowly and gently. I will stand by to watch in case she needs help. Her pain has led to several injections and she may suddenly need another.'

'Thank you, nurse,' said Teddy. 'I cannot tell you how grateful I am for all your kindness. How do I wake her, just to let her know that I have not forgotten her?'

'She knows that already, Sir. She always calls out for you and John when she is in pain. Just touch her arm.'

Her black, tired, sweet eyes opened drowsily as he gently nudged her. Her first concern was not for herself; it was an amazing manifestation of selflessness.

'How are you and John, Edward?' she asked.

'Never mind about us, love. It's you we are thinking about.'

'I doan think yer will be thinkin' about me more nor a short time, Edward,' she said feebly but with feeling. 'I'm nigh on gorn.'

'You can't go, Mary, you just can't. You can't leave us two boys!'

Mary smiled her sad and glad acceptance. They held hands, their eyes closed. They were married then. Teddy had tried to put a little jolly humour into what he said and how he said it, but it did not work. They both knew the truth. It was the end of a love that would never die, for her in Heaven and for him in his life. He did not know how extraordinary that would prove to be.

She was soon tired, so he considerately left her, after the tenderest of kisses. He felt the sourness of the damp that signals ill-health on his lips. Her eyes had closed upon his departure before he had made it. He went out into the street with the desperate feeling that he would like to die with

Mary. Hardly had the thought flashed through his mind than he realised its futility and wickedness. His boundless love for his son excluded all further timidity. In living for him, he would live for Mary. He would never let either of them down again, he promised himself. In some ways he kept that promise in a special love and in sacrificial duty; in some ways he did not. He was a very human man. There are, unfortunately, frailties which accompany humanity. He never let his son down, however; he was part of him and part of his Mary.

*

The next day, Doctor Seymour called early in the morning. Teddy was still in his dressing-gown and unshaved. He had only just made himself a cup of tea. Eating was out of the question. He had already smoked endless cigarettes and the house smelt stale with exhaled tobacco. He admitted his friend immediately. The bad tidings were written in the elder man's eyes.

'Tell me quickly, Doctor,' Teddy blurted.

'Mary will not last out today. Do you want to come and be beside her, even if she may not constantly recognise you? John will be at home with my wife. He must not be there. We will think of what to tell him later.'

'Give me ten minutes and I will be with you. I think that I will put some whisky with my shaving-soap. I shall try to think up some prayers at the same time.'

He was not joking. He was crying.

By five in the afternoon, Mary was gone. Everyone had done their best and Teddy recognised this. He had sat on her silent bed for seven hours, with only short absences for personal needs. He had been offered food but could not eat it. The dear old sister had even rustled up a drink for him. He thanked her but asked her to take it away. Two hours before she died, Mary looked into Teddy's eyes. She whispered something which he did not catch. He leant a little closer.

'Kiss me, Edward, my old boy. It will be for the last time. Remember that I doan' never regret nuthin'! Kiss my John for me, too. You're such a good man, you'll care for him.'

Before Teddy could reply, she had lost consciousness for the last time in her brief life. Teddy made a promise that he would never forget. He kept faith.

The funeral, in a Brighton cemetery, was deliberately brief. This fact denoted no disrespect. Only Doctor Seymour and Teddy attended. They drove back together to the doctor's wife and John. The little boy did not know where they had both been or why. His father realised that he would have to tell him about everything as soon as he could find the words and the courage.

*

By August 1937, Edward had to go back to India. He was rather disorientated. He had no prospects in England and few in India. He could hope for nothing from his family. He had no inheritance, no friends and now, no certain love. Yet, that was not quite true. He had the love of his son, for whom he pined, and the extraordinary care that Mary's doctor and his wife were giving John. Above all, he could not let down his son, even if he had disgraced his own family. But then he refused to admit that he had done that; he had only to look into his growing son's eyes. What a fine man he was going to be! It proved that he would be exactly that. Teddy could not have known it yet. His son was to be a brilliant man with a marvellous, if rather adventurous, character. How could his father blame him for that! The genes must have spoken.

The doctor and his wife said what they hoped to be a very temporary farewell to Teddy in late 1937. Not because they wanted to be rid of John; they loved having him at home, where he trusted them and they taught him to speak without a London cockney whine. They taught him all sorts of other things too; how to eat properly, how to study and how to

106

read and write really well. He was an extremely apt pupil. Doctor Seymour realised that, by the time John was seven, he ought to go to a good school.

War was looming in 1938. The doctor wrote to Teddy and told him that he must come home for urgent consultations. The father obtained immediate leave from his kind colonel.

'You go home, my boy, and fix the lad up. You'll have to. Your brave doctor has been all too good. You'll never forgive yourself if you don't arrange things properly for the lad. Tell him plenty of tales of India; tell him how you love the people; tell him how proud and kind they are. Tell him, above all, that God loves everyone. Go home and have a wonderful leave, although there must have to be sad parts of it. We have both told one another about those. Dealing with them makes the man,' he ended abruptly.

Once again, they turned their heels upon each other. Before he reached the door, Teddy heard a gruff command:

'Step here, Captain.'

Teddy did not know what to expect.

'I lost my son, but that is no reason why you should lose yours. Don't do that, ever. I will help you financially, should you need that.'

Again they shook hands. As equals and friends, which they were to remain.

*

On April 3rd 1938, John was seven years old. He had now begun to write to his father, whom he adored. Doctor Seymour and his wife had taught him at home, but it was now time to make further dispositions. He had not forgotten his sweet mother, and he felt the lack of parental company. But he was a stoic lad. He still attended a little, local council school, but his studies with the doctor had taken him far beyond that. They loved each other's company and John, advanced for his age, had begun to ask questions about his origins which his guardian was wary of trying to answer. This made it all the more urgent that his father must return soon. He was the only one who could tell him, very gently and possibly in palatable instalments, all that he ought to know. Teddy knew this, having been written to by the doctor very often, and he dreaded having to tell the complete truth. He need not have worried. John had the understanding of someone beyond his young age.

Late in the evening of April 2nd, Teddy arrived at the house of his son's guardian. He had not gone to see Joan first because there would not have been time and second because he thought that it would be a betrayal which, he thought, was henceforth and for ever forbidden. He felt that he could not sully a young life with the impurity of another love, although of a different type. He wanted to be just himself when he met John and for ever after. He did not then know how much his son would understand him and help him in later life, nor how much he was to forgive. For the time being, Teddy was strong and resolved.

His welcome in the old, suburban house in Brighton was quite unbelievably warm. They all kissed each other and Teddy hugged his son until he nearly squeezed the breath from him.

'John has already had supper,' announced Ethel, the doctor's wife 'but we have got a little cold curry for you, in memory of India!'

'I don't want to remember India at the moment,' said Teddy with good humour, 'but anything at all would be fine after a bumpy journey in an ancient aeroplane. No food and nothing to drink! Could I have a wash and a nice gin afterwards?'

His face was lined, drawn and tired, but his eyes flashed love for them all.

'You go upstairs and take your time, my lad,' said Stephen Seymour. 'We will all wait for you. But don't be too long. John has school in two places tomorrow! There and here.'

He went upstairs and unpacked all that was immediately required, dashed water over his face and scrubbed his hands. He did not even spare the time to put on a pair of slippers.

He combed his abundant hair which, he noticed with some amusement, but with no surprise, was greying early.

As he sipped his drink, in which Stephen joined him, to Ethel's feigned disapproval, he sat next to John on a sofa. Each of them thought that he was sitting next to God. Perhaps they were. The son told his father all about what he was doing, all about his friends, of which he appeared to have many, and of how much he wondered about him when he was away. This made Teddy feel sad, but he determined not to show it. Tonight was to be the happiest of all. It must not be spoilt by anything.

'I have to be away sometimes, John,' he said, 'because I must do my job and pay for you in the future.'

Here he stopped lamely, not knowing quite how to proceed.

'You see,' he continued, 'we have your future to consider. I think that we will have to discuss that together tomorrow.'

He already realised that he could take his son into a man's confidence.

'I would like to do that, Father,' replied John. 'You see, I have been wondering about it all such a lot. I loved my mother. She wanted me to be an educated man like you. I don't want to disappoint her memory. I want to be like you. I think I want to be a doctor, not a soldier though!'

He smiled indulgently.

'I never wanted to be one either, John. We'll talk about lots and lots of things in the morning. I think that you are old enough to know that your father is not quite the perfect man that you think. But I love you, my son. Above everyone else in the whole wide world!'

'I know that you do,' said John trustingly. 'I have always known that because mother kept on telling me how grand you are!'

Teddy felt ashamed of the trust of both his loves. He felt meagre, stained and paltry in his soul.

'We'll have a long chat and that's a promise, John.'

Teddy was determined to make everything open, clear, plain and honest. He could not wait to do his duty. He was to do it well. He could not have counted on the success of it without the help of his son.

'Now, up you go to bed!' said father.

'Not if you don't come up with me! I'll stay here until the daylight comes, otherwise!'

Teddy went upstairs, tucked his son into the covers and hugged him until both of them were nearly asleep. Then he went downstairs again.

'Ethel has gone to bed,' said the doctor. 'She could not stay up any longer and gave her apologies. But you will have a few days in which to chat. I waited up. I just wanted to say a few words to you. First a question. How long do you think you are going to stay in the Indian Army?'

'I think that it will not be for long, Stephen. I may be sent to Europe for the war which is bound to come or, more likely, I shall be kept on in my boring administrative post in Bangalore. I can now afford to come home more often than previously and I am sending you money regularly for John. India, I hope, will secede soon. I shall then be free of the army. What I shall do in that event I do not know. Let us address the problems of the day on the day – or a little before!'

The doctor thought for a moment. He had to compose his words.

'I know that you will forgive me for being frank, Edward. What I have to say is by no means intended to hurt you. You have not led an altogether circumspect life, although you have a heart full of love and a gentle soul. In terms of the severe practicalities, that is not always enough. You have nothing much to fall back upon, as you have told me.'

'All that you have said, Stephen, dear old friend, is absolutely true', answered Teddy. 'I am certain that what I have to do now is to be done without delay. I could never have done without your magnificent help. Nowadays I am a responsible, if not very happy man, in some respects. In one way, however, I am and more than ever. It is my son. I am going to send him to a first class boarding school and I will visit him once a term. The only thing is that I cannot take care of him on my own in India. My servants are wonderful but I cannot expect them to look after a small boy for too long when he is on his own. I trust them implicitly, as they do me; I feel one of them, which accounts for some of my undeserved unpopularity. I have told them all about Mary and John. Their faces lit with love. "We must see the young Sahib", they all said. Yes, I will take him for short holidays and he will learn Hindi. What of the rest of the time, I wonder?'

'You have no need to ask,' answered the doctor, kindly. 'We love having him here at home. It is not as exciting as India would be, although I have never been there, but there is mutual trust and a pillow of love. I will ensure his safety and the reliability of his education. It is up to you to arrange it.'

'I will broach the subject tomorrow, Stephen. Thank you infinitely for all your voluntary solicitude. There are no words that may frame my gratitude to you and Ethel. I could never have managed without you, and without your help it would have meant an institutional home for him. You have given him a home which is not an institution. He will always love you and writes to tell me how kind you always are.'

The two men looked into one another's eyes with trust and understanding.

'Go to bed, Edward. I certainly need to. I have been so excited about seeing you, particularly you and John together, that I'm quite tired out. You must be also. Get up whenever you like. Ethel is yours to command as to breakfast!'

'I would hardly dare to command your wife!' added Teddy, still with a twinkle in his eye; Stephen knew that he loved Ethel as a son does a mother.

*

The next morning, Teddy was slow to awaken. The journey and the emotions of the last two days had drained him, but his energy returned quickly. Ethel gave him and John a fine breakfast before Stephen drove John to his rather dismal school. His father did not go with him, partly because he was ashamed to see his lowly place of education and partly because he was simply too tired. He thought that a slow recovery would arm his mind best for the task that lay before him. It weighed upon his mind all day. He appeared to be relaxed when, in fact, he was as tense as a piano string. He wanted above all things to prevent the necessity of intimidating his son with a different mode of life and of shocking him with truths that he would not understand – perhaps even not forgive. He underestimated his own blood. This his son possessed in full.

The day passed quietly enough. Ethel was uninterfering but attentive. She was a calm lady, nothing ever seemed to ruffle her inner peace. She, at first, appeared not cold but a little unfeeling. In fact, she was the reverse.

'I know that you have got much to think about and to do today, Edward. I would be the very last to interfere and I shall make myself scarce, so far as that is possible with my girth! I wish you all the good luck in the world. I think that, from what I know of our little John, you will not find your passage too hard. Just take your time. He will come home at about four and then your tea and biscuits will be ready. Stephen will go up to his study. He is not on call this evening, just for a change. I do want him to retire soon. We are never going to move, so you needn't worry about John at the times when you cannot be here.'

'Ethel, apart from my Mary, no one has ever been so kind to me. I want to …'

Here he was cut off. Sharply too.

'I don't want any more talk of that sort, Edward. I'm well used to putting up with ghastly men. I am devoted to them! Cheer up, you old idiot! Above all, don't look so worried. It doesn't do with the young.'

Teddy tried hard to take her advice. It took him all his guts but he was still apprehensive.

At about four-thirty, John leapt out of the doctor's car,

hardly able to wait to see his father for their promised talk. He tripped over the patient dog and fell into the drawing room where Teddy was waiting.

'Father!' he exclaimed, 'I've been waiting to see you all day! I've hardly been able to do my lessons, although they were neither interesting nor particularly difficult. Most of what I know has been taught me here. The doctor tells me that my Latin is not too bad, and that is praise from him! I have written a few poems and I am already reading about human anatomy. I want to be a doctor – a surgeon for difficult operations on poor people who cannot afford them, I hope. I cannot wait for my first visit to the operating theatre, but the doctor says that I shall have to wait for a bit yet! How are you, father? You still look tired.'

All the words came tumbling out of his lively mind without pause for comment or reply. His eyes were bright with the expectation of he knew not what. They fell into each other's arms.

'God, it's splendid to see you in such fine form!' said Teddy.

'I've been looking forward to seeing you all day – and all last night, Father. I have a feeling that there is something you are going to tell me.'

'There certainly is,' replied Teddy, feeling unaccountably far more at ease than he had done all day.

'Go on, then' goaded John, his eyes glinting.

'You may not like all of it, but I think you are grown-up enough to take it, and I've got to tell you sooner or later, anyhow. I think the sooner the better.'

Then Teddy began, haltingly at first and then with a fluency that surprised him. He told him of the circumstances of his birth, of his deep love, powerless at times in terms of material help, for his mother and of her tragic death. He told him of the dire lack of love from his family. The boy listened with attention, interest and respect. He stayed very quiet. He had already suspected some of it, but without according any blame.

'Finally,' began Teddy, 'for your best interests, you must go

113

to school, to a good school and away to it. You will have to board there. You will be well looked-after and you will, I know, have plenty of friends. You will be taught really well. I will come and see you as often as I can afford it. It will cost me a lot, but there is nothing that I would not spare myself for you.'

It took a few moments for the stammered words, which were uttered practically all of a breath, to sink into John's young mind.

'You just send me wherever you think best, Father,' said John. 'I know that you are full of love and mean the best for me. Probably your life, like mine, has not been always easy. I understand that kind of thing. I know you already and love you because you are my father. Please never forget me and keep on helping me. I trust you. I used to be known as The Gypsy at school, but I've beaten them all! I'm proud of my mother and my dad. I'm proud of what I am, even if they did call me a bastard and a fatherless child!'

The tall, upstanding lad leapt into his father's arms. They knew then, that whatever happened, whatever the vicissitudes of life, that their love and understanding would last them always. They were never to be disappointed.

'God, John!'

'God, Father!'

They said hardly anything else to each other that day.

*

The next morning, John went off more than usually joyfully to his not-very-distinguished school. He had high hopes of his father, who, it was promised, would not disappoint either of them. He did not, either. It would have crucified his heart and his integrity not to have done the best for his son, his only link to Mary, his only link to life. He remembered Mary in every glance of his son. His father loved and respected his son's surprisingly mature understanding. He was, although he could not have framed the same thoughts in his young

114

words, proud to be a true son of love. He would come to know the meaning and the beauty of that later. In the meantime, he just adored his long-absent father. He already knew things about life which his years would not have portended. He was not precocious, merely understanding, grateful and forgiving of anything. He had a deep, trusting soul. For the moment, he would wait; it was quite enough that he had a loving guardian and a father who promised him a future.

That Teddy embarked upon without delay. He went to see the headmaster of his own preparatory school in Kent. He was kindly received but unimpressed and disappointed by the run-down condition of it. The whole place had a shabby, fusty air about it. True, he wanted a demanding education for his intelligent son. In which case, he could only accept the best. The next day, for he was never a man to delay long, as the prompt induction into the world of his beloved son had demonstrated before, he went to see another place, this time in Suffolk. It was in beautiful countryside, which could have been painted by Constable. It might have been, for all he knew. Even before he saw the building, he felt the softness of the grasslands and cornfields that he had known himself as a boy. He knew at once that his son would love them as well. Hadleigh House was just what he wanted. It was a small, Queen Anne manor with modest grounds and a gentle, firm headmaster.

Their interview was brief. Teddy, never one to hide anything, told him his whole story. He was touched and impressed. He said that he would take him without interview and upon trust.

'No,' said Teddy, 'I would not have that. You must judge his merits. Otherwise you might regret it. But don't forget that, although I do not want any favours, he is the core of my heart. I can already tell that you will look after him as a son. Forgive him if he does not speak in a very refined way as yet; do not disparage him for that. Think about what a fraught life he has had to endure. It is my fault. I'm still proud of the fault though! It has given me a wonderful son!'

'And so you should be proud, Mr Osmond. Love is no fault.'

Teddy knew at once that he had chosen the right place and the perfect setting. Mr Kenwood was, he thought, a wonderful man. Indeed, he proved to be exactly that; his wife, Grace, as he came to know her later, was stern, matronly but infinitely kind. She obviously stood no nonsense either from her husband or from the boys that she adored. She never tried to let them know it, although they all did!

'Just the place!' exclaimed Teddy to himself, as he drove back to Brighton and his friends on the rainy, yet somehow sunny, April night.

By the time he returned, John was already in bed and he was not to be long out of his own either. He felt an inexpressible relief that he was at last doing his loving duty for his son. Not that he had intended otherwise.

'Tell me all about it tomorrow,' said the tired doctor, who had waited up for him. 'I want to know everything. His home will be for always here for as long as you and he need it. That is our promise. Ethel is ready with needle and cotton for the name-tapes already! All that you have to do is to come home as often as you can, because the lad will be needing you, you know, possibly more often than you may imagine!'

'I shall be needing him, too, Stephen, more often than ever. My arm will be around him, even from as far away as Bangalore! I know that you won't forget my strong, intelligent gypsy lad, any more than I will. I am so tired that I cannot say any more. I must go to bed now. I won't even disturb my son.'

'That was something to promise, in all conscience!' replied the doctor.

*

116

Doctor Seymour and his wife were delighted to hear the news that, for the time being at least, John's future was settled. He promised Teddy that he would take the boy out at least twice a term and that his holidays would be secure. Stephen refused the cheque which he was offered for his keep.

'You just pay the fees and we'll do the rest. John need not know that. Besides, to give us a rest from his liveliness, he may well go and meet my grandchildren, some of whom are of about the same age.'

It all sounded ideal. For once in his recent life, Teddy was not disappointed. Everything had worked out perfectly; at least, as perfectly as it could have done with his protracted absences from England.

Teddy had to return to India. He took John to see his new school and the visit was a splendid success. John felt the beginnings of a new world; the broad horizon seemed to open for him. A new, very blue sky cleared over his proud, hoping head. His father immediately signed a cheque for the fees that he could not afford, but did so nevertheless with gratitude and delight. Grace said that she was well practised in organizing boys' uniforms and that Teddy was not to trouble himself with that side of it. As all men would be, he was immensely relieved!

The new captain returned to India on April 10th. Both he and his son were as brave as possible on the railway station at Brighton. The flight was long and uncomfortable; uncomfortable in more than one way for Teddy.

Over the next few months, he had letters from John and from his guardians, to which he replied at once. In the last one from his father, Teddy told John that he would not be able to obtain leave in the summer, but that he would arrange for him to come to India in August. He would stay with an Indian family that he knew well not far from his station. The father was a doctor and he had three sons and a daughter. Two of the sons were of about John's age. The letter that he had back from John was full of excited anticipation. He said that all his many friends envied his luck.

Meanwhile, Teddy's life continued in a dreary kind of way, buoyed up by the thoughts of August. John's life progressed with growing excitement. He was doing incredibly well. One of his friends was an Indian and had started to teach him Hindi, as well as about the Indian way of life and Vishnu. John drank it all in.

The holiday in India was a revelation. He made firm friends of the family in which he was so welcome and insisted upon wearing borrowed Indian clothes. His Hindi was already becoming fluent by the time that the holiday ended and, with his dark skin, he sometimes passed as one of the doctor's sons. He was proud of this. So was his father, but, apart from the dear old colonel most of his brother officers looked at his broadminded attitudes ever more askance, made stupid and hurtful remarks, and one idiotic little snob once told him that he was performing a miracle.

'Who could have thought that anyone could transform an illegitimate gypsy into an Indian? Only you, Osmond.'

This was disgusting, but Teddy bore the insult, in all its ignorance, with a certain kind of courageous pride. His love was without frontiers, completely cosmopolitan. After all, he had loved in three cultures.

The war drew ever nearer. Teddy was to remain in India, which he loved, and retain his post which he did not. His visits to England became necessarily rarer and more interspaced, but he returned as often as he could. First stop Brighton, where he reorientated himself after the journey; second to Suffolk. He even managed to watch John playing cricket matches on the odd occasion. They both loved that. John made several visits to India in perilous times and stayed with his beloved "family". When his father came to the school, everyone was kindly amused that, especially if they did not want anyone to hear what they were saying, they both spoke Hindi!

In 1944, John was thirteen and took a fine scholarship to

118

his father's public school. He went to the same House, as well. He continued to achieve highly, vowing early on to become a doctor. As he was a lively fellow, he got into a good deal of mischief, none of which was destructive. Teddy hoped that he would not go off the rails – at least, not with the results that had attended his first forays into the love of women. He told him how to be careful. The boy looked at him with an understanding twinkle in his eyes.

'Don't worry, father,' he said simply. 'I've found out a bit more than you did! Actually, I am rather glad that you hadn't,' he added in a charming, gentle and grateful way.

During John's time at school and until he left in 1947, Teddy made as many visits to England as he could manage. In 1946, he realised that his military career was at an end. He did not care for the idea of going to an English regiment, so he accepted the lump sum as he was released from the army. After he had tidied up his business in India, it was January of 1947 that saw his return. He was only thirty-six. He was seriously worried about his prospects; and he had need to be. He had no particular qualifications, yet he still had an enormous responsibility. This weighed heavily upon his mind.

With the burden of impending unemployment and his duties to his son, he decided to see both his father and Foley. He dreaded both of these visits. He had foreseen the problem and he came over in early 1945. The weather was dank and grim, the skies grey and his heart greyer. He had promised to try to see John, saying at the same time, that he might have to disappoint him because of the necessity of attending to his future. He told his son everything. Neither had a single secret one from the other. John wished his father luck, without extending much hope. He understood the priorities. His father had been so good to him at immense personal cost that he could not possibly be selfish about just one visit.

He went to Devizes first. He had written to his father a few weeks beforehand and hoped that he would be able to stay the February night. Charles had replied that one night would be enough, but that he could expect a cold supper, with luck. He arrived at Hetherick in driving rain and by a taxi that he could ill afford. No car had been sent for him. A maid, whom he did not recognise, opened the door.

'Come in, sir!' she said. 'We had been expecting you. The master is in the study.'

'Thank you,' returned Teddy. 'I will find my own way.'

The house smelt stale and damp. It looked none too tidy either. He wended his uncertain way along the dimly-lit passages, eventually reaching the study. A flood of memories, the more recent ones none too friendly, streaked through his anxious mind. He knocked, almost a stranger, upon the door. His father, when he entered, was sitting in an armchair by a dying fire. He was now aged seventy-two and looked ten years older.

'Good evening, Edward,' he said without warmth and hardly a glance at him. 'What is it this time?'

There was something in his voice that stifled any emotion in his son. The coldness of it invaded his heart. He thought of Mary and John both at once, but his father's glare seemed to exclude them. Teddy felt a chill which he would always be incapable of giving to anyone.

'I came to tell you about my plans for the future, Father. I thought that you ought to know them and I wanted to ask your help.'

'You can tell me your plans, boy, but you can forget the help. I thought that I had given enough of that to you in providing for your woman and your illegitimate son. I fancy that I have done enough in that regard to get you off my back.'

Although he half-expected such a reception, Teddy was hurt and deflated. His dead wife and his son seemed to be for ever excluded, taken down from and denigrated by his family. In a final, desperate bid, he decided upon a last throw.

'Father, please listen to me. I shall be coming home for good in 1947. John will be sixteen. He still has two years to go at school and then will go on to medical training or university. Possibly both. I cannot expect Doctor Seymour and his wife to look after him for ever. They have been wonderfully generous. I have no savings because I have to pay for his keep in the holidays and for his fees for the terms.'

'That's your look-out,' said his father gruffly.

'I know that it is, Father,' said Teddy with ever-growing premonitions of unsympathy, 'but I have few prospects in England and I must live here to look after my son. I am determined to do everything I can for him. He is a very bright and winning lad.'

His pleading eyes met no response.

'If you think that I am going to take you back, even as a labourer on the farm, you are much mistaken. You have made nothing of your life so far and I don't see much prospect of improvement in the future. You're not much better than a bastard yourself. You were born in wedlock, but that's about all. I want to see you and your brat no better than I want to see a wet Sunday.'

'But you have never seen John, Father. It would be wonderful for him and his health to spend his holidays on the farm. He would work hard. He's a strong young man.'

'I've never cared much for gypsies. They're a dirty bunch.'

'I have never said this to you before, Father, but you and Foley are the dirtiest people that I know.'

That signalled the end of the interview and the end of their meetings in life. The next one would be his father's funeral. His father's last remark would be the penultimate one. It wounded him as much as the next.

'Your supper is in the kitchen. There are no attractive servants there.'

He went down to the lower regions, took his cold lamb scrags, a couple of potatoes and a glass of beer with which the kindly old maid supplied him.

'I'm sorry it ain't better, sir,' she apologised. 'I just did what the master told me.'

Teddy thanked her kindly and said that she was not to be

121

concerned. He went up to a small, cramped bedroom where he slept fitfully. He was too tired and upset to formulate any positive plans. The next morning, he was graciously driven to the station by the chauffeur.

Still, he was determined.

Two days later he made an appointment to see Foley in London and at his home. Joan was away seeing her elderly mother. His visit was grimmer than even he expected. He was given some rather tired sandwiches and a glass of indifferent sherry by a maid, while he waited for Foley, who had evidently been at a meeting in the city. He was offered no dinner. It would have choked him anyway, he reflected afterwards.

Foley was now forty-four. When he entered the drawing room, Teddy could hardly recognise him. A tall, thin man, unlike his brother who was broad and stocky, he was stooped, round-shouldered and almost smelt of ill-health. Unaccountably, despite his skinny frame, he had an early and inelegant pot-belly, due, Teddy could only suppose, to chronic lack of exercise. He was right. His hair was sparse and not too well groomed. His suit was expensive but its occupant looked dirty, as dirty as his nature. Although Teddy had to speak with him, the adventure made him feel sick. How clean, in contrast and in every way, were he and his son! It was really for the latter that he was here at all.

After perfunctory greetings, Foley asked Teddy to sit down.

'I know why you are here,' he began coldly. 'You are soon to leave India and you want a job. Get a job as an untouchable, is my advice. I have nothing to offer you. Take your peasant of a son with you.'

This filled Teddy with unquenchable fury. He could never have imagined so vile a way of talking. He thought suddenly of the doctor and his family and felt sadder and angrier than ever.

'You never know, Foley,' he announced with some feeling, 'when you will ever need help. Physically you look nearly at death's door. No wonder you get everyone else to do your work for you. It won't be long, I shouldn't wonder, till your brain packs up in disgust as well.'

It was a savage jest, bitterly made, but there was some truth in it.

In spring, 1947, after he had tidied up the administrative loose ends, Teddy returned to England for good. He was to go back to his Indian friends, with his son, for holidays. Neither wanted to forget them. They still spoke Hindi together. It made a kind of bond. Languages often forge those, and the links do not break.

He went back to his small hotel by taxi, crying for his friends, for India, for his son and, he realised, for himself.

6

Reward and Retribution

At the end of April 1947, Teddy installed himself in a small hotel in Swanage, where he had managed to obtain a job as a bank clerk. His experience in administration in the army probably had enabled him for this unenviable post, which held from the start no interest for him. He had, however, to think of his beloved John and he would do anything and everything for him. After about two months in the hotel – rather more like a boarding house – he found a little flat in a peaceful avenue. It consisted of three rooms and an apology for furniture. The first thing he bought, apart from saucepans, was a put-you-up bed for his son. The landlord and his wife were kind. He had given them both an abbreviated version of his life. If he had told them everything – and he liked to unburden his heart, because it helped – they would not have understood. They did not seem to worry about his rent being a month or two overdue. They must have recognised his essential honesty. Even his worn-out clothes breathed that.

He visited John whenever he could and the lad came to stay in his cramped place every holidays. He always hoped that they would be able to depart for India each time, but he understood that his father was fully subscribed financially in regard to his education and he realised that this was an important sacrifice that he was making. For this he was boundlessly and quietly grateful. During the holidays, he studied for his examinations and the floors were strewn with books and papers. His father was delighted with this academic chaos and stepped carefully over it. In the meantime, during the day, John went shopping and made his father's and his own beloved curries, at which he was now expert. He had been taught in India!

In July 1948, John left school. He won a fine award to an eminent Oxford college, where he was to study medicine. His father was restless in his dreary employment and decided that they would both go to India for a bumper holiday with their friends. He had saved up for his leave for a while now and neither of them could wait with any kind of patience for their welcome from their doctor, his wife and his family in Bangalore. They were not to be disappointed. There were all sorts of things in store for them both in life, about which they could not then know. Some were good and where others looked good, they were not. All was good in India. Their Indian family was so close, loving and kind to them both. Teddy and John were at home and recognised their inestimable privileges. They had known them for several years. They had shared their lives. None of them sought any particular reward. When that is the case, it usually arrives.

*

The summer holiday, which lasted a month, went all too quickly. There was so much news to exchange. Politics, frankly discussed, took up much of the evenings. After the doctor returned from his busy day, a lazy al fresco dinner relaxed them all. The whole family attended. As in all eastern and asiatic households, everyone drifted off to various parts and at different times. No one sits glued eyeball-to-eyeball discussing unimportant things such as the incidence of rubbish collection in suburban areas. They sit quietly telling anecdotes, recounting ridiculous stories or

125

talking about the philosophies of life. In a Jewish or an Indian garden, it is often enough to enjoy the peace of loving silence. That is perhaps the best part. In quietness all is spoken.

John walked up and down the gardens with one of the doctor's daughters. Radhika was eighteen years of age, the same as himself. John loved her on sight and he hoped that she felt the same about him. As it happened, she did. She was petite but beautifully shaped and formed; she had oval, loving eyes and a hazily dark complexion. Her hair rippled down her neck. Her lips were the loveliest enticement that John had seen. They smiled to each other and held hands. They spoke Hindi. But they also spoke another language, that of the heart and love. They told each other a thousand things. John told her everything about himself and his father, besides a good deal more without words. The parts without words they both felt came from Heaven. They did.

'I can tell at once,' he said suddenly, 'that I want to marry you. Heaven knows what your father and mother will say. I'm the illegitimate gypsy son of a gentleman, but I'm proud of it. My only fear is that your parents may not be, although I love them, as my father does. Do you think that something could be build on respect?'

'I respect you,' she said, 'but I will have to tread carefully. So shall we both. My parents are very traditional and I respect that code. I think that love can overcome every obstacle, but you must realise that patience and tact are more powerful than force.'

It was a wise remark.

'You get qualified first, John, and I will see that we marry afterwards. I want your dark children. You are dark, like me, but your soul is full of light. I love the Indian side of it and all its other sides too. Until the time, I would rather that you did not have another woman, but I expect that you will,' she said with a twinge of mischief.

'That is in the way of things,' replied John, with a little regretful shame, 'but I am really reserving myself for you.'

In the quiet, cool shade of a huge Indian oak, they

embraced. There, their promise was made and it was one that was never to be broken.

'You are going to make a good Indian,' she said simply.

John was more heartened and flattered by that than he could say. His horizon was beckoning and wide in the sky. As they went to the table in the garden, where dinner was about to start, they both felt warm inside.

The doctor's eye's looked into John's. It was clear one to the other that there was mutual acceptance. No words passed because they were not needed. Indeed, they might have spoilt a deep, silent trust. They both looked up to the sky, which seemed benevolent and kind.

Teddy came to say good-night to John after the lovely, peaceful evening. He sat on his bed and held his hand lovingly. No words were spoken for a few minutes. Mutual faith was enough communication.

'I do not know quite what to say, John,' began his father. 'All I can hope is that you have as much happiness as I had with your mother, but with better judgement. I do not wish to say that I regret a second of our wonderful, if brief, relationship. It will be for ever in my heart. She was a wonderful lady. You have the blood of both of us in your veins. Don't forget that.'

His sentences became more and more staccato. He was so near to tears of love, not regret, that he could hardly speak.

'The tragedy is, my son, that I am a failure.'

'You cannot say that, Father. You have given me everything that a man could want, and all your advice, too. I am only sorry that I am still a burden on you.'

'Don't say that, John. You are my lifeline. I live for you and for your life and its success. I hope only that you will learn from the mistakes of your father. You are the best mistake I ever made!' he added.

'Do not cry, Father. I'm more than glad that you made it! I've promised myself to my girl. No, my lady. I'll have to wait a bit though.'

They kissed each other on the forehead.

*

Father and son returned to England in the summer of 1948. John got his traps ready for Oxford and his father slaved at the bank. It was all he could do to afford the books that his son initially would need. He sold his pocket watch in order to do it, but he did not let on. He yearned for a woman in one way and for the love and success of his son in quite a different one. He sometimes wondered whether he loved people too much. He decided that this was impossible. Immensely proud of his son, he was equally unproud of himself, at the same time. He did not know where to turn. It was true that he had no debts, but he also had no assets. He wondered how on earth he would foot the bills for his son. He must make life respectable for him and, if possible, enjoyable. Teddy went to bed puzzled, every night. Sometimes he drank too much whisky and became morbid. He often asked himself how life had gone so wrong. He blamed himself for everything and then, after another drink, thanked God for all the decent and lovely things.

Some things calmed his restlessness. These were letters from Joan, Foley's wife. They had always been very fond of one another. They shared mutual regrets. They could sympathise about some of the unlovely treats which life had spread before them. Occasionally, they met in a restaurant, somewhere modest, while Foley was away in France titilating his now jaded palate with the next import of wine. They went to bed together sometimes. They shared a very tender love. They did not wish to hurt a soul; they were so discreet that they did not do so. Joan was desperate. She did not see any escape from her bondage to her husband. She said that she could hardly support any longer his stale and unhealthy smell. She regretted her marriage, although she had joined it not only for her own selfish interests but to help her parents. She told Teddy that it was the biggest mistake in her life.

'I have a bit of news for you, Edward,' she said to him on

128

the pillow, one night. 'I think that it might be a break-through.'

'Whatever could that be, Joan? Apart from the memory of my Mary, to which I know that you do not object, as you have a lovely nature, I can't imagine any rip in the lining of the sky.'

'I think that I had better tell you then, Teddy.'

This was the first time for ages that anyone, including himself, had called him 'Teddy'.

They had made very soft, gentle love. They were reciprocally respectful one to the other and innocuous gratitude played an important part in their craving relationship. They did not crave crudely; they were just begging for love. This they gave to each other delicately and with fond consideration.

'I think, Teddy, that I had better tell you that Foley is failing. He makes love about every few weeks, but it is a feeble and hardly ennobling experience. I oblige him for duty only. But there is worse to come. His mental and physical health are declining. There are some days when he is intellectually vastly alive; others when he seems to be in a state of collapse. I think that it will not be long before he retires and sells everything in the firm. We will be very comfortably off, except spiritually!'

'I understand that,' said Teddy, 'but what are you driving at?'

'You must not tell anyone this. He wants to sell Hetherick and buy a small estate in Hampshire. He told me that a hundred or two acres will do. The trouble is that I do not think that he will be able to manage it.'

There was a pause while they both held hands and thought about the import of Joan's announcement. Suddenly, their hands squeezed together in a certain understanding.

'That might solve the problem for both of us,' said Joan.

It was to prove to do so in some ways but not in others. The path was delayed and tricky, the effects of fate a brutality made true.

Before any permanent change, there were to be two more wearisome years in the bank. John was the light in Teddy's life. He and Joan were the two people in the world that he was not going to let down. He let down both of them, with the best will in the world and quite unintentionally. They both forgave him and with love.

*

John was doing well at Oxford and was pleased to share his father's shabby flat in the vacs. He even had some of his friends to stay. They slept hugger-mugger on the floors and everyone was delighted to see one another. No one made a disparaging remark, because John had told them all about his family life. They liked him for that so much. He was very popular, so was his father. The lads loved his honesty, his dowdy clothes and his enormous respect. Everyone seemed to barge in and out of every room without the slightest embarrassment. It was all poor but homely. Everybody who knew him respected John for his intellectual prowess and for his open heart. He could have put them all down any day in an argument but, smiling gently, he never did. They teased him unmercifully. He liked that.

'Fancy a gypsy marrying an aristocratic Indian lady! You lucky old bastard!'

'I'm lucky and a bastard but not old yet!' he would reply. 'You just wait! I'll have lots of sons and they'll all beat yours at cricket at Oxford!'

They loved being able to rib John and he enjoyed it because he knew that it was harmless and meant out of somewhat envious love. They knew about his Indian promise; they hoped that it would be fulfilled; they respected what he stood for. They would all go to his wedding. And they did, although it was not to be quite yet.

Foley's health declined rapidly and his nature with it. Joan wrote regularly to Teddy and kept him abreast of events. Her husband's filthy temper made their life a disgrace, but Joan could do nothing about it. She had her daughter to consider. She also had to think about her aged parents. She was trapped by the foulness of her husband and the poverty of her parents. Foley was still sexually a brute at times; she looked forward only to the occasional visits of Teddy when life would be restored to some kind of normal sweetness. Sex, a crude word, was made into Love, a beautiful one.

'Why can't life be better? Why can't it, for God's sake?' she cried to Teddy. 'At least, you had proper love, even if the end was sad!'

'Wait awhile, my love, and we'll see what happens,' he answered feebly.

'Something will, my dear,' said Joan. 'Something will.'

In January 1950, Charles Foley Osmond died. He was seventy-seven. He had suffered a sudden heart attack brought on, it appeared, by nothing in particular. It could have been caused by one of his now more frequent fits of bad temper or because of his increased consumption of whisky. His doctor did not know. He had grown so tired of his patient's moods that he did not much care either. The two had fallen out. He had tried to make his patient more forgiving. And now Charles had fallen out with the world. No one regretted his death, but they thought that they ought to be present at his chilly funeral. Chilly it was, the chillier still because he had been a man who had been at once loved and loving. He was now despised, and without any affection and hardly any care.

The cold was the old man's beckoner. There were drifts of snow in the Saxon churchyard, the tombstones seemed to wish to claim even the living. Those present at the interment seemed urgent to retreat. Were they fleeing or merely standing back from the flight of an embittered soul?

Teddy had arrived early. He was given a kind glass of brandy by one of the servants. He could not understand why any of them had stayed with his father. Suddenly he thought of India with regret. He thought of Mary and of his son with even more emotion if that could have been possible. He soon left the gathering, without sympathy, without love.

The night before, he had gone into the church where his father lay in his shining, dark oaken coffin. Before entering, he had thought that he should pay a tribute. He opened the case of the little organ. It only had four stops. He did not know quite what to play. His thoughts were unframed and nameless. He closed the case on the two little manuals and played nothing.

He could not have spoken to Foley and he did not dare speak with Joan. He simply left.

As he returned to the house across the yard, he saw an unfamiliar car. He was going to call for a taxi. There was a tall figure beside the car and in front of the gates.

'Step in, Father,' said John.

It was a magnificent moment.

*

It was not long after his father's funeral that Joan wrote to Teddy. She informed him that Foley had sold Hetherick and that he had bought a two-hundred acre farm in Hampshire. It was small in comparison with Hetherick. She told him also that he had sold his huge share in the wine importing business and that he now wanted to become the gentleman farmer. Teddy thought that the word 'gentleman' was hardly applicable. He knew that Joan did not either.

Foley was now unfit for nearly anything. His brain seemed to function only upon various favoured days. Joan was becoming desperate, not for resources of which there were plenty and in abundance, but for life and its strength, vitality and beauty. She was still a very attractive woman – what made her even more attractive was that she had no vanity. Vainness in a woman never draws a decent man. Teddy was decent, if impoverished; he was not vain either.

In the meantime, Teddy was becoming desperate about his life and his future. He was devoted utterly to John, but needed, as he knew that his son must now, someone to caress and hug in bed; and the bed, the sweet bed, of gentle love. There is nothing else like that in life, although there are other loves which are its equal. The only other equals are the love for your sons and daughters. There is a particular love for your only son. Teddy experienced that deeply and it was reciprocated fully by John. God, how Teddy looked forward to his son's marriage, even more than his own happiness! His own well-being was a paltry consideration beside that of his son. He said his prayers now as he had never said them before; not in abject self-pity, rather in thanks for the gifts that God had given him, in thanks for his son and in humble penitence for his own failings. He was to be answered in two or three curious ways. He prayed for John and Joan.

Foley bought New Farm in August 1950. He proved not the slightest bit interested in husbandry, offended all the labourers and generally had no idea what he was doing or supposed to do. The house was delightful for Joan, only spoilt by the presence of her husband and the absence of Teddy. She started to have ideas. She so badly, in her kind heart, wanted to help Teddy and his son. She wanted to help herself, too, but by giving rather than taking.

Joan wrote to Teddy in October. She was desperate for his love and help. She was not a mean, selfish woman, she wanted to help John as well. It seemed that to Joan, Teddy and John that love was craved for, longed for and sacred. That is, of course, the way it always should be. Sitting up alone one night, she wrote:

New Farm
October 21st

My dearest Teddy,
My husband, if that is what he may be called, is in bed. I am therefore in peace to write you this letter. Things are even worse than usual at home. How I envy you, poor though you may be, in your tiny flat, with the sweet

memory of Mary and her lovely son to care for! Suffering is worth the reward if it is positive and for the good. I suffer for nothing. The bills are paid but the mental cruelty seems endless. My only company is the hope of you and John and, of course, Fiona. She is a plain girl, but she has a lovely nature. I don't think that she will ever marry! Does it matter, anyhow? For people like you and me it does. For John it shouts at you! Don't think that I am being vulgar. It's just a loving heart speaking too loudly. Give him my love, if you dare!

Now, unfortunately, to business! Do not think for a moment that I am writing this out of self-interest, other than in the aspect of love, about which we know already. I am writing because I need your help. I also want to help you, Teddy. I think that we could well serve one another, if that is not too dreadful an expression – it was not meant like that! Perhaps, after all, it was? Business. Yes, I have become distracted again. The fact is that the farm is beyond Foley. The whole thing is chaos. I much prefer living in this nice old house than in the smart one in London. At least, the air is clean and the people are homely. But the administration is beyond me and my knowledge of agriculture is nil. I think that I need hardly ask the question, but I shall have to! Will you come here and manage the farm? It is all grain, so there are not many labourers to employ. The foreman has stuck by me and he knows everybody. He will be able to find able hands. Whatever Foley says – and he says little these days – you and John will have a quiet, loving home. Do not think that I am patronising you. In one respect, you have had the worst luck in the world. I do not know whether or not I shall succeed, but I am going to try to reverse that awfulness. Tell John what I have said to you both, but make sure to destroy this letter. All my love, Teddy.

Joan

*

134

Teddy thought about Joan's proposition for a week. John was up at Oxford and he did not want to unrest him. However, he thought that a decision such as he would be about to make must concern the one person for whom he was totally responsible. He still thought of his natural responsibility with the greatest love and tenderness. He was so honest that he never even dreamt of any kind of escape. He and his son were partners now. It was a partnership that would never be broken.

Teddy went up to Oxford a couple of days after he had had the letter from Joan. He had no need to explain the situation to John, but he did feel that he had to talk with him and to ask – yes, ask – his advice. They met in a little pub in the Broad. It was rather crowded and full of jolly students, but they ate a filling wad for lunch. They also downed a few beers, perhaps one too many!

'John,' said Teddy when they got outside, 'don't call me Father any more. Call me Edward. I would rather like that. After all, we are two men together now. I just wish that your father were a better man, but he has got just as many faults, even more perhaps, as anyone else.'

Speaking stopped. But the interval was, graciously, not long.

'What to you want to say to me, Edward, my father?'

As they strolled up and down the Broad and the High – they could never after have counted how many times – Teddy told his son absolutely everything, concluding with his offer from Joan. He even told him about their love and sweet John was completely unshocked.

'Good for you, Edward!' he exclaimed, 'but be careful, not of love but of your half-brother. He is a snake. Don't go and get bitten in the grass. I am on the way to being a doctor, but there are some wounds that no man can heal. Permanent damage is one of them.'

'Shall I accept the offer then, John?'

'You are miserable in your own work,' replied his loving son. 'Try this. Try to be happier. But I hope that I can tell you something that you may not like and from which I hope that I will never have to suffer. Nor you, either. You have given love, but never accept slavery.'

As it was to happen, he accepted both. He wrote to Joan at the end of October.

7

Bitterness, Guilt and Love

Teddy wrote a long letter to Joan in October 1950. In it he told her everything about himself and John; particularly about his deep aspirations for his son. He knew that Joan would understand him and she did. Neither she nor Foley had ever met John, but they soon would, although only Joan would know the beautiful truth as John and his father did. That was the sharing part and it was equal and available to all three of them. Foley was outside in the arctic cold of his heart, in the despicable shabbiness of his nature, in the total lack of beauty in his soul. John was soon to know his father's half-brother; his father's half-brother never knew who he was, his lovely nature nor what he stood for. After all, his father's half-brother had never known the immediate, compulsive love that gives true and honest life. He thought that mistakes were a pity. He would never know that the making of mistakes out of love were, and always had been, given by God. He did not think that he had ever committed a sin. The man who thinks that is deprived.

In his letter, he told Joan that he would come to New Farm as its manager. He said that he did not think that this would be until December. He would have to tidy up his affairs and settle things with the bank. Beforehand, he would have to have an interview with Foley in order to arrange terms of employment. He would have to see that he had adequate quarters. He wanted them for John too, but he almost dared not ask. However, he had an idea which was at once pathetic and ingenious. It was also loving.

Because his son was at university, he had to have somewhere to lay his tired, loving head during the vacations. He would also need some pocket money. Foley had never seen him. He would never know who he was. He resembled Teddy only in his physical strength and in his heart. They could never have been taken for father and son. A good, close look might have revealed this, but people do not go about with magnifying glasses! Hearts join people, not looks.

Joan had told him that there were two or three cottages on the farm for labourers and their wives. There was one which was very small and dilapidated and which sometimes casual labourers used. She said that, without any disrespect, this one would be ideal for John. He could work on the farm and have his private place, modest as it would be. She added that she would, unknown to Foley, make sure that it was both habitable and clean. Faithfully, she did both. Father and son were to spend some lovely times there together, both alone and with Joan. They all needed each other greatly. That need would become far greater eventually, but they were not to know that yet.

Joan warned Teddy that Foley was not only beastly but unreliable. She could not give him any indication whatever about his financial remuneration. She said that he would never go without food and that he would have a small flat at the top of the house. It would be modestly furnished. She added that she suspected that he might have to work all hours that God sent and a few more besides.

She proved to be right. She made him a promise in the course of her very kind letter: *'Don't worry about love. I'll look after that for us both'*. This she did and to fulfilment.

The next step was going to be the rickety one. Teddy had to go and see Foley. Before that dreaded interview, he wrote to John.

'Be with me in November,' he wrote. 'I am working for both of us. I am going to see your wretched half-uncle Foley about the farm manager's job that he wants me to do. He does not know, and never will, that you will have a guaranteed holiday job on the farm. I shall, I expect, be in charge of hiring labour. He does not know you by sight, so he will never guess that you and I are partners! Joan is going to see that a tiny cottage for you is clean, tidy and well-provided. As one slave does to another, I shall boss you about! Let's just pretend! I sometimes wonder if my luck will turn.'

John wrote a wonderful letter back. His father to him was an unsung hero. Most of all, of course, he was his father. The strong ropes of faith would always tether them one to the other.

'Keep the faith, my Father Edward,' he concluded.

*

It was a bleak November day. Teddy had thought that it would be best to visit Foley before he burnt his boats at the bank. There did not prove to be much tinder in either heart. Teddy had the correct premonition that he would get a bad bargain. He felt trapped. He had no fine thoughts other than those for Joan. His son lived on for his Mary, so that he thought about them at the same time. He wondered quietly whether God would ever give him a break.

Teddy found his way to the Hampshire farmhouse, conveyed by a taxi driver who was none too sober. As he was the only one available on the windy station, Teddy had to accept the risk. It was eight o'clock at night when he rang at the door. The lantern above it was swinging in the wind. There was still no answer. He tried the stout door, but it was locked. He rang again. This time, he heard the scuttering of footsteps in the flagged passage and the door was at last opened by an old woman, obviously a servant. She was none too gracious, either.

'Who are yer then and what does yer want?'

'I am the brother of your employer, I have come for

supper and I shall be attending an interview,' replied Teddy with little grace but with some sarcasm. 'I have already wiped my feet, so you may let me in without peril to your situation.'

'Sit in the 'all. I'll see the mistress.'

'Tell me the way and I'll see her myself. You may take my hat and coat.'

Sourly, she obliged.

Joan leapt up when Teddy, unannounced, came into the drawing room. Her face was a picture of happiness and misery at the same time. At this moment, happiness seemed to assume the dominant. She was obviously both anxious and thrilled.

'Teddy!' she exclaimed. 'It is more than wonderful to see you. I don't think that I can tell you quite how wonderful it is. I think that we had both better have a rather large glass of sherry to wish each other good luck!'

She smiled engagingly and with beckoning. They were in love.

The evening passed without event. Foley was not, apparently, well. He was in bed. Teddy did not go in to see him. Neither did his wife. Perhaps his absence had been contrived deliberately to make Teddy uneasy and timid. It certainly achieved the former, but not the latter. Joan and Teddy were not slow to embrace, promising a rendez-vous the next day. Caution would have to be the watchword. She wanted Teddy on the farm; to ruin this opportunity by an early and overt indiscretion would have been madness.

After a long and lasting hug, they went their separate way to bed with some regret. They both had that giving nature and inclination which is never taken away. Love is not subject to the subtraction of time. All men feel the same and so do decently-loving women.

*

Teddy got up early the next day. He did not revere the face which greeted him in the shaving-mirror, although it was his

140

own. It was lined with an anxiety which he could only regret and strained with hopes which he longed to be satisfied. It was also striped with dread. The bank job was a penance. Would helping Foley set him free and give rein to the generosity that he would like to extend to his son? He did not know what the answer to either of these questions might be. He merely tortured himself with a sense of duty, with a sense of pride and with an extreme sense of the loves which he had known and knew keenly still. He knew his helplessness. He knew that his fate was in the hand of another. Even worse, the fate of his son. He dared not think of the consequences of his failure. His poor heart was filled with shame for himself. It was filled with ineffable pride and hope for his son. It was filled with great love for Joan. He loved her well beyond the sheets, the comfort and exhilaration of which he hoped John would be experiencing, but without any pain. When he thought of John, he automatically thought of Mary. The sweetness of love never sours, neither does it perish. Where on earth was love?

It certainly was not in Foley's study at eleven o'clock on Tuesday. His heart was fixed in November. It never moved from there. It was to die in it, but not during the next few years.

The maid told Teddy that the master was ready to see him. He walked to a rather cheap-looking little study, where he was, without grace, invited to sit down. This he did opposite a shining, almost unused table, untainted by the ink stains and glass-marks that had covered that of his father. Foley sat in a velvet dressing-gown on a velvet chair. Anyone less like a farmer one could never have imagined. Teddy's strong, healthy hands contrasted conspicuously with his half-brother's weedy, crab-like claws; his firm, if worried face was a contradiction of that of his brother, which looked, for all the world, like a concave dish of porridge. The room smelt of stale and unhealthy sweat. Foley looked as mean and as ill as he was – although he could have helped himself.

'I have called you here,' he said arrogantly to Teddy, 'in

order to make some dispositions. You may accept what I have to offer, as you may happen to choose. You seem to have made choices without much regard to wisdom for most of your life. It occurs to me to wonder whether I am wise in asking you for your help now. I have not made many mistakes in my life, but I think that this ought not be one of them.'

Here he paused. He looked not only ill but supercilious. His hooded eyes shed scorn and contempt. He knew full well that he could not tread on any other farm manager as successfully as he could upon his brother. He was going to make capital, in the most beastly way, out of his necessity. Dreadful people rarely know what is in store for them.

The fleeting thoughts of both men were but the matter of seconds.

'I will come here to manage your farm, Foley,' said Teddy without love. 'You will have to accommodate me, feed me and pay me. You will also have to accept my son and to pay him for his labour on his vacations from university.'

'I did not know that gypsies became doctors or that they would be accepted as such,' said Foley, with a revolting sneer.

'God made everyone just as good and bad one as the other. You cannot leer like that when you talk about my son.'

'You will never present him,' answered Foley pompously, 'upon my estate. I don't want any bastards here. You can run the place as you wish, as long as the profits don't fall. You will have a free billet and three thousand pounds a year. That is the end of my generosity. I shall pay you monthly. I know that you have to work for your bastard, but you'll have to work your balls off to do it!'

'Thank you, Foley,' said Teddy, with the tears of rage and pride starting in his eyes, 'I shall arrive in December and I will work hard.'

'That is indeed what you will have to do,' said sickly Foley.

Teddy went to his cold bed and said his prayers. Some of them were for himself and most for John. He made God a lot of promises. As it happened, he was able to keep them all. Everyone would keep all of theirs for him. He was lucky, but he did not know it now.

*

Teddy returned to London. The day was grey and cold. He felt despair and hope both at the same time. It was a strange sensation.

John was soon to come home, if that is what it could be called, from Oxford, where he was doing brilliantly. His gentle nature never derided his father. He would not have minded to have shared a barn loft with him. They were like brothers. They had and shared the same kind of pride.

What worried Teddy was where John would live. He knew that Joan would fix up the cottage for him; what he dreaded was the suspicion of his contemptible brother. He prayed for the power of deception. He had his prayer granted. Joan and his son were able as his accomplices. The situation was urgent, since John still had at least three years to go before becoming fully qualified. Besides, because he was pledged in marriage, he could not let the family down. Radhika occupied his heart and the thoughts of his mind and soul; her dear father and mother, Roshan and Varsha, could never be betrayed, particularly after the trust that they had given him, a foreigner; although neither did he feel one nor did they hold him to be so. He knew that to marry an Indian girl was an immense responsibility. He had to have a proven position in life before he could possibly join her in the final step. He was striding forward to take that. His father was going to be a great help. He could not count the cost; it did not matter.

The day after his return, Teddy handed the bank his statutory month's notice. His employers showed little regret, for he had never been particularly apt, often having made embarrassing, if unintentional mistakes. They had been kind to him in some ways. They knew that his life had not been without its hardships, but nothing personal had slipped between them.

'What are you going to do now?' asked his manager on the last day.

'I am going to be a farm manager for my brother in Hampshire,' replied Teddy, without enthusiasm. 'I am not cut out for banking and I must give my son a home and more support.'

'I did not know that you had any family,' rejoined the manager, looking slightly surprised.

'I had one when I was eighteen, actually. He is the best mistake I ever made! You'd like him. He's got far more brains than both of us put together! Oh, sorry, I shouldn't have said that! I suppose it was just fatherly pride.'

'That is more than understandable, Mr Osmond. But don't you think that leaving the bank is rather a false move, if you don't mind me asking?'

'I don't mind at all Mr. Evans. John's mother is dead and I love another woman. I want to give John some healthy fresh air. I think that I may be able to oblige both our needs at the same time!'

Emboldened by the manager's sympathy, he told him a little of his history. The little man told him to sit down. Unexpectedly, he produced a small flask of whisky and two glasses.

'Edward,' he said with some affection, 'have a drink with me. You are a better man than I am, although not perhaps such a careful one! It may be that carefulness does not fulfil the heights of a man's ambitions. Your life has seen so much more than mine. You might experience hardship, but you'll never be as dreary as me. My book of life is short and nearly closed.'

'I think the next few chapters of mine may be a little difficult to read,' replied Teddy with a humourous inflection in his voice, 'but I hope to enjoy some of the paragraphs!'

'I bet you will, too! Good luck to you Edward. Good luck to your love and to your son.'

It was a very gentlemanly farewell, on the part of two very different men. They would never meet again but, curiously, they would always think of one another with respect.

144

Relief and anxiety invaded his mind. Relief that he was unburdened of a job that he loathed and that he was to return to his beloved countryside; anxiety that his life at New Farm under Foley would be a tale of tortured muscles. He would have very nearly no money. He would occupy a degrading position. But there would be John beside whom he would work anonymously in an unspoken bond of pretended unrecognition but of deep, silent love; and there would be Joan, whom he would love in a different way. He could not wait to take her in his arms. Two loves, he told himself, were worth all the bank pensions in the world. They were worth slaving for as well.

He returned to his lodgings and started to sort out his clothes, papers and letters. He had decided to go to Oxford for the weekend. He could not afford it, but he was determined to do so. He wanted badly to tell John about the new turn that life was to take. He also wanted to ask him for his love and advice. He craved love, above all from his own flesh and blood. He needed the warmth of someone who cared for him. He knew that John did this. He would have liked to have made his visits a surprise, the encounter of wide-eyed recognition and delight. As he knew how many and demanding would be John's commitments, he realised that he would have to tell him by telephone.

He managed to contact him and they met in their pub in the Broad. They consumed a modest lunch and a couple of pints of quite decent beer. It was obviously not the place for conversation, so they mutually agreed to leave that until after the meal. As it was raining heavily, they went back to Magdalen and up to his rooms. He welcomed the smell of books and papers, the regulated chaos of his studious son and his handsome and cleanly appearance. They took an armchair either side of an unlit fireplace. The fires in their hearts were alight, so the physical side of things did not come into consideration.

Teddy told John everything. He told him about Foley and

145

his revolting treatment of him; about Joan and her kindness to him; about his secret dispositions for his work on the farm. He told him that his health, with all the work that he had to do academically, was of prime importance. He told him about the little cottage. He told him about his heart. He had to tell someone everything; he chose his son, who enjoyed being told.

'I am going on December 10th,' said Teddy.

'I am coming on the 17th, Edward. Make sure that you need a new farmhand. You must go home now because of your train. I've got some news for you which might mend a dismal Christmas. But I'm going to keep you in suspense!'

'What do you mean?' asked his father, with half an idea that his son was just like him although, he hoped, more sensible.

'You think about it, Edward! It's the greatest news of my life! I'm saving it up until I come to the cottage.'

'You're a rat, John! I shall just have to enjoy guessing.'

'Guess kindly,' said John, with warm eyes that twinkled with love for his father. Teddy did not have to guess anything.

*

Teddy's arrival at New Farm was not accorded the accolade of his brother's presence. He had been in bed all day, an absence that no one seemed to regret. He had been in chilly sweats all the previous night and subject, intermittently, to nameless terrors in dreams. He even drank a glass of port, on his own, of course, at about three o'clock in the morning. His pyjamas were smelly, cold and damp. He had not shaved for at least two days, but his growth was so feeble that he only looked dirty. He loathed his brother, but did not see what he could do without him. He was jealous of his convivial character and the charm that he appeared to exercise upon everyone that he ever met.

The same rather dismal maid opened the door to Teddy.

There was a stiff wind and it clattered to, seeming to shut out the positivity of any definite future. He was left, chattering with cold in the hall, until Joan was fetched from upstairs.

'We both look dreadful,' she said, with her usual sardonic humour. 'Let's go and get better-looking by what's left of the fire in the drawing room. Do you want scrambled eggs or brandy or both? If the latter, in which order?'

'I love you, Joan,' wept Teddy, without answering either question.

'Don't cry, love. I'll take your coat which that miserable old wretch of a maid had not even the manners to lift from you, and we'll both start with a decent cognac – it's not going to be mere brandy tonight!'

Dear Joan. How vivacious she had remained, even after tribulations about which Teddy could never have dreamt. When she brought in the glasses, they hugged with tears of new wonder. They were not going only to be lovers again, they were going to be friends. They talked about a thousand things. They made promises. They were generous and fine in the sight of God. Their shoulders straightened as they braved the world. Love mended so much for both of them, and in such a few seconds. Teddy went up to his little flat, washed as he always did meticulously, said his desperate prayers, gave his love to the world, besought Heaven and went to bed. Joan did much the same. Foley stank quietly on his own. John could not wait to see his father. He could not wait to see Radhika. He did not exactly know it, but she could not wait either.

*

Teddy lost no time in showing a faked enthusiasm for his new job. A rather rotten-looking labourer drove him and Foley round the farm. They passed the cottage where John was to live in his university holidays. But had Teddy done what he would have liked, it would have drawn down upon him a suspicion that he could never have allowed. He let the

147

weeds grow rank and the tiles slip, he did not plant the little garden, which it would have delighted his heart to have done. As they were passing, (he and Foley), he thought of India, his son and his future daughter-in-law. Radhika was beautiful, gentle and giving. Teddy envied his son but in the kindest and most sympathetic way. Had not he loved out of his race as well? He hoped with his whole heart that everything would be a fragrant success. There were, for him at least, a few unfragrant moments to come, however.

The estate was absolutely run-down. The hedgerows were overgrown and untidy, the fields were manifestly ill-fertilised and the buildings, cottages and sheds in a state of deprivation and disrepair. Teddy said nothing as they drove through the December afternoon back to the December heart of the house. He had appraised everything. He knew what he could do with the land. He knew, furthermore, that what he could do would enrich Foley but not himself. But he had two wonderful secrets which he enfolded in his heart that night: he would make this painful gate open for the love of Joan and for the help of his son. How pleased Mary would have been to see John a son of the soil, her beloved soil! How delighted she would have been to see him growing into the fine man that he already nearly was! How he became so happened not very long afterwards. His honest energy made him burst into the world, a glad man. He would have to admit what he had done. In fact, he had done it for Radhika; he was desperate not to let her down on their first time. He had to have knowledge not to do that. He was to start with not a great deal, but that was more than enough. The rest was in the future.

After a rather frugal and somewhat unrewarding supper, Foley and his half-brother met in the dim study. Joan decided upon an early bath and went to bed. Foley stepped uncertainly down the corridors on his stick. He was thin and his hands trembled. His voice was none too steady either, and this was not because of drink. He was failing, but slowly. Far too slowly for Teddy.

Once they had uneasily installed themselves, there

appeared to be no immediate prospect of conversation. They sat in unanimated silence for about ten minutes. Neither of them could think of anything interesting to say. Foley knew what he wanted to talk about. Teddy was determined to wait for the opening gambit. He did not, at any cost, want to be on the defensive; he had too much to defend. He would have to do that with some dexterity and skill.

After what seemed an age, Foley broke the crust.

'What do you say about the state of things as you have seen them, Edward?'

'I suppose that you want my opinion, Foley? Do not answer the question, I will give you the reply,' he said dismissively. 'The whole place is in the hell of a mess, the buildings are in a dreadful state and the land is agriculturally deprived. You obviously have not nearly enough labourers. I have noticed that the dusty cottage windows show no occupants. For two hundred acres you only have a foreman and two elderly workers. I know that you only grow wheat and barley, but is this enough? You need someone – possibly several able hands – to restore the buildings and cultivate the land better. I think that I had better employ a few more people, even if they are only on a temporary basis. Leave it to me. I will do you the cheapest deal possible. If you do not cheesepare them too hard, they will pay you dividends.'

Foley listened with dismay but with a surprising respect.

'I leave it to you, Edward,' he said weakly.

Without nearly the trouble that he had feared, without even any at all, he had opened the way to his beloved bastard. Bastard! He was a king to Teddy!

On about December 20th – Teddy could never remember dates – a stranger arrived at New Farm. It was an extraordinary performance by two men – a father and a son who had to pretend that they did not know one another.

'Edward,' said Foley, even before they had thought of supper, 'will you take your temporary labour to his shack?'

Father and son got into the Land Rover.

There were no words that needed to be spoken on their

way to the cottage. It was one of the best of all the long journeys that Teddy had ever made. It was short, but he could have wished that it had lasted for ever. Mary and John were beside him both at once.

*

'Here you are,' said John. 'Open the envelope and look!'

They had only just opened the door. Miraculously, there was a fire in the grate of the small downstairs room. A card was on the mantelpiece. In bold writing it said: '*Have a wonderful homecoming!*' It was from Joan.

Before even unpacking his bags, John sat down.

'Go on, Edward!' he said. 'I told you to open the envelope!'

'Obedience is all, I suppose. Actually, I can't wait.'

The contents were a wonderful surprise.

'Photographs from India! How lovely they are! How wonderful your future wife!'

'I have been given a promise that I could never have deserved. They definitely are going to allow me to marry her!'

'What an inestimable privilege and what a grand hope you have in store, my son. Love her, hold her and keep her.'

'That is a lesson that I have learnt from you, Edward, my Father. Some people may deride you, some despise you, but I know your real worth and your true father's love. I would not change you for anyone. I know the sacrifices that you have made for me born of infinite concern. You don't forget that kind of thing!'

Teddy sat mute. He sat mute for some minutes. So did John. They did not need to say anything. They simply sat in the far domain of love. It was without horizon yet filled with hope.

'Sit down again, John,' said Teddy with authority. 'I am the chef tonight. I'll see what Joan has put in the kitchen and I will give us both a surprise!'

Neither of them minded what he ate. I happened to be heated-up cottage pie. It was just what Joan thought that they would need. A good old wad. They followed this with stewed apples and cold rice pudding. They both thought that they had eaten fit for kings. They were kings to each other, which is what mattered.

At about midnight, Teddy left the cottage. His heart did not but only his body. The farmhouse was cold upon his return and so was he.

The next day, father and son would sweat it out as strangers. Their toil was made the better for vision and promise.

*

John's first night was full of thought, loneliness and yet gratitude. He had brought quite a number of books with him for his study, but he knew that his stay would be short this time; he would have to return to Oxford in barely a month. He knew that he would be returning to the farm in early spring. He wondered when his next trip to India would be. Then he would be betrothed and make his promises. He could hardly wait for those. He was waiting for Radhika just as much as she was for him. Whilst she was keeping herself a virgin for him, she hoped that he had burst the bounds; she would forgive him and ask no questions. She did not have to, as it happened, for he, with his honest heart, told her everything. Experience is not the same as love. It helps, but it cannot compare with the bonds that can never be broken. John had the honest heart of his father. Even in his early life, he wanted to be husband and father of children.

So John went to bed. He said his prayers in Hindi. Although he did not know it, but just simply hoped, so did Radhika and her parents. He was not to know then the degradation which would be afforded him the next day. All he wanted to be was a kind, open, giving doctor and the father of his beloved wife's children. One day, he would be

151

both. It was the waiting that taxed him, and which gave him even more determination.

On the day after John's arrival, they both set off in the morning to do hedging and ditching. Layering a thorn hedge an acre long makes the hedge look beautiful but flays your hands. Even if you use a thong to secure the hook, you cannot wear gloves. The hook can slip from your grasp and you can cut yourself badly. Across the fields they both went, and for days afterwards, across and across again. They worked all day with the other workers, of which there were now a few more, Teddy working and supervising at the same time. Some of the farm lads helped. They broke for lunch and took out their bent tins. These usually contained a large peeled onion, eaten like an apple, a hunk of bread and a big slab of cheese. They all drank cold milk tea out of a bottle. Teddy knew this classic, sustaining meal from his days as a boy. John came to like it too. At the end of the day there was often a naked dip in the river, refreshing and with no shame, a quick dry in the grass and back for cider or beer. This happened in winter and summer. That's how you got tough! John liked the life, though he knew that he had to look after people rather than crops. But he thought that there was dignity in both callings. That was until he met Foley for the first time.

It was a cold, damp morning with no wind but a bite to the air. Teddy and John were at the ditches. It was a messy, hard job, without interest. The ploughing and sowing had naturally been done. Ploughing was a fine task behind a great shire horse, gentle and so strong. The single ploughshare and the guided animal, almost like a person, were as one. The lad had to know how to guide and when to step on the bar to make sure that the share kept its depth. John had to learn the art of the straight furrow. This morning, both father and son were filthy and cold.

Foley shambled up to them. They stopped work in order to hear what he had to say. With their hooks in their hands, they stood cowed like two peasants from the middle ages.

152

Foley looked somewhat dismayed about the mud on his thin shoes.

'I see that you are progressing well,' he said without interest.

'It's coming along but it's a long job, this,' replied Teddy.

'This lad is one of your new labourers, I suppose?' enquired Foley.

'Yes. His name is John. He is a student.'

'John what?'

'John Adams,' John lied.

'Well, John Adams, what are you studying and where?' asked Foley in a rather contemptuous tone of voice.

'Medicine, Sir. In London.' he lied again.

'Well, try not to murder too many of your patients! I would never trust a dark-looking doctor myself!'

Foley walked off.

Father and son looked at one another.

'Don't be hurt,' said Teddy. 'It's not worth it. I have had experience of that.'

'It makes me laugh Edward, my Father. And it makes me all the prouder, too! Let's get on with this bloody hedge.'

They smiled broadly. They finished the 'bloody hedge' with the promise of a supper together that evening, in the cottage and after a bath! Teddy notified Joan about some promising leftovers and asked her if she could possibly join them. Broadminded John was delighted. He liked Joan and he wished his father some consolation and happiness. Teddy realised how good it was to have such a wonderful son.

*

In 1950, Edward was aged thirty-eight, Foley, forty-nine, Joan thirty-seven and John twenty. They all looked fine for their age except Foley, who looked as if he were made of mediaeval parchment.

John returned to Oxford and his jolly, chaotic lodgings in January. He was glad to get back to his work and his friends, but he hated parting from his father. They instinctively grasped both hands and turned quickly away on the draughty station. They were both emotional, giving, loving men who hated farewells. They immediately said their prayers for each other. Then there was, for both of them, that inexpressibly empty space created by the sense of absence; the absence that you hope will be transformed into presence as soon as providence can manage it.

Teddy worked on, and alone. From time to time he had letters from India. Roshan and Varsha told him of the love that Radhika had for John. They said how very glad they were that John was to become a doctor when he would be a fine man for their daughter, bring up wonderful sons and daughters and be a true son to them. Teddy wrote back. He told them about his situation. He did not think it would be prudent to say that he loved another woman after his first wife, although they had not been married and she had died. He did not know that John had told everything, in his typically honest way. He had said that gypsies are next to Indians. This was not in any deprecating manner; it was just to say, with deep respect, that they shared the same heritage in certain respects. They shared some of the same looks; the same kindred and the same liberality of mind; the same, tough tenderness. He said that he would now be experienced enough to make his future wife happy and that he would honour her entirely ever after. As it occurred, they would never break faith in the gratitude of long pleasure, a pleasure that would last all their lives.

Life on the farm was hardly ennobling. Teddy saw less and less of Foley, as did his wife. She and Teddy were practically thrown together. She was still a verdant young woman. She and Teddy often embraced before they went their separate ways to bed. It was to be that they were not going to be separate for much longer. After a couple of months, they slept together. They made deep and relieved love. They savoured each other's body. They also had the respect that real love gives. For Teddy and Joan it was not just a common jerk in the dark. It was a bond of respect. John was going to be the same as his father – a wayward and eventually faithful gentleman. Never was he to betray his wife, he had no need to; she would be his perpetual splendour. The thought of their everlasting bond enhanced his intentions to study. He was working for Radhika.

At the other end of the world, or so it seemed, Teddy and Joan were forging their own fetters. They were fetters that they wanted. They both knew what would happen. They were bound together by an indissoluble metal. In October 1951, Penelope was born. Foley was immensely and disgustingly proud because he thought that he was the father. He was now nearly impotent at an early age, but Joan could still aver that her husband was the father. The latter was at a stage when he could and would believe nearly anything, no matter how improbable.

Teddy had taken Joan for many a walk across the improved fields during her pregnancy. He loved, as many artists have, the beautiful shape of a woman with a coming child. He was longing, as Joan was, for the fruition of the ripe corn of his seed. They now loved one another as never before. In the woods, he felt her belly and the already moving child. His hands were now rough from his undignified work. Mercifully, they felt softened by the touching of his Joan's body and by the thought of the littler one inside it.

Foley did not show much interest. He merely displayed a haughty proudness for a gift that he had not given.

As a cheap student hand, John came down for labour the following December. He lived in the same cottage that his father had deliberately kept free, although it could have been occupied by others. He had worked harder himself for the lack of one less labourer, in order to reserve the vacancy. Earlier, he had made up his mind to tell John about his tiny Penelope. He wondered how his son would take it. He wondered whether he would be jealous – all the love had been given only to him before. Teddy felt nervous because

155

he dreaded offending the son of his life. He drove rather shakily to the station, without any clear idea of what to say.

*

The wind blew Teddy's greying hair untidily. Equally untidy was John's prolific mane as he veritably leapt out of the train. He looked at once tired and eager. He obviously could not wait to meet his father. They crashed into an unembarrassed embrace.

'God, Edward, I've wanted to see you!'

'Lord in Heaven, John, I have longed to see you, you old sinner!'

All of a sudden, Teddy thought about what he had unintentionally said. Holding himself back, he decided that, although honesty was what he intended, he would have to leave the admissions until later. For the moment, it would be more than enough to get home, forgetting about what some people might have called sin.

The little cottage was already warm and there was a hot-pot on the stove. A bottle of wine graced a little side-table. There was even a corkscrew beside it. Joan had been more than kind. She had also placed a note on the mantelpiece:

'I can't be with you tonight. Penelope will need her mother and her feeds! We never neglect those whom we love. Have a tremendous evening. I bet you'll sit up till all hours! You men are dreadful!'

Teddy had to return to the farmhouse, pretend to eat something in the kitchen to which he was consigned for his eating needs and crash shut his bedroom door. This he reopened silently, as silently as he left the house and strode down the lane to see his son. In his pocket was a flask of stolen brandy. He felt guilt but did not apologise for it.

The two men sat down.

'I've got something to tell you, John,' said his father

156

without ceremony. His heart was beating hard. He did not want to offend the person whom he loved best in his life. He looked ashamed and abased. He poured them both a drink, asking if the meal, which would not spoil, could be delayed by a few minutes.

'There cannot be a problem when you are here, Edward. Get it off your chest. I don't think that either of us could be shocked by anything, could we?'

'No, John. But this could hurt you.'

'You could never hurt a fly, Edward, and I'm bigger than that!'

With his heart in his mouth and in other places as well, Teddy told John that he had just had a daughter by Joan. John got up without a word and poured his father another brandy. Himself as well.

'Stand up, Edward, my Father!'

Edward obeyed, looking rather vacant.

'I want to see my little sister as soon as I can. You great old fellow! I'm so glad for you. When I can manage it, I shall see Joan. Medical advice is free!' he added in a spirit of levity.

'God, it's kind of you to have taken it all like that, John.'

'Not kind at all. It's a joy and an honour, Edward.'

They both enjoyed a huge supper. The brandy disappeared and so did the wine. They were both happy and forgiving men. At the same time, they knew that they had nothing for which to forgive one another, only that for which to thank.

Much later, the two paupers, rich in hope and love, said goodnight. They both returned to toil, not all of which was rewarding.

8

The Thread and the Windfall

Life at the farm was grim. The gardens were large and the
land was under-supplied with labourers. To make up for
Foley's parsimony, Teddy had to work until dark, when he
returned, filthy, to the house. He would go to his bathroom,
which was unheated, and descended to the dimly-lit kitchens
for a pauper's supper. His sole delights were his loves: Joan,
his little daughter and his son John. He lived for them all,
and only for them. Sometimes he wondered whether he
even lived for himself, but he realised that he had to because
that was his solemn duty to his kin. He remembered that a
Jewish friend had once told him that man's prime duty was
to survive. It was his duty not only to himself but to his family
and to those whom he loved. He never forgot that message,
even though he had often thought of taking his own life. He
did not know quite how he would do this, or even if he
would have the courage. Would it be tablets and the bottle of
vodka or the knife? He decided that it would be neither
because, although he was now wallowing in a dismal, cold,
muddy pool of depression, he had to live for those whom he
loved so deeply.

He felt ashamed of himself whenever these thoughts
assailed him. His hands were crooked now and his back bent
with toil. He received no thanks, other than from Joan, but
he had love (which his brother could not really understand)

from his daughter and weekly letters from John. These he opened privately. His torn hands trembled. The letters were always loving, grateful and thankful. They were not addressed to the house but to one of the cottages, which was sometimes his but unoccupied during his absence at study. Teddy would unlock the door and find, regularly, a damp letter on the boards in the little hall. Having read what John had written, always in thanks and consideration, Teddy shoved the pages into his coat, where they became even damper during his day's work. Still, they were where they should be, next to his heart. At night, he put them under his pillow. Sometimes he slept gratefully with his head on another pillow in the main house. Those times were when Foley was too debilitated to know anything. They were sweet nights. Then he always kissed little Penelope and thought of his John. He and Joan would love each other before his dawn departure for the dismal farm.

And so the Thread of Life, although it appeared broken at times, spun its inevitable way. For every vacation, John worked, unidentified, at New Farm. He did not yet know about The Thread. He was soon to do so. When he did it was to be most wonderful moment of his life. In the meantime, his studies continued apace and he was already wondering whether he might specialise. Although he and Radhika corresponded a great deal, and lovingly, they did not see each other particularly often. John's studies and the lack of money restricted this but she was more than calmed of her desires in the thought that she must keep herself for him. She knew that he would not be able physically to do this, because he was a very immediate, giving man. Despite this, she knew, and she was right, that he would inwardly never love another woman in the same way as he did her. They both dreamed of one another and they seemed to know, across the infinite miles, that they did so. Their souls and bodies joined in the distant nights.

These days, Foley was scarcely ever seen. The sight of him was hardly regretted. He kept to his stuffy and rank-smelling bedroom more and more and only came downstairs for the odd frugal meal and to do his accounts. Sometimes he even neglected these and Teddy had to call him to task. Foley's desk was always locked and his brother was never allowed access to it. One day, he was to break it open, antique as it was. But that was not to be quite yet.

Whenever John came down to slave away, Teddy paid him out of his own meagre pocket because he did not trust Foley. In various ways, he got it back from him afterwards. The two men were always delighted when Joan came down to the cottage for an evening of affection. John said to her one night, quite unexpectedly, after a homely supper: 'I'm going to tell you something now, Joan. Don't be embarrassed, will you! You're my new mother and I mean it. That sounds silly from a man of twenty-one, doesn't it?' There were tears in his big, dark eyes.

'"Silly", you dear boy!' she exclaimed. 'No one could have been more silly than I! I'm proud and honoured.'

'And I'm just the same about Edward, you and Penelope. I know, you see.'

There was a silence. Then they all embraced. The bond was sealed for ever.

*

In late 1951, there was a not-too-unexpected shock. It came at just after nine o'clock at night. Joan had taken up a tray of light supper to Foley who had been spending one of his many days in bed. She did not linger long in the fetid room. Teddy was reading the paper in the large old kitchen, seated in a farmhouse chair. The old-fashioned range, which they refused to replace by a modern oven, warmed his damp, chilled body after yet another unrewarding day's toil. The ploughing was done and he had been mending fences. All he had done to improve his personal appearance was to wash his face and hands in the stone sink. He would have a bath upstairs after supper and then he destined himself to an early bed. He had not the energy or the will to go

160

through the dark with a torch to The Three Trees; it was raining anyway and he had had enough of that since seven o'clock in the morning. He preferred a rather longer encounter with the warmth of Joan's eyes to the jollity of the bar at the inn.

All was quiet in the house. It was just before eight. Joan produced a splendid steak and kidney pie topped with crisp pastry and placed it on the big pine table. Teddy had poured himself a pint of beer from the pin of ale which he always kept in the cellar and Joan had a glass of sherry. It was a homely scene, loving yet with sad undertones. Little Penelope, their privately shared joy, had been long in bed and Teddy had returned too late to give her the kiss goodnight that he always enjoyed as much as his daughter did. She would be sleeping soundly because the remedy that her mother had given her for her sore throat, a mixture of brown sugar, blackcurrant jam and glycerine, had ensured relief and peace.

Without many words, the two ate their sustaining meal. There was so much between them that speech was rarely necessary. They just felt warm together, physically and in heart. After the pie, there were stewed apples and cream. They both felt tired and sleepy, but decided upon another drink. Teddy poured Joan a sherry, of which he bought her the occasional expensive bottle. Then he went to the cellar to draw another pint of his excellent ale. He left the door above the stairs open while he did so. Suddenly Joan appeared at the top of them just as he was about to come up.

'Teddy, come up quickly! There has been a crash upstairs, above the kitchen where Foley's bedroom is.'

'All right, Love, I'm coming,' replied Teddy without much urgency.

'I think something might have happened. We must go up and see.'

'I'll go up and you stay here, Joan.'

He put down his beer on the table, silently regretting that a quiet, peaceful evening had been interrupted. Still in his heavy farm shoes, he plodded up the staircase and knocked on Foley's door. There was no reply. He turned the handle. It did not move. It had obviously been locked. His brother usually kept himself very private but Teddy did not know until now that he incarcerated himself in such security. The fact was, as he was later to discover, that he kept a considerable amount of money in his bureau and trusted no one in the house. It was a ridiculous precaution.

Teddy knocked again without response and then set his broad shoulder to the door at the end of a short charge. It gave on the third attempt. He switched on the lights. There was Foley on his back on the floor a few feet from the bed. There was vomit scattered between him and the covers. His brother turned him on his stomach immediately in case he choked, although he would not greatly have minded had he done so. He sat him against the bedside and felt his breast and pulse. He was breathing feebly, alternately deeply and then scarcely at all.

He went downstairs and, without a word to Joan, lost no time in telephoning the doctor. He told him to keep him sitting upright and to wrap him in a blanket. In the meantime, he would at once get an ambulance.

By eleven that night, Foley was taken to hospital. He had, the family was informed, suffered a serious infarction (or blood vessel blockage in the heart) and would be detained, if he survived it, for about three weeks.

He survived it and was soon home again, this time more debilitated than ever, but more grim, dim and fractious than before. He was also more demanding. Everyone suffered from this and he showed no gratitude. After a few weeks, Teddy forced him to.

*

By January 1952, Foley was walking about rather more, although scarcely ever outside. He was pallid and frail but yet seemed determined to cling on to life and on to his money as well. One morning, when his brother looked a little more vibrant with life, Teddy told him that he must talk with him. Even though the farm could not have functioned without his strength of mind and physique, he felt nervous. He knew that Foley could do without him financially and that it would not matter to him whether the farm went down the drain or not. As it happened, the younger brother had misjudged the elder and he need not have worried as he did. Foley would spend a fortune not to lose a farthing. The full incongruity of the rapacious miser was something that Teddy had not realised.

It was just after lunch when he addressed the lord and master of his tribulations.

'I must now speak with you,' began Teddy uncertainly.

'I hope that it will not be for long,' was the reply.

'It won't, Brother! You are going to have to pay me better.'

Here he stopped. Suddenly his determination and resolve strengthened him to make a bold throw. He awaited the effect of his opening gambit. His brother looked vacant.

'Did you hear me, Foley?'

'Yes.'

'Well, you can now hear me a bit longer. I have slaved for you for over five years and I'm bloody well sick of working like a mere labourer for nothing. I know that I get my pauper's place at the kitchen table, but there's little grace in that. You have had all the advantages in life that I have been denied through what I have always considered to have been merely a youthful mistake.'

Here he thought of John and bit his tongue in shame at his last word. What he had meant was the contrary, he needed more money to help his son. He hoped that God would forgive the unfortunate way in which he was forced to go about things.

'You will have to double my salary, which you can well afford to do, or your farm will go to ruin and you won't have any labourers left. When you next have a heart attack there won't be a strong man to pick you up. You will be alone with a couple of old servants, a wife and a small child. You'll still have packets of your filthy lucre but no help. No one has any respect for you and you know it. I know that I have gone off the rails in the past but you would not know even how to misbehave properly!'

He rather savoured his last remark, thinking at the same time that he might have been foolish to have made it. As it happened, Foley was abashed. He gave in at once.

'I will double your salary as from the beginning of this month, Edward, but don't expect any more favours.'

'I don't recall ever having had any from you,' he replied as he quietly left the room to gloom and despond.

*

The rest of 1952 and the whole of 1953 passed much without event until June of the latter year. Until then life went on. As Teddy was rather better off he was able to give John a few more things to make his existence less spartan. He got him fitted up with a couple of decent suits, bought him a reliable watch, some shirts and three pairs of good shoes. John was tremendously grateful. He also told him that he need not come to the farm to work any more as that would not be necessary. He added that he could be henceforth freer to go to India with his father's help and that he would try to join him when he could. This they did several times together and thus the family bonds grew closer and became firmly cemented. They both longed for these spiritually free intervals. John took various jobs in his vacations from Oxford, but they allowed him to continue his studies without too much stress. He was a born worker, obtaining distinction after distinction in his studies. He missed his future wife all the time and, in a different way, his beloved father. He was devoted to them both.

He often came to stay at The Three Trees, as he could hardly have come to the farm to do nothing. He stayed under the name of John Adams, of course. It was not long before Nancy, the barmaid, guessed who he was, nor the locals either, but they pretended that they didn't! When

164

John was there, Teddy was such a frequent visitor that they could hardly have been in much doubt. One day, Teddy told Nancy the truth. There was nobody in the bar at the time. She had the kindest of hearts and said:

'Teddy, you old fool, I'll never let on! He's got just the same nature as you have! I can see the likeness in your faces. I bet you're proud of him, a doctor and all!'

'Well, not quite yet, Nancy,' said Teddy, 'but soon.'

They both had a tear or two to dash away.

'Never you mind, Teddy, I'll make sure I feed him up dinner times and slip him a double portion. I don't suppose he's up to four-course meals as a student!'

'I do my best, you know,' said Teddy with a twinge of self-reproach.

'I know you do, my love. Shall I tell him I know, otherwise he might wonder?' she asked suddenly.

'That would be lovely of you, Nancy, my old dear,' said Teddy.

They gave each other the hug of two old friends; they enjoyed an affectionate complicity. When John knew, he felt much more comfortable in another avenue of trust. Nancy used to wink at him in a saucy way which meant no more nor less than a motherly affection. When he told her about India and his 'family' over there and Radhika, she cried into a sentimental handkerchief.

'Wish I was a bit younger, John. You wouldn't stand a chance!'

'You'll always be young, Nancy,' he said kindly and gallantly and he meant it, too.

She and John became great friends and his visits were always extraordinarily welcoming, but Nancy was the only one who knew about his photographs of which he was evidently so proud and which he never failed to show her in quiet moments.

'Be a good boy until the wedding!'

'I'll really try,' said John.

'Well, don't try too hard,' laughed dear Nancy, with the arch smile of worldly knowledge. She had a fund of that.

John smiled back. He loved and respected earthy friendliness. He was more like his father than yet he knew.

*

In June 1953, John qualified. He had a special interest in cardiac surgery. He knew that there would be at least two more years of study and practice before he would achieve his goal. Before this, he wanted badly to get married to Radhika because he could not leave her faithfully waiting for any longer. For that matter, he could not wait any longer either. But he was plagued by the fact that he could not call upon his father or his future father-in-law for more financial help. They would have given the couple anything, as they had already given John all that they possibly could, but to set up a household would have been too much for them to be asked to subsidise.

In uncertainty and doubt he tossed and turned in his bed. He had determined to go to India in July. He had not seen Radhika for months. She had understood, but you can't always overstretch understanding.

Then, at the beginning of July, just as John was preparing to go, the windfall came. It would mean release for everyone except Foley, who did not deserve any mercy, and unhoped-for happiness for the young couple. The event delayed his departure by a month, but it would be worth every day of absence from his future wife, every day of the anxiety that he, his father and Joan had suffered.

Late one morning in July, Foley did not come down to breakfast, which he had just taken the habit of doing. No one took a great deal of notice until about midday, when Teddy returned for lunch. Joan was busy in the kitchen and the old maid was still floundering around among the furniture, redistributing the dust.

'Where's Foley?' asked Teddy.

'He hasn't come down yet,' replied Joan, 'but that's nothing to be worried about!'

Eventually, as the minutes ticked by, they became suspicious, although not exactly worried, that something was amiss. Once again Teddy went upstairs. The sight that greeted him was not pretty. It was as ugly and distorted as his brother's soul. He had had a stroke. He lay on his bed a victim to paralysis, his hands inert and his face twisted to the left with the mouth in an inarticulate rictus.

If one is to recover from a stroke, it takes about ten days before even partial restoration is confirmed. Symptoms of this did not present themselves. His eyes rolled, semi-hooded, in their sunken sockets. He could not help himself in any way. Definite and drastic measures had to be taken, both medically and legally. These Teddy saw to with little ado. The tragic circumstances were to lead to a free path for everyone at New Farm and for the worried John. No one would exactly have wished things this way, but there was a touch of poetic justice about the outcome.

This took less time to realise than anyone would have thought. Teddy immediately contacted their solicitor and, in conjunction with the doctor, managed to get the power of attorney into Joan's name. This was not as difficult as might have been expected because Foley was not even able to make his mark, let alone understand the spoken or written word. The large realms of Foley's monies were now at Joan's disposal. She disposed well. The first thing that she did was to employ a full time nurse. She gave her a flat at the top of the house and unburdened herself of her husband for good. It was an effort for her to go up aloft to see him, not that he could recognise her or anyone else anyway.

From this time onwards the farm went well and without any interference. Teddy employed more men. Joan looked after him in every way. She told him, without any idea of requiring gratitude or further slavery, that he and his son, for whom she had an enormous regard and sympathy, could ask her for anything they needed – and a good deal more besides. She was never to let them want and they, for their part, never exceeded the bounds of decency in their requests. In fact, John never asked for anything; he was to be

167

given much, but he left the asking to his father. He hardly had to do that either.

It was not until early September, then, that John and Teddy would go to India. Joan would look after the farm and let her 'two boys', as she called them lovingly, go and look after themselves for a whole month! They did not have to fend for themselves very much, as they both suspected, even knew.

The two men were both tremendously excited. It was all going to be wonderful. It was. John and Teddy could hardly contain their mutual joy. They felt the approach of fulfilment and holiness. There would be much to learn.

*

It was therefore on a rainy day, but a bright one for them, that father and son boarded the plane for Bombay. They stayed a night there in a very pleasant hotel. Their nerves were tingling with anticipation. They devoured a very pleasant vegetarian curry and retired to their bedrooms early. There would be the long journey to Bangalore the next day. The train was packed and it took hours creakingly to reach its destination. The countryside was unutterably beautiful in many parts, but both men were so tired and full of thought that they hardly took any notice of it. They took sporadic meals at long, hot halts. There was no need for either of them to travel with much clothing, for they knew in advance that everything would be provided by the doctor and his wife, Roshan and Varsha. Their house in a cool suburb of the small city where they lived would gush relieving waters and be fragrant with the scents that they knew so well. They arrived hot and dirty. The fatigue of the journey seemed to dissipate itself suddenly upon their arrival. The distinguished doctor and his elegant wife greeted them warmly, especially John's Radhika. They all embraced. They were all at once at home. Their arrival was like a bathe in deep grass.

'My two sons!' said Roshan with feeling. 'It was about time that you came to us. Everything is arranged quickly, because I know that John has only a month here. Before we talk of that, you must drink a refreshing orange juice and go up to bathe. Then we will have dinner quietly and afterwards we will talk and I will explain many things to you and my daughter. To her on my own, as with you. You give us both great joy.'

'Father,' said Teddy and John at once, 'we have so much to learn from you all.'

'You will know it,' replied the doctor quietly, and with a longing, proud kindness in his eyes.

After dinner the three men sat down. They talked of nothing in particular for some time, until John wondered when the eldest man would come to the point. Suddenly he said, almost in a peremptory way:

'You must both go to bed now. I am tired too. I shall speak to you, John, alone, tomorrow.'

The next morning, Roshan was patient. He did not disturb his friends (he did not call them guests or think of them as such), leaving them to sleep in refreshing peace. At nearly midday, John made his tardy appearance. Radhika, more elegant than ever, was waiting for him on the verandah with a light meal. In the sunshine, she teemed with beauty and they made visual love, without words.

'I won't keep you waiting long, my love of loves,' said John.

'I don't want you to, but everything in a family such as mine has to be done properly first.'

She laughed teasingly and he joined her in this anticipatory mirth. They were both enjoying each other already, looking forward tantalisingly to the same promise. John felt incredibly honoured and equally impatient. He knew that he would have to suppress the latter sentiment, but it would be only with difficulty. Offence would be unthinkable.

After having allowed the two lovers to talk, even if with few words for a while, the father came out on to the verandah. He looked at his most distinguished in his white clothes and silver-grey hair and his bristling, immaculate moustache. His appearance and bearing breathed authority. This morning, he looked almost severe. Obviously, he had much upon his mind and had been waiting to unburden himself of his urgent information. Radhika went into the house, knowing that the two men must be left alone.

'That you are going to marry my daughter is without question,' he began. 'You will do this with my blessing and with my love. I have been praying for you and Radhika.'

'I have been doing the same, my Father,' said John reverently, 'and for your whole family.'

'That is as it should have been. Prayer is not always enough. It is steadfast intention that really counts. We have lovingly accepted you and you must never depart from the loyalty which that commands. You are about to take some very holy and serious steps about which I am about to tell you.'

There ensued a pause. John wondered what was to follow and felt slightly uneasy. He had the impression that the doctor did as well. He had judged correctly

'There is something that I have to say before I start on the proper parts. You have, I expect, had experience of women. That is quite as it should be; it will help you to make my daughter happy in that she will know that you are a man. Myself, I had never doubted it. I myself was not exactly innocent before I married my beloved Varsha. Since that time I have stayed, whatever casual temptations may have presented themselves, entirely faithful to her. It is difficult for a man sometimes, I am the first to admit it. But you, John, must promise me that you will do the same. After you have been accepted by the rites and ceremonies, you reserve yourself to your wife only and forever.'

'I understand that, Father, and I promise it.' Roshan smiled trustingly and held his future son's hand.

'I accept and believe that,' he said simply. 'Now to the real

170

things, since I have got that off my chest!' They both laughed the laugh that mutual relief brings to anxious people.

Roshan's talk was long. John sat quiet, honoured, interested and silent. He knew that he could not miss a word of it, nor disregard anything that he might find strange. As it happened and because he was so in sympathy with the Indian culture, he did not find anything strange at all, just fascinating, honourable and valuable.

'The idea of an arranged marriage may be difficult for Western peoples to accept. I know that you have some different blood in you, if you forgive me for saying so, which will make things easier for you to understand. I know that your mother was partly a gypsy and that this people came from northern India. Your looks and colouring, distinguished this to me straight away, even had I not known. I am not insulting you, I am honouring you, my son.'

Here he paused, not only to order a further fruit juice for them both, but to measure and assess John's reactions. They were, as he had predicted, totally open and receptive. He sat and waited with deference.

'Your marriage to my daughter will not be accepted by all my friends; most of them are very traditional. As for me, I sometimes think that tradition can be blended with understanding; we may both see that we have that quality. Compatibility among Indian families is of the essence. Your father is accepted here and so are you. I know that you have a fine career ahead of you and that you will look after my daughter properly. You will be able to support her and the children that she bears you. But there is another responsibility which you probably will not have realised. You have a duty to the whole of your family, not only in England but here also. I think that it will be unlikely that we should call upon you financially, once you have fully launched yourself upon your career, but it could be so. In such cases, it usually does not devolve upon one member of the family

171

only, but everyone has to rally round and take the toll. Are you willing to do this in the proportion that you can afford, John?'

'Of course, my Father. My wife and children will come first and then my family the closest next.'

'It did not occur to me that you would not agree, but I had to put the question. We will now be your family. Have a rest for three days after which all will have been arranged. You will be more than a little surprised and, I hope, delighted. Sacred ceremonies and promises do not have to be dismal, you know!'

The elder man's humour showed through. Both men shook hands warmly, in understanding and trust.

*

After the three days of promised rest, John and Radhika went to the temple. The priest, a distinguished and kindly man, extended his hands to them. His welcome was sweet. He smiled benignly upon the couple about whom he had been told by the girl's father. John, by his voice and appearance, could not have been taken as any other than a devout Hindu. He felt as such and was soon to become one. The priest asked no questions. He knew all about the groom and trusted him.

He was about to preside over the couple's complete yet devoted severance from their families to the end that they would henceforth take entire responsibility for themselves. A person cannot be married until this ceremony has been performed. The two were blessed by the priest, who then tied a thread round the left wrist of the bride and groom. This was to purify and protect the couple prior to their wedding. Between then and the wedding, they were told that they might not touch or shake the hand of somebody with the hand bound by the thread, in case this might bring bad luck to the marriage.

The Sacred Thread was tied, so were their bodies and

their lives. They both had a feeling of divinity in their soul, the expectation of future wonder and enlightenment. Neither could speak for some time. There are certain things which are beyond the expression of words.

The engagement ceremony was lavish, more than convivial and bedecked with presents. There were evening snacks of chicken tikka with mint chutney, fish foods and mushrooms. All relatives and close friends were invited. Varsha and Roshan gave them both jewellery and clothing, as is traditional. Everyone was decked in their finest national dress. Rahul, as everyone was later to call John, wore the Indian clothes, contrary to what they expected, and he felt as completely at home in them as he did with the people that carried them ordinarily. The red tikka was put on his forehead between the eyes. He considered this the ultimate honour before his marriage. The same was put on the bride's forehead. The couple and their immediate family then went to the temple again to be blessed by the priest and to say their prayers. After this, they exchanged engagement rings, putting them lovingly upon one another's finger. Their smiles were as deep as their souls. It was a profound moment, which neither of them would forget for the rest of their lives.

The next day, the Mehndi Ceremony took place not long after midday. It was traditionally late. The fact was that it took place. And it took place with love. At the far end of the hall, there was a stage with a double mattress and bolster pillows. Behind this was set a collage of fresh flowers which depicted a tranquil garden. The tranquil garden that their love and life should be. In front of the stage, there were rows of mattresses upon which the female guests were to recline, while their feet and hands were decorated.

The bride arrived with her mother and several close friends, who joined her and sat around the stage. The bride had one artist to decorate her hands with henna as another decorated her feet. As the painting dries, the surplus cream crumbles, leaving a reddish-brown stain on the skin. Once the decoration of the bride had started, there was a veritable brigade of artists to decorate all the female guests' hands and feet if so they wished. At the entrance to the function room where the ceremony was held, there were two large baskets of coloured bangles for the female guests to take as gifts. They chose them to match their saris. There was also a supply of tikka to decorate their foreheads.

Once the ladies had finished decorating themselves, John, the groom, came in with the majority of the male guests to see how attractive the bride had been made. He did not even have to imagine, let alone see. After that, everyone joined the ladies for lunch.

It was by now early evening when the Sangeet began. Everyone was relaxed and joyful. Songs were sung to the beauty of the bride and to the hopes of the groom. The sitar was played by a great Indian musician. The bride and groom were clapped into the room late, for they were not supposed to arrive too early. They sat on cushions as the dancing began. They drowsed happily a little while in the scent of jasmine and in the dreams of love. They both knew that it would always be as pure as the night air. John knew that this was not a mistake; suddenly, the word hit him hard in the heart and he was all the more grateful for the privilege of his acceptance by noble people. He would never lose his sense of duty, love and respect. He would now never be a 'mistake' any more. He was accepted. He felt that this honour was beyond price.

He, in his Indian clothes, she in her beautiful wedding sari, scarlet and woven with threaded gold, presented themselves to the priest. It was the greatest moment of their lives other, that is, than the birth of their children. The Nikah, or wedding ceremony, is fairly relaxed because all the vows and promises have been taken beforehand. This is the culmination of all the hopes, not only of the bride and groom, but of both families. Both fathers made an exchange of gifts in front of the priest. They placed some rice, with reverence, on a purple fan while the priest read from the

174

Holy Book. The priest then lit the fire. Each father in turn dipped a stick into a bowl full of ghee, then added it to the fire. Rice was then added to the flames. Each father then warmed his hands and guided the warmth of the fire over the bridal couple. The senior male members of the family all did the same. Teddy was the only one on John's side, but he felt as proud as a crowd of twenty. This ceremony symbolised the sharing of the warmth and the prosperity of the united families and the bridal couple. John, now Rahul, and Radhika felt fused together in that warmness which can only be born of spontaneity of feeling. They had never doubted one another and would never have needed to.

As they walked round the fire, as bidden, they performed the Phera. They walked round it seven times; at each time, Rahul proclaimed that he would accept the bride as his wife. Roshan, the father of the bride, placed a sweet into each mouth. Finally a garland of flowers was hung around their neck. At that moment they were married. The couple could hardly see for joy and thanks.

*

Finally, the time had come for the bride to leave her father's house and to go to that of her husband's parents. But where were they? One was dead and the other had, or almost had, a farm in England. The distances made tradition impossible. Everyone understood this and they were given a small garden house for the time being. There, surrounded by the lovely gardens, they made their first love. It was a wonderous time for both of them. Neither had ever known such high dignity or such tender pleasure. The breaking of Radhika's virginity sent a flare through John's brain. He was now Rahul and for ever. With a pulsing heart, he knew that he would love her for always. He was more than ever glad about the 'mistake' which was himself! Where would he have been without it? He was gentle with her and they washed each other. They went to bed again, clasped together. Just as dawn

175

was breaking the next morning, they made love again.

'Let's call him Prakash,' said her Rahul into Radhika's ear.

'That is what it will be,' she replied, sinking beautifully into another sleep.

That was when Prakash was made.

The departure from India was not easy. Radhika knew that she would have to say farewell to her whole family for ever. Rahul, or John, if you like, tried to persuade her that they would all meet again. Although she knew that this was true, there was the inevitable parting of loyalty and of souls, a transference of spirits and adherence. John told her that love never dies and that she must sustain it. Bravely, she did. They all kissed the new wife good-bye with a touch both of sadness, gladness and envy.

The long journey began. Bangalore to English Hampshire is a fairly long stretch. The couple kept up well. They were both full of apprehensions. These, as they had hoped, would be immediately dispelled upon arrival. Her Rahul would help her, thought Radhika. This he did and her integration was far easier than she had anticipated. Prakash was to be born to an English farm, although he was never to forget his origins, of which he would be as proud as his mother and father were of theirs.

9

Fulfilment and Shame

The arrival in October was as rainy as the departure in September. However, for all three of them – or would it be four? – the sun shone in their souls, obliterating the dismality of the weather.They all felt an inner warmth that nothing could chill. The vagaries of the English climate could never dismay their joy. And Radhika had not been to England before. She was a little timid. She spoke perfect English, but her Rahul had to hold her hand in the 'plane all the time. When he had to get up to fulfil natural obligations, then Teddy did the same. He was proud of her.

'Do you think everything will be all right for me in your country?' she asked him. She asked him this more than once.

'Yes, of course it will, you lucky love. We two boys are going to see to that and everyone will love you.'

'You are so kind to me, Edward,' she said quietly.

'Do not mention kindness, my dear. That is our duty. We embrace that with our heart. Remember the faith that I kept in the face of all opposition. You won't have any of that.'

She looked into her father-in-law's eyes and realised that they loved one another as father and daughter. There was in their gaze a mutually honest appreciation.

'There won't be any trouble in my being accepted, then?' she asked, in a still timid way.

'In a minute, I'll give you a good smack,' replied Teddy good-naturedly.

They both smiled the smile of trust as John returned. It was his time to take her hand again.

They were all excited, even after the very long journey. They did not arrive at New Farm until late at night. But Joan, ever considerate, had prepared some light snacks for them and the champagne, Moët et Chandon, no less, was awaiting their homecoming. Teddy and John heaved in the baggage, which was now considerable because it contained all the wedding gifts, including some fine silk rugs, with a thousand stitches to the square inch. They had been forbidden to walk upon them in shoes! Not that they wore shoes in the house anyway.

They hammered at the door; but they did not have to wait for long, for faithful Joan must have been waiting very near. Even little Penelope, now aged four, could not be kept out of bed. She had decided that she was going to be part of the celebrations, too.

Everyone embraced. Foley was ill upstairs and he would not have been interested anyway, especially in the new family. They all felt so very deeply part of one another. For a time, until the words came tumbling, teeming out, they could hardly speak. Joan gave Penelope a tiny glass of champagne and a little piece of fruit cake and then took her up to bed. She kissed everyone goodnight. They all kissed her fondly as well. Then the long evening continued. The presents were displayed and the account of all the lovely, elegant and holy ceremonies was told. Joan's eyes opened wide.

'I'm going with you to India next time!' she exclaimed.

'You have got to, my Mother,' replied Radhika, with a spontaneity which touched Joan to her heart. 'You don't mind if I call you that, do you? I did it automatically!'

They all laughed. It was the laughter of love and respect. Any ice that there might have been was immediately broken and they all knew it. The two women got up and hugged tightly. The great friendship and acceptance was made in that second. They already knew all about one another.

178

The little party went on until far too late. It was not until two or three in the morning that Joan drove the young couple down to the cottage. She had got everything ready for them. It was a wonderful and generous surprise. She had had it decorated and fully equipped throughout, their bedroom was delightfully comfortable and the fire, although almost out now, made the place homely. Radhika was in tears of joy.

'I had been so nervous,' she said to Joan, 'but now I know that I don't have to be any longer. I feel as much at home here as I do in India!'

'That was how it was supposed to be, my dear,' said Joan, with feeling. 'The cottage is yours whenever you can make it down here. If you cannot come too frequently, I shall know that it is only because of John's work. By the way, what do you call him?'

'Oh, you heard, did you? Rahul. I hope that my first son will be called Prakash. I'm going to have another one, too, I hope. He will be called Ashok, after one of my favourite uncles.'

'Don't be in too much of a hurry, will you,' replied Joan. 'But your ideas are splendid and I love your children already.'

Joan left them and drove back to the house. She felt rather empty in one way, but tremendously fulfilled in another. Her beloved Teddy was back and she, in her motherly soul, was to have the joy of another family. It was an additional comfort to know that Penelope loved both John and his wife. Joan at once knew that she would never be able to do enough for them. After years of deprivation with Foley, her heart was overflowing with the generosity of love and gratitude. She needed to be wanted and now she was. When she went to bed with Teddy, they both held hands and said prayers, silently and with fervour. They loved, almost as if it had been for the first time.

'I'm so glad that you are back, Teddy.'

'I am too, Joan, love. But you know that I had to go.'

'I'm unutterably glad that you did. How wonderful for you

and John! And what a beautiful homecoming. I think that we are so lucky.'

'I do too,' said Teddy, as they hugged each other to sleep.

After only just three beautiful days, John and Radhika, with the future little Prakash inside, warm and beloved already, went to Oxford. Thanks to Joan, they had a lovely flat, well-furnished, clean and quiet, not far from John's college. He did not study there all the time, having to go to one of the main hospitals for lectures and to observe surgery. This would continue for two years. In the intervening vacations, they always went back to New Farm, where they were intensely happy. In 1953, they had Christmas there, although neither of them were Christians. John had embraced Hinduism. He felt that this was a duty not only to himself and to his feelings but to his wife and his future children, as well as to his family in India who had not only befriended him but accepted him. He had a great sense of honour and was determined not to betray it.

At Christmas 1954, the couple went back to New Farm. But the two were now three. In July, Prakash was easily born and was a fine child. His parents were proud and delighted, first because he was the first son and second because he looked completely Indian. He was going to be handsome. You never forget your origins; his father was half-gypsy, dark and swarthy; his mother of the sallow and lovely complexion of her race. They were both intelligent and cultured. There was every hope that their children would be the same. They were not to be disappointed.

Joan was delighted and so was Penelope. They billed and cooed over Prakash until his mother told them to stop. She already wanted him to grow up to be a man like his father; she did not want him to be pampered. Everyone, except his father, of course, took the hint and left him to his mother. His father and mother bathed him proudly together.

'I want to have another son as soon as you will,' said Rahul.

'Give me a bit of time, Rahul. I want another one, too!'

In 1957 Ashok was born. He and Prakash were

immediately friends for life. But 1954 had not ended yet, and the life of Ashok had not then begun.

*

It was just before Christmas when Penelope, the darling daughter of Teddy, was scuffing the leaves with her father down the frozen, sunlit drive to the village. They both loved these times and Teddy looked forward to when Prakash would enjoy them also. He had loved so many in his life that he hardly knew where to turn, he could hardly believe one man's luck either. He was now devoted to so many people. They all mattered to him. Although he knew that he could not deserve it, they all loved him. He thought of them all in a frantic simultaneousness.

Father and daughter both had a convivial time in The Three Trees. Nancy sat the little girl down with some other small friends in a cosy corner. They all had lemonade and giggles. Teddy felt expansive and chatted about his family. Everyone was eager to see the couple. But they could not stay too long. There was a special lunch on the way and he could not inconvenience Joan or his son and Radhika either. It was going to be a special roast of lamb; Indians do not eat beef. That did not matter to Teddy. After all he had had his pint; the two strode up the hill again, their hands gripped tight in love. Their smiles were warm in the cold, yet intimate, sunshine of winter.

They walked straight inside the house. John and Radhika came directly into the hall as soon as they had heard the door open. They were strangely mute. They seemed to be standing there with no reason and with nothing to say. There was no smell of beckoning Sunday cooking. There was an empty silence as Joan arrived.

'Foley is dead,' she announced dully. 'John has verified his death.'

All four of them went into the drawing room and sat down. The curtains were open upon the already dimming, wintery scene. Depression, not sadness, seemed to be their key emotion. Joan was the pluckiest of them all and suggested a good, large glass of sherry all round. Radhika did not drink alcohol, so she had a fizzy orange. There was silence. No one seemed quite to know what to do or say next. They did not feel particularly enlivened by the corpse lying above them. John was the first to speak.

'Let us be practical,' he said. 'We must get his own doctor to sign the death certificate. I will telephone him, if you give me his number. He will take my word about what has happened. You, Edward, my Father, you must arrange the funeral at which I do not wish to be present and I will not allow my wife to go to it either.'

Teddy consented to all these sensible arrangements. The doctor arrived early the next day and provided the death certificate. The half-brother went to see the local vicar, who found a patch for Foley in the churchyard. The undertakers did everything with dispatch.

The service and burial took place with scant attendance. Teddy and the maid were the only ones in the unbidding churchyard at the interment. Joan and the rest could not face it and Penelope was too young to be exposed to the grimness of deathly disappearance. It was a dismally windy day. The clouds scudded greyly across the sky and Teddy wondered where among these would be Foley's soul. Frosty autumn leaves, still unswept, fluttered on to his coffin, almost like notes of farewell, but without either feeling or charity. The earth was as cold as his body and his heart. When all was at an end, the two went back to the farm rapidly. They did not talk, but they probably had the same thoughts, although they might have expressed them differently. Foley was unloved because he had given no love. Lack of love brings its own hollow reward.

Very shortly after this event, Joan went to Foley's lawyer and saw the will. Everything had been left to her. After the sale of Hetherick, his father's legacy and the profits from the wine business, the amount was more than considerable. The present farm was worth quite enough, too. She decided to make a will immediately. She had never made one before because she had had nothing to leave to a soul. She immediately wrote notes for the solicitor who approved her dispositions.

When she returned to New Farm, everyone had a cold lunch preceded by hot soup. Joan was very quiet. No one wanted to disturb her, so that the meal was eaten in friendly and considerate silence. At the end of it she said:

'I want you all to come and sit with me in the drawing room. I have an important announcement to make. Parts of it may take you by surprise, but remember that I have thought of the good of all of you, of your best interests. I do not in the least regret Foley's passing; he was foul to me but I have been the sole recipient of his money. Perhaps I don't deserve that. I made a terrible mistake in marrying him and I'm glad that he's gone, although I would have wished suffering upon no one. Now I want to help you all and I hope that you will not find my dispositions strange or hurtful.'

There fell an awed silence. Everyone loved kind Joan. They had no idea what she was going to tell them. Their nature was anything but avaricious and they only hoped for her content and ease after the life that she had suffered with her extraordinary husband.

'For once, I am going to have a glass of port,' she announced, with a humourous glint in her eyes. 'I think I deserve one! Help yourselves, as well!'

They all did, even – and she felt pleasantly wicked about it – even Radhika.

'This is what I have done. I have left this farm to my daughter Fiona, with all the cottages, apart from yours, John. That will be for you a peaceful retreat from your heavy and demanding work and will give your children a breath of fresh air. It will be fine to see them running about with the country lads and will make sure that they will never become snobs!'

Here she paused and everyone laughed. They realised that she had more wisdom than they could have guessed.

They sipped a little more port, not in greedy anticipation, but just for comfort. They all admired her composure.

'As for the rest,' she continued, 'I have left half of my liquid money to Penelope and the other half to you and Radhika, John. Teddy, I have not left you a penny.'

She waited for the impact of this statement to take its effect. Placid Teddy looked rather stunned, but smiled and said nothing.

'I know what you are thinking, Teddy. I have left you ungratefully out.'

'What is yours is to do with what you wish to,' he said quietly.

'I don't think you have quite understood, all of you. I will explain. Edward, as you call him, is going to live with me as the husband he has been to me for years. Penelope, as you know is his daughter. He's a wonderful man. He's been, and still is, a wonderful father to you, John. This is the point. I cannot marry him because he is the half-brother of my late husband. Therefore, were I to leave him money, he would have to pay inheritance tax. Then, upon his death, when he would leave his share to you, you would have to pay it as well. I know, and damned fine, that you will look after him if anything should happen to me. He has this house for his lifetime.'

John stood up and said:

'You stand up, Edward, my Father. I promise you that I will look after you for ever. That is a very small gift in consideration of the fact that you gave me life itself and helped me.'

It was a moving moment and there were no dry eyes. Suddenly, someone thought of Fiona. She was thirty-two and living in Cheltenham, where she was the high-powered personal secretary to the senior manager of the largest bank there. She was trusted, respected and slightly feared, even by her rather suave boss. She had plans and answers by the torrent; she could have run any department; some said, not without justice, that she ran the manager.

She went to a secretarial college in Winchester. She

accomplished the course in record time and, immediately afterwards, joined the bank where she still was. She rose from an obscure juniority very rapidly to the position that she occupied today. She was not without humour as she frequently wrote caustic letters, the wit of which often neither the manager nor his clients fully understood. 'Miss Osmond wrote it, so it must be quite proper and just what they need' was the normal verdict.

Her hair was scratched back in a bun, a style which tended to make her look rather on the severe side. She liked Cheltenham, where she had been sent to school, and would not have looked out of place, even at a young age, numbered among the rows of primmish schoolmistresses. Fiona seemed to be the possessor of no particular age. At first, she had shared a flat in a quiet backwater with a friend, who did much the same job for an accountant, but soon she decided that living on her own in moral and physical solitude would be preferable. Occasionally, she played bezique or chess with her former flat-companion, but generally she like the lone life best.

Sometimes she payed a brief visit to the New Farm where no one understood her, but liked her all the same. Joan used to send her sporadic letters which were reciprocated in the same manner; neither had much to say that would greatly interest the other. Joan did not regale her with the more gripping events of her life and that of the family; she would definitely have been seized with shocked pity for the earthy zest of its members, although the origins of John were never to be disclosed to her. They all awaited with amused anticipation her discovery that her nephew, a doctor no less, had 'foreign' children. They all thought that, when she knew, which would be soon, that she would drop to her knees in prayers for his restoration to what she always called The Way! By this she meant the firmly guided path to Our Saviour. Everyone who had not embarked upon this passage ran grave risks of the loss of The Eternal Goal. All of them ran these cheerfully and enjoyed life all the more for that.

Fiona had not been able to attend her father's funeral, not

on account of any particular dislike but because there had been a vital business conference for which sentiment should be cast aside selflessly. Her selflessness won the day. She wrote a kind but formal letter of condolence to her mother, with a brief word to Teddy appended as an afterthought. Had she known the truth about him, she would have consigned him with a doubt to eternal darkness in the great beyond!

'You must tell Fiona about the will,' said Teddy kindly.

'Oh, of course, Teddy! How awful, I nearly forgot. Poor old Fiona!'

She wrote to her the next day. The reply came almost by return. It was in the nature of a surprise.

> *My dear Joan,*
>   *What a very kind thought you had in leaving me New Farm, under certain understandable conditions, but I am not interested in farm life, so I will sell it to you at a kindly price when the time comes.*
>   *I hope the garden is looking tidy. The daffodils will be out any minute, I imagine.*
>   *In busy haste as usual!*
>   *Love*
>   *Fiona*

This reply, rather fusty as it was, did not worry Joan, or any of them in the least; she would split the proceeds between Penelope and John.

*

Meanwhile, John had returned with his family, to spend most of his time either in private study or in the hospital, where he was under the guidance, apart from having to attend some lectures, of Doctor Gordon Macrae. He was a brilliant surgeon though not the most biddable of men. His appearance as well as his personality betokened not an endearing oddness as much as a grim gracelessness. He had a red face, a peaky inquisitive nose, cold grey eyes and a ratty little moustache. This was topped by thick hair of an indefinite colour, which looked as if it had been controlled by a sheep shearer. His clothes indicated a perpetual disregard for any form of smartness. His brown suits were shabby and looked as if he had slept in them, his shirts were rumpled, his only two ties like chewed string and his shoes were never polished. He had a brutal manner with students and patients alike. However, both put up with him; he was one of the most highly-regarded in his profession. He possessed boundless skill and energy. His lectures were of the most skillful, his commentaries, while operating, profoundly understandable. He was modest about himself in an arrogant sort of way, because he knew he was equalled by but few.

John worked under his aegis with a dedicated will, but he looked forward first to his family and second to the occasional convivial dinner evening, as changes of scene. Life at home was idyllic and the jolly times at his college fun. Then there were the warm visits to the family in Hampshire, none of them these days as long as he would have liked. Nor were they long enough for Radhika, whom he sometimes 'allowed' to have a change of air for a week down there.

The next year he would qualify completely for his chosen calling. He had promised the whole family a holiday in Bangalore in September 1955. He could well afford it because Joan had told him that she would pay, that he and Teddy would be the guides and that the rest of the family would leave all arrangements up to them. Meanwhile, the farm went on at a pleasantly lazy pace, Joan and Teddy were completely happy and the sun seemed to shine every day upon the fields. Penny was going to a nice little village school, where she was happy among laughing friends. Fiona was learning Japanese whilst Prakash, in Oxford, walked well and was just about to learn the pleasures of getting into mischief.

Radhika wrote frequent letters to her mother and father;

all of them were full of the family news and of the great visit in September. Equally, Varsha and Roshan could not conceal their excitement. Their news was often humourous, telling of peculiar or charming patients, poking good-natured fun at the government or recounting the idiotic blunders of their servants, which last amused their frequent guests.

August changed everything. John had decided to give himself a day off and take Prakash with him. That would give Radhika a little time entirely to herself, when she could decide which saris to take on the holiday, which shoes, which jewellery. Or simply, if she wanted, to do absolutely nothing. She decided to do a little of both. The saris came first. They were all beautiful, some sewn with gold thread on a cobalt-blue background, some with interesting borders containing little jewels, some again just patterned or completely plain. She kept them in a large, perfumed wardrobe in the bedroom, into which she had just gone at about half-past two that hot, close afternoon. She thought that it would thunder, after which it would rain like the monsoon, and then the air would be cool and fresh.

Because she was singing quietly to herself, she neither heard anything nor was able to take precautions. She was leaning over the bed and laying out the saris when, too late, she realised a presence behind her. She was grabbed roughly round the waist and hurled to the bed. In a trice, Radhika was turned round and flattened by a heavy, burly man of about forty. He had a cruel, smirking face and a sickening, bad breath. He had obviously been drinking beer for a long time and had just rolled out of the pub. She started to kick and shriek; until, that is, the man produced a sharpened screwdriver. He threatened her face and eyes with it. She was terrified. With one knee on her left shoulder, he pinned her down, ripped her clothes in order to savage her cruelly. He then secured her with his left elbow. She was bruised and hurt all over and he mangled her tender breasts. When he had finished, he knocked her out by a colossal blow to the chin to ensure her silence. Then he left without a word and without precaution to ensure any particular stealth, making a clumsy exit through a kitchen side-window which she had left open by mistake.

*

They had all enjoyed a modest lunch. Afterwards Radhika strapped Prakash into the pushchair and he and John set off for the local shops. They felt fresh and happy. John had already decided to buy some presents, a few little toys for his son and some favourite biscuits for his wife. He had also been given a modest list of shopping, things which had been forgotten on the large list of weekly purchases the day before. It was a pleasant time, and the golden sunshine reminded John of New Farm. They must go there soon and then there would be India. How everyone was looking forward to that! So were Radhika's parents. All the family letters contained almost nothing but things about arrangements and the manifold enjoyments that they would all relish. Joan and Penelope looked forward to the opening of a new world. John smiled to himself in already excited anticipation; he would be as proud of his family as they would of their hospitality and heritage. Teddy was so enthusiastic that he read in Hindi again and wrote to the Mahendras. A lively newsy correspondence was joined.

It was at about three-thirty that they returned to the cosy little house. John unlocked the front door, wheeled Prakash in, released him into the kitchen and started to unpack the small things that they both had bought. When he had done this and looked round the ground floor, he was not surprised to find no one about. Radhika was probably asleep upstairs. He was grateful for the day off that Doctor Macrae, acid as he might be, had given him. It was to prove to have been a bitter gift, but neither man could have known this. Wondering what to do next, he realised that he had forgotten to get any flowers; things like that were awkward to buy when you had a child to look after whilst making a tasteful choice. It was during this silent interval that he

189

heard moanings from upstairs, then loud groans. John was puzzled. He was about to go up when he heard cries of anguish.

'Rahul, Rahul! Where are you? Come here, Rahul!'

He had not even had time to wash Prakash's grubby hands and face. A voice of pain had called him and fear struck his guts. The boy was safe in the kitchen, as he verified before answering the call, but he heard, loudly calling, the pleading cry.

'Help me! Help me! Come quickly, John! Rahul! Rahul!'

He rushed up, in sick anticipation of something dreadful beyond description. It was exactly that.

The scene in their bedroom, the place of their finest love, was beyond imagining. Radhika was on the bed with her clothing partially rent and writhing in pain, shame and anguish. Her face was contorted with grief and agony, both physical and mental; her lips were bleeding and bruised, her neck, too; her breasts were bared; her underclothing removed and discarded; her thighs were bloodied from her vagina. She sari beneath was stained with cruelty and sin. John stood powerless, mesmerised for a few seconds.

'What on earth has happened to you, darling?' he asked needlessly, kneeling at once. Sickened, he knew exactly what had.

'I will try to tell you, Rahul.'

At this effort her voice failed. She retained a dazed, terrified silence, her eyes staring into her pain.

'Say nothing. Leave it to me. You have been raped. Tell me later. I have got to act.'

Radhika was so comforted and safe in his presence that this even relieved some of the pain. Trust was with her again.

He drew a large bowl of warm water as quickly as he could and found some sterilised gauze. Then, with sterilised scissors, he cut off her clothing, in order to avoid as much as possible moving the body. He swabbed her as fast as he could because he knew that speed was of the essence. He had to get her to hospital without delay and see about Prakash as soon as he could. Her beautiful breasts were tender and bruised and she hurt incredibly between the legs. He was white with terror, fear and compassion at the same time. He did not dare show any but the last feeling to his wife, now his patient. Once he had got rid of the clothes and the sari, which he later burnt in an incinerator, he wrapped her in a blanket, placing pads of gauze where temporarily necessary.

'Now,' he said, 'I'm going to take Prakash next door to Mrs Hall, who has had lots of children and will look after him. It will only take a minute. Keep as calm as you can and don't move. Then I shall ring Dr Macrae.'

She moved to object, saying that she would be fit in a minute, but John knew better. The shock and realisation of possible shame and despair would come later. He must hurry. He gave her a glass of sugar and water.

'Drink some of this if you can,' he said hurriedly.

Next door lived Mrs Hall, fat, sixty-five, motherly and mother of six, grandmother of ten. He knocked and entered.

Mrs Hall was doing the weekly wash, by hand of course. She loved her new neighbours and got on well with Radhika, having given her invaluable and old-fashioned tips about bringing up children, telling her all the time to have as many as she could. She was a really good-hearted Yorkshire lady of immense experience.

'If you want to 'ave the next one at 'ome', she once told Radhika, 'I'll be first on the spot. Should be like shellin' peas out of a pod fer a bonny lass like you, wherever you come from!' Her dear bluntness did not offend, rather the reverse. Radhika liked her enormously.

'Hello, there, our John! Yer looks a bit flurried. What's up, lad?'

'Mrs Hall, something terrible's happened. Radhika's been raped at home while I was out shopping with Prakash to give her a bit of a rest. She's in a bad way. I have cleaned her up, but have got to get her to hospital. Would you and Frank like to look after Prakash for the night? I can bring over some things for him. I will ...'

'You'll do nowt at all, John. It's bloody terrible. Yer can tell me about it later. I'll take care of this little soul for as long as it takes and longer. Yer knows me – mother of the world!'

'I'll go and get him, then, Mrs Hall.'

'Wait while I take off me apron. There's nowt I can't look after. Wait on, I'll just tell Frank.'

They rushed next door and in no time Mrs Hall and his son had gone. John was both confident and inexpressibly grateful. Mrs Hall was a real brick.

With his mind cleared of one anxiety, John addressed himself to the next, but equally vital consideration. He decided at once to telephone Gordon Macrae. It was by now nearly four-thirty in this desperate afternoon. John kept his head above a breaking heart, bursting with hope and doubt at the same time. He rang the right department immediately after having been up to his wife. He gave her sad face a loving kiss, tried to reassure her and said that he would arrange everything in next to no time.

'Thank you, Rahul,' she said weakly and with a lovely, hurt smile.

Composing himself quickly, John went to the telephone, forced himself into a sort of disembodied calm. He rang Dr Macrae's department.

'This is Doctor Osmond. I need to speak to Doctor Macrae, please.'

The rather icy voice of one of his secretaries replied that Macrae had been doing urgent operations all day and for some of the night previously and was just about to go home. It would be better if he were to call tomorrow.

'But it is a matter of the utmost urgency, Miss Aitken. 'I must, I really must speak to him at once.'

'This is all very inconvenient. Will someone else do?'

'No, they will not,' replied John, becoming more emphatic. 'Only Doctor Macrae will do.'

'Very well, then,' she replied testily. 'I'll get him.'

'Thank you, Miss Aitken.'

He waited only about thirty seconds.

'What is it Doctor Osmond?' asked an abrupt Scottish voice.

'I need your help urgently, Sir. My wife has been raped and she is in a bad way. It was while I was giving her a day's rest from the boy on my day off. I returned to find something almost indescribable. Please will you come! I repeat, this is a plea for help, Doctor.'

'I'll be with you in ten minutes, or less, if I can manage.' That was the end of the conversation.

It was within the promised ten minutes, or less, that Gordon Macrae arrived. Looking his usual shabby self, tired yet alert, he faithfully kept his word. He carried a small case and a worried look.

'Don't explain anything to me. Take me to her. Have you cleaned her up?'

'Yes, Sir, immediately, and I have wrapped her up in a blanket. I have arranged for my son to stay with Mrs Hall next door. I'm terribly worried.'

'Of course you are.'

They went upstairs. the young doctor was told to leave him.

'Get yourself a glass of whisky, laddie, and bring me one too, if you have enough.'

John did as he was bid. Meanwhile, the old doctor's tender hands and a surprisingly soft voice, to which his often terrified students were unused, allayed the fears of his patient and helped her to feel less ashamed and more relaxed. He examined her with infinite care, respect and solicitude.

'You will be as right as rain, my dear, in no time at all. In absolutely no time at all. We will have you safe in our hospital in no time at all, my dear, no time at all. And you'll forget in no time at all.'

'What shall I do, Sir?' asked John.

'You, me boy, are going to do absolutely nothing. Leave it to your old uncle. Just you bide with your girly awhile and I'll fix the rest. Be off with me below!' he told himself. He took his whisky with him.

Mutely the two held hands. There were no words needed.

Downstairs, Gordon Macrae displayed his finest telephone

manner.

'Is that you, Jenner?' he asked needlessly, when a sleepy voice answered.

'Er, yes Macrae, but I'm in bed. It's my day off and I have had three days' emergencies. I'm not available.'

'If I want a decent gynaecologist, I call you. I'm calling you now. John Osmond's wife has been brutally raped. You're the man I trust. So bloody well get out of bed but put something on over your pyjamas. Donna bother to even clean your teeth! Just be quick!'

'I'll be there in fifteen minutes, Macrae – don't drink too much of your filthy whisky in the meantime!'

Both men were gruffly respectful to one another. They each knew that there were few their equal in the profession.

'While you rumble into some sort of clothing, I'll terrorise the matron in to getting an immediate bed.'

As it was Doctor Gordon Macrae, he had no difficulty in this.

He then finished his whisky and immediately stole another one, rather stronger than the first.

John came downstairs for a moment to see what had supervened. The doctor told him not to worry about anything now, except his wife. All the administration was taken care of. He told him about it.

'We will leave in five minutes, John,' announced Macrae.

Thank you infinitely, Sir,' replied John, with a near blank mind.

For the first time it was 'John' that his mentor had called him, by his first name; a first for everything, he thought. He saw a new side to the tatty-looking, weather-beaten Scot whom he had thought hard and without the more obvious effusions that affected him. His usually grey eyes, the eyes of the one-minded concentration that his calling had always demanded of him, changed to a sort of deep, soft blue. With astonishment, he saw that he had a tender heart.

'My dear boy, she'll be all right. We'll see to that. It hurts me to say so,' he said mischievously, but sincerely, 'but I respect you. What you have done in your short life has taken will and courage. I trod the same path myself.'

During those anxious moments before Radhika's transport in Gordon Macrae's ancient but comfortable car to the hospital, full of pain and foreboding, their relationship changed from that of master and student to that of friend and friend. Their eyes met in trusting faith.

'Let's go upstairs and get her down. Before we go, John, I must tell you something that you must keep a secret. Soon you will be ready to join me as my assistant.'

They shook hands.

'I had a wee laddie myself, but he and my wife died at the same time. That's why I'm such a gruff old bastard!'

They both dashed a tear away and shook hands again.

When they arrived at the hospital, Radhika was immediately taken care of and installed in the right place by the Matron, of whom everyone had a secret fear but an infinite respect.

'I expect Dr Jenner will arrive at any moment,' she said, with an emphasis, which only a lifetime of efficiency could have given, upon the word 'any'.

Dear man, he did, clad in assorted clothing put hastily on over his pyjamas.

'Thank you,' said both Macrae and John at once.

'I shall be in contact as soon as it is possible. But you two get some rest now,'

Gordon Macrae took John home and then went to his own. Food did not seem to matter. Before he left, the doctor said to John:

'I forbid you to come in tomorrow, John. Good-night and God bless you!'

'The same for you, Sir, and thank you.'

A mutual glance of confidence spoke for them both.

*

By the time that John had shut the door of the lonely house behind him, it was about half-past six. As he poured himself a drink, which he sorely needed, thoughts like a stream of ants teemed through his head. He prayed for his wife, hoping that her terrible experience would not alter her sunny personality and calm confidence in love and motherhood. Then, a sudden and ghastly thought assailed him, worse than any so far. He wondered why he had not seen the desperate possibility before. Would she become pregnant by this monster? He shivered. He could hardly hold his glass and put it down on the kitchen table. God! Whatever then? He knew that Jenner would give her post-coital contraceptive pills, equally, that they were not one hundred percent certain to succeed. Even then, three weeks must elapse before a decision could be made. What a three weeks they would be! His examinations were to begin a week from today, as well. They were all supposed to go to India on September 1st. Now they would not be able to, since the three-week period would take them past that date. He could rearrange the flights once they had been given assurance that Radhika was not pregnant, but what if she was? What if she were too shaken and in too much mental disarray to wish to go anyhow? For the matter of that, he felt half-crazed himself.

He was a man of courage. He must keep everything together. He knew that he must do well in his examinations for the sake of his future and his family. To this end he must keep all the different calls upon his mind and energies in separate compartments. It would be difficult, but it had to be possible. It was imperative.

The first compartment now was to see Mrs Hall. Prakash would be in bed and mercifully ignorant of what was happening. He knocked on the front door. Mrs Hall waddled comfortably to open it.

'By, it's our John. You look washed out, love. And that's not a wonder. Come in, deary, and have a sit down. Shall I get yer a cuppa tea?'

'I don't want anything, Mrs Hall, thank you, but I'll sit down for a minute.'

They went to the homely kitchen, of course; only formal

196

visitors went to the 'parlour', as it was called. John preferred the kitchen. To be invited there was to be one of the family, as distinct from the Man from The Prudential. He certainly was not that! Frank was in there, braces and collar-stud complete, supping a milk stout, whilst studying form for tomorrow's races. He hardly looked up.

'I heard all that load of old rammel,' he said unceremoniously. 'Bloody 'ell fire, what 'e wants is owt a site stronger than that, missus!'

'Now then, Frank, none of yer dirty talk,' admonished his wife, without the slightest anger and with no hope of correcting the blunt but harmless expression of her husband of forty years.

'By 'eck, then, if you prefer it. What's it to be, lad, a stout or summat stronger? I've decided. Don't answer. Get that rum out of sideboard, Mrs 'All, and I'll fetch down a glass.'

Before he had drunk anything, John felt comforted. Frank poured him an immense tot. He had been a Navy man all his life and had long retired. He had never lost his earthy way of life. They had come down from the north, their Yorkshire birthplace in Malton, near York, only because they wished to be near their son and his family.

'That'll perk yer up a bit, lad. Yer might even go home market fresh, as they say!' he chuckled.

'Market fresh? What does that mean, Frank?'

'Well, in Malton, on a market day, the pubs was open from nine in't' mornin' till 'eaven knows what time at night. The drovers and farmers went in at all times an' stayed till all times. When they rolled out a bit cale-eyed, as they say, they was what you called market fresh!'

'I think that'll do, Frank' said Mrs Hall.

She knew that he had done it all on purpose to put John at his ease and to take his mind off everything, even if momentarily.

'I think that we had better discuss things for a minute Mrs Hall. I had better tell you everything. I had better admit the lot. I'm desperate and I don't know which way to turn. I've got these tremendous exams to take, Prakash to look after and Radhika as well. All at once. Whatever am I going to do?'

He then told her and explained all the medical details. For the first time since it all happened, he buried his dark handsome head in his slender surgeon's hands. There was a slight, but unembarrassed pause, encumbered and met by nothing but understanding.

'Stop 'angin' about, Missus,' said Frank, 'and tell 'im!' He never called her Joyce unless they were alone.

'Well it's like this, our John. By the way, even if Frank can't bring 'imself to do it, you must call me Joyce,' she said with a little laugh that she hoped would make things completely informal, 'and I'll come out with it. And there's not to be an argument. I don't 'old with them and never 'ave!'

'No arguments, Joyce,' said John, raising his head.

'First go off, I want yer key to yer 'ouse. Yer can go get it after. Next, when yer out tomorrer mornin', I'm coming in. I'll bring all me own things and sleep in yer spare room with the door open. Little Praki can sleep in his bed beside me. 'E can look after me!'

'You don't mean it, Mrs Hall – I mean, Joyce?'

'I nivver says owt as I don't mean, my lad!' exclaimed Joyce, whose accent became broader with emotion and excitement. 'It'll be a right pleasure to get shot of that old bugger, any road up!'

'Now then, our missus, 'o's talkin' about ripe language!'

Joyce disregarded this admonition and went on:

'I've not finished. I'll look after the little lad, look after Radhika while she mends at 'ome and clean the 'ouse. I'll cook for everyone, including our Frank, and we'll all eat together with yer. Fer as long as it takes. No arguments. It'll be an honour. Now then, 'ow's that?'

'God in Heaven! said John, 'I can't believe it.'

'Well you'd best make a start to!'

'I've got a few calls to make on the 'phone, Joyce, so I'll see you tomorrow.'

'That's not good enough. I know that you want to be alone fer a spell; but tea'll be ready in an hour. After, you and Frank can go down the pub and you'll sleep better – though I don't approve, mind!'

She did, of course, otherwise she would not have suggested it.

Feeling a little stronger, John went home. The first things that he did were to wash his face and brush his hair. He supposed that this made him feel more at normality, more up-together. He was overwhelmed by the blunt, unutterably selfless kindness shown to him and his family by his friends next door. Colour and class were so obviously and completely irrelevant to them. He thanked God for that.

First, he rang the hospital. Mr Jenner had gone home, the Matron told him. The Matron liked him, so that is why she consented to answer, instead of allowing him to be put on to the ward sister. She secretly admired his abilities and liked his character. She would never have told him this, however, other than through acts of consideration. John admired her also. Equally, he never said anything, except that he always cooperated with her. The Matron of a senior hospital is no mean figure.

'Matron,' he began with trepidation, 'I ring to ask you how my wife is. I hope that I do not disturb you. Early evening is a busy time for you all there.'

'Doctor Osmond, it is a pleasure to hear from you and thank you for not having rung sooner. It has given us a chance to settle and so on and so forth.'

'So on and so forth' was one of her many favourite expressions.

'You obviously want and need a full report and so on and so forth.' This was not a question, but a statement. 'Well,' she continued,' without waiting for a reply, 'I will give you all I know. Here it is. Your charming wife is quiet and meditative, but is rather more comfortable than when she arrived. She is in a quiet ward and I have told the nurses and the sister that they are to sit on her bed and talk with her whenever she seems to need company and attend to her every need. But she is very undemanding.'

There was a pause.

199

'Thank you Matron, but please, I need some medical details.'

'I was about to give you those and here they are,' replied the Matron, crisply but kindly. 'Let's start at the top. We have soothed her bitten lips, but the contusions will take a week or two to subside. Her breasts are bruised, particularly the right one and there is nothing one can do about this. I have told her to sleep on her sides. Due to the nature of the case, I called in a police surgeon who was in attendance while Dr Jenner examined her and he received a full copy of his report. Everything that Dr Jenner did and wrote was accepted. This is quite natural in the case of a man of his reputation and standing.'

'Upon Dr Jenner's advice, she has been given the usual medication, which we all hope will be effective. She is not too severely damaged in the vagina, merely uncomfortable after a brutal assault. There is nothing that will not mend itself. What she needs is a couple of days with us and then you can take her home and look after her. So, set your mind at rest, Doctor Osmond. Our sympathies are with you, your wife and your son.'

'Thank you all so very deeply, Matron' replied John. 'May I come and see her tomorrow? Doctor Macrae has been wonderfully kind and has allowed me a day off so that I can collect myself. Believe me, I need a bit of collecting!'

'I can understand that, Doctor, but what are you going to do to look after your wife and son whilst you are working and taking your all-important examinations? Is there anything that we may do to help you?'

'It's very kind of you, but I have some wonderful neighbours. We are all in the care of a Yorkshire grandmother!'

'I don't think you could do better than that, John! Oh!' she added, 'perhaps I should not have called you that! You may not know it, but we all do behind your back! It just slipped out!'

'I would not dare to call you anything else but "Matron"!' said John with a laugh. 'Thank you so very much anyway.

May I come in after lunch tomorrow?'

'With the greatest of pleasure, Doctor,' she said warmly.

Hardly had he put down the receiver than the telephone rang. This was the last thing that he needed; he wanted to get back to Joyce and Frank. He had actually planned to ring Roshan Mahendra in Bangalore. He had been thinking about what to tell him in regard to a possibly delayed start to their holiday; possibly no holiday at all until much later. He was wondering how he would disguise the truth so as not to distress the distinguished old doctor; he did not wish to cause him anxiety or to bruise his heart. He dreaded the thought that he might think that he had not taken sufficient care of his daughter, had even been careless of her. This haunted him. However, all such considerations were interrupted by a cheerful call from New Farm.

'Thought I'd just give you a quick buzz, John,' said Teddy's voice. 'How's things? Are you all ready for the exams? Knowing you, I expect you are. Tell me how everything is with you both and Prakash.'

'Well, Edward,' began John haltingly and rather taken by surprise, 'not so bad. Prakash is well and doing fine, my work is complete and I am taking a day or two off to relax my mind a little before the big days. I have been offered the post of Doctor Macrae's assistant afterwards.'

'That sounds absolutely fine, John. But you have not mentioned Radhika. How's she? Lovely as she always will be, but tell me her news.'

This is what John had dreaded most. He paused for mental breath.

'Edward, I had better come straight out with it. We will probably not be able to go to India on September 1st, possibly not this year at all. As we have never shared anything but the truth, however painful and distressing, I will tell you the whole story, on condition that you tell no one at home. My today has already been as long as a lifetime. We will have to concoct a story between us so that it will be converted from a tragedy into a mere disappointment.'

He then proceeded to tell his father everything. Teddy was

aghast. At the end of the long tale, he said that he would cooperate in anything that John would like him to.

'Would you like me to come down and help?' he asked plaintively.

'No, Edward, my Father,' replied John, in the familiar yet strange way in which he always addressed him. 'I have some wonderful neighbours and the wife is looking after us all. I will keep you posted as events unfurl themselves. I will ring you again in a couple of days.'

'Very well, John, I shall keep quiet and pray my funny old prayers for you all – particularly for Radhika.'

'I know that you will. I've got to go now because I must ring her parents, although what I shall tell them I have no idea. God bless you. Good-bye.'

With that he put down the receiver. He girded his loins for the next step. Against his habit, he poured himself yet another drink.

His heart beat hard and his hands and brow sweated. He felt seedy and exhausted. He could not wait for Joyce's tea and a change of scene. Still, he had to persevere. The accomplishment of his telephone calls might herald a short release, of a certain kind. He dialled Doctor Mahendra's number in Bangalore. It took, unnervingly, several attempts before he got through on a bad line.

'Roshan,' he shouted, 'it's me, John, Rahul, from England.'

'Rahul, my son, how wonderful to hear from you! We cannot wait until you arrive here on September 3rd! Hurry up!'

'There is rather a problem, Father,' replied John in agonies of dishonesty. 'Prakash is not very well and has to go into hospital for an intestinal operation. Do not worry, it is quite frequent in small children and I know, as a doctor, that it is not serious. Provided the operation is carried out now, he will never have any further trouble in his life. The only thing is that we will have to delay our arrival. Do not prepare, in your usual generous way, anything at all until I give you further news.'

'I shall pray for him. I shall go to my prayer room now. I am very sorry, my son, but I understand. The main thing is his health. Our love to you all.'

With that, the telephone went dead. John was relieved to have staved off the immediate problems of family relations with relative ease. He wondered whether Roshan had really believed him, if, perhaps, he ought to write him a letter to explain all. His mind was too tired now; he would leave that until tomorrow.

He walked straight into Joyce's, without even knocking. He just sat down wordless at the kitchen table, in one of her big, Yorkshire farmhouse chairs.

'God, I'm whacked!' he said. 'I'm late too. I've had to talk to both families. It wasn't fun.'

He told them about it all.

'You did right, lad,' said Frank. 'Best thing is to have the tea, with a drink first, o'course, sit and smoke fer a while and then we'll go, no'but us two, down to the Greyhound fer a nightcap.'

'I'll settle for all that, Frank, you old pal,' said John warmly.

A splendid northern stew was ladled out of the traditional brown pot, the vegetables all included, kept piping hot on the old range that Joyce would never get rid of.

After he had finished, John said: 'Don't think I'm being rude or ungrateful, Frank, but I don't think I could go out now. I just want to go to bed, early as it is. I just haven't the energy left. Perhaps tomorrow.'

'That's all right, lad. Joyce is always glad to steer me away from temptation!'

'There's one thing, both of you. I'm an honest man. I know that I must pay for your care of us. Will you accept this?' He drew out of his pocket five five-pound notes. Joyce was shocked.

'You'll do no such thing, my lad!'

'Joyce, I've got to. Things cost more and more every day and you'll have to do our shopping for us and there's all your trouble, too. And what about the meals that you will be giving me?'

'Get away with yer! If I have ter buy a deal in, I'll let yer know, but yer pays fer nowt in our 'ouse. Isn't that right, Frank?'

'O'course it is, love. Now, off with yer, John, lad, and sleep the sleep of the righteous, like me!'

He bad his friends goodnight and asked them to give his love to Prakash first thing in the morning. He went home and straight to bed. He was so tired that he fell asleep immediately, to awake shortly after nine the next morning.

*

The next day, at about ten o'clock, he went to see Prakash. He was in fine form and rushed to his father. He took the boy in his arms and swirled him round in an enormous hug. He sat him on his lap afterwards, where he stayed in silent contentedness. When John looked into his eyes, he saw his mother; equally, when he saw his mother he saw his son. They were all so much a part one of another. Father and son chuckled happily together for a while, until they were interrupted by homely Joyce, who declared that it was time that the lad had his dinner. John left them to it and sat and read the paper with Frank. Then, he looked miserable again.

'Take up, lad,' said Frank. 'Yer missus won't think a deal of a long face. A bright 'un will make 'er a site better than the one you've got on at the moment, take me word on it. When yer see 'er this afternoon, don't thee look down; look up, and she will an' all.'

'Alright, Frank, I'll buck up.'

'That's it, lad. Even an' if yer don't feel all that grand, just pretend. It does a world of good sometimes. I remember when Joyce was badly with our Robert. I 'ad a glass or two of stout and braved the wave; she did an' all. They both pulled through. With your girl, it's injury to 'er soul and the shame which she did not deserve. It's different, but you must treat it the same ways out. The more normal yer treats folk, the

204

more normal they becomes! Hard but true!'

'I'll take your advice, Frank.'

After cheese, home-made bread and pickles, he did exactly that. He had the two bottles of stout, too. He blessed dear old Frank's homespun advice. It worked.

He arrived in the Matron's office, waved through all the way, at two o'clock. His heart was thumping, his soul contorted. His only hope was that his wife's life would not have for ever been spoilt by her terrifying experience. He wondered whether she would ever be the same again. He remembered her insistence that they should have another child, in particular a son, whose name would be Ashok.

'God,' he said aloud to himself, breaking the silence of his many other prayers, 'answer us all!'

The nurse who had shown him the way knocked for him on the door. The Matron's voice responded immediately; she knew who it would be.

'Good afternoon, Matron,' said John quietly. 'It's good of you to see me. I will not detain you long.'

'It's good to see you, Doctor Osmond. I am glad that you came. Please sit down. I am in no hurry and I know that there are a great many questions that you would like to ask me.'

'Not really, Matron,' replied the young doctor. 'I would rather you told me your thoughts first.'

The Matron appreciated that, for she hated arrogance, especially in doctors. After all, she had had more experience than many of them put together. It happened that, in common with so many, she liked the promising cardiac man. Doctor Macrae had told her a lot about him, although John did not know that.

'Well, to begin at the beginning,' she started crisply and with merciful economy of words, 'your wife was naturally in some state of shock yesterday. Doctor Macrae has told you all about it, and so on and so forth, I am sure. There is nothing wrong with her that time will not cure, fortunately, except that she is desperately worried that she may have been fertilized. To be safe, we gave her the appropriate medication about which you obviously know. The next three weeks will be a trying time for you both. With your examinations and a small child, you are going to find things a little fraught. She aches everywhere, particularly in her heart; she feels that her soul had been damaged and her purity spoilt. You will have to heal all that.'

'I know, Matron,' said John.

'She has spent a good deal of time crying tears of shame. We have tried to comfort her, but it is best to let the grief come out because the release of deep feelings is the first step to mending a broken heart.'

'I know, Matron,' said John again, in wonderment at the compassion of someone whom everyone would have thought traditionally hard.

'Now,' she said, after a pause, 'what about the arrangements at home? She must not be left alone in the house for the time being, until she can banish fear and regain confidence. She's a strong girl with plenty of character, so I don't think that this process will take too long. What are you going to do?'

'I have already done it!' replied John.

He told her all about Joyce and Frank.

'That's absolutely splendid!' exclaimed Matron. 'Now let's go and see her. Oh, there's something else. Radhika's very lucky. In the small ward in which I was able to put her, there's a splendid, cheerful cockney lady. Her language is a little on the earthy side, but she has been a wonderful companion already for your wife. Cockneys can make you laugh about anything, however dire!'

'I'm glad about that, Matron, but can I take her home today?'

'No, John, you can't. Probably tomorrow evening, after Dr Jenner, with or without pyjamas, has had another look at her.'

His first name had slipped out again, which did not escape his grateful notice. He liked the bit about the pyjamas, too.

'I'll leave you to it now, Doctor. Stay as long as you like, but not too long.'

'I understand Matron, and thank you.'

He entered the small ward. There, beneath a window, lay his wife. She looked tired, but her eyes were shining with delight.

'Rahul! Rahul! It's you!'

'Who else, my love?'

He immediately sat on her bed and kissed her face and her swollen lips with the utmost tenderness. They held together hand in loving hand. They were wordless for several minutes, just gazing with love and respect into each other's eyes. It was with those that they spoke their deepest thoughts.

'I wanted to take you home today,' said John, 'but Matron said that it would be better if it were not until tomorrow evening. Doctor Macrae said that he would take you, because I shall have exams until at least half-past six. Do not fear. You will not be alone.'

He told her all about the arrangements at home with the Halls and Prakash.

'Aren't people kind!' she exclaimed in gratitude. 'And look at what you have been through, Rahul, and at a time like this!'

'My sweetheart, do not think of me. Just get better quickly. Try to forget the horrors and life will mend all the more quickly. I'm thinking of you more than anyone. And, oh, my goodness, I forgot to bring any flowers! What an idiot I am!'

'All men are!' said a cockney voice from behind him.

John turned round. There, propped up on numerous pillows, lay Mrs Bates. She was heavily made-up and her hair was obviously dyed.

'Life's a bastard at times,' she declared, 'but I don't give a brass bugger for no one and I'm bloody determined to come out of this lot alive and kickin'! That's what I told yer Missus. "Come on, ducks", I said, "show the sods what yer made of and stuff all them criminals!" That's what I think, and she's got the guts and she'll bleedin' well do it an' all!'

This magnificently colourful piece of counselling made

them all laugh.

'Thank you for having cheered up my wife, Mrs Bates, it's really nice of you,' said John, and he meant it.

'Not a bit, my love,' said Mrs Bates, 'laugh and the world laughs with yer, weep and yer weeps alone. That's what I says. Never mind about them bloody flowers, dear. She's sharin' mine, ain't yer ducks?'

'So I am, Mrs Bates, and thank you,' said Radhika, laughing already, 'doctors are so forgetful.'

'What! Not another one! You ain't really a medic, are yer?'

'Well, yes, Mrs Bates, I'm afraid I am.'

'Gawd All-bleedin'-mighty, wonders never cease!' exclaimed Mrs Bates good-naturedly. 'You lot's every-bloody-where! Want a drop of old square-face?'

'A drop of what Mrs Bates?' enquired Radhika.

'Gin, dear. I've got me make-up box 'ere. What they don't know is that underneath the top tray there's 'arf a bottle. A nip now and then keeps yer going and one of the porters keeps it filled up for me. Tricks of the trade. 'Ere we are, my dears, take a swig out the neck!'

'That's very kind of you, Mrs Bates, but neither of us is really supposed to drink.'

'Oh, well, never mind. Each accordin' to 'is taste.'

John and Radhika were amused. They kissed good-bye until the next day and John gave Mrs Bates a kiss as well.

'Thank you,' he said, 'for looking after my wife.'

'She's lovely,' replied the old lady, 'What a lucky old bastard you are, doctor!'

He kissed Radhika again and left the hospital, not before thanking the Matron. He told her about Mrs Bates but, loyally, not about the gin-run!

After the first day of his testing examinations, John arrived home at about six-thirty. He was greeted by Joyce and Frank. They were delighted to tell him that the Matron had released Radhika and that she was safely tucked up in bed and happy. Little Prakash was in Joyce's room and contented too. John immediately went upstairs and poked his anxious head around the door of the main bedroom. Radhika was asleep, her long, tousled hair tumbling over the pillow and her face. He listened to her breathing for a moment, but did not wake her. She would waken when he got into bed beside her. Just at the moment, he felt tired and decided to go downstairs to supper.

Everything was ready and waiting. There was Frank in his braces and Joyce in her busy apron.

'Wait on, our John, it's on the table in two shakes,' announced Joyce proudly. Indeed, it was. They started with the traditional Yorkshire pudding and treacle, followed by the beef and vegetables. Apple pie was to follow, with its warm, clovey taste. John was slow to start, but Joyce enjoined him to feed the inner man, although she did not quite express herself thus, and he set to.

Afterwards, although there was the prayer room in the house, which should have forbidden the dispensing of alcohol, John sometimes disobeyed the rule; this time, he forgave himself entirely. The three had a welcome nightcap. They did not feel the need to speak much. At about half-past nine, Frank left.

' 'Ere goes the deserted 'usband,' he said good-naturedly.

'Nivver you mind, our Frank, you'll survive and I've got the dishes to do,' replied Joyce. 'And you, master John, 'ad better get up ter bed. There's someone waitin' on yer, thou knows!'

'I do indeed, Joyce, and thank you for a lovely dinner and for all your invaluable help!'

'Get away with you, you silly boy!' she said.

John did as he was told without a second bidding.

He first went and kissed his son gently upon the forehead. He held a small, brown hand above the bedclothes. He stood and said some silent prayers, both of supplication and thanks. Just pride welled in his burdened heart. He prayed for himself too, that the powers would take some of the weight and help him.

Then he went to the bathroom to make the essential

ablutions. There he prayed for a clean life and that the waters of heaven would wash Radhika's soul from any imaginary guilt. He tried not to cry, but he could not help it. Perhaps it did him good...

In the bedroom, with the door ajar to admit just enough light for him to see his way, he divested himself of all clothing, as was his wont, and slipped into bed beside Radhika, naked as God had made him. This made him feel honest and unashamed, meek yet proud. Radhika stirred and turned towards him.

'Rahul, put your arm across me,' she whispered.

John did not answer, because he was going to do that anyway. He caressed her with infinite gentleness and said: 'You are home and healed now, my love. All I want to do is to kiss your sweet face and hold your little, loving hand. Do not think of anything else. Be warm beside me.'

Suddenly, she spoke, passionately, loudly and with definition. It cost her a great deal to say what she did: 'John, you are my Rahul and always will be. I'm not half so scared of a rapist as I am that you may never want me again because I have been made impure. I feel a defiled woman. My heart and body are full of dirt.'

She was crying and her body heaving with painful sobs. She was rending her poor heart.

'When you are better, which will be soon,' said John softly, 'we are going to make Ashok.'

They fell into the embrace of trust. All problems fled away, dispelled for ever, except for one, which John had to keep to himself. Radhika was still and would always remain beautifully innocent. She had evidently forgotten about the three weeks, or if she had some forebodings, they were ill-defined.

10

Release and Hope

Life at New Farm continued its even tenor. The harvest was in without mishap, the stubble burnt and the outbuildings repaired and painted where necessary. One or two gates had to be rehung. The gardens were rich in late summer colours. Teddy mowed the now weedless lawns, where he and Joan, sometimes with a few dinner guests, played croquet inefficiently but with harmless enjoyment, in the warm evenings. The farm was producing reasonable profits. Joan told Teddy that he was to keep these; she gave him a good deal more besides, because she knew that he helped John and his family. The couple was, then, very comfortably off. There was, however, one thing that plagued Teddy; he was in agonies of frustrated honesty. Eventually he could stand it no longer and the banks burst.

'You're very quiet this evening, Teddy,' said Joan after dinner.

'Well, sometimes one feels like that,' he countered, thinking inevitably that Joan had smelt a rat. 'I have one or two things on my mind at the moment.'

'You always tell me everything, my dear. I know you, you're keeping something to yourself, aren't you?' asked Joan more in the manner of a statement than a question, whilst still knitting a pullover for Prakash.

'You'll get it out of me eventually,' replied Teddy, 'so I had better tell you. Be prepared for a shock. And put down that knitting. This is not going to be easy for us.'

There was a pause whilst Teddy fetched Joan a port and himself a rather unseemly-sized whisky. Twisting his fingers, he began:

'The truth is that I had, for once in my life, to tell deliberate lies. Both to you and to the Mahendras. John told me the truth about the family and I did not really know what to do about it.'

Joan looked apprehensive as a thousand unwelcome thoughts scudded through the skies of her mind, casting dark patches upon the lives of those she loved so deeply. She sat perfectly still and waited. Teddy told her everything about the real reason for the delay in their Indian arrangements. Joan was truly horrified.

'We may not even get to go on holiday this year at all, Joan,' he concluded.

'Blow the holiday, Teddy. That's not important. You should really have told me before now. I would have gone straight up to Oxford. Shall I drop everything and go now?'

'No, my love, you have Penelope to look after. I shall go as soon as John lets me know the verdict of Dr Jenner. Radhika is to see him in three days when the three weeks waiting-time will be up. That is what I was looking so quietly glum about. Now you can understand. I'm sorry. You are right. I should have told you before, but I thought it was a terror that John and I should bear on our own.'

'I shall write as soon as you tell me, Teddy.'

In the meantime, Radhika was gaining her self respect and confidence. At first, she did not want to go out of the house, but Joyce started her rehabilitation by going shopping with her and eventually she launched out on her own. She felt rather cruel about it, but she knew that the young wife would have to take the plunge. She waited for her return to the house, when she was delighted to notice that Radhika was confident and smiling with evident relief.

'There, love, that weren't too terrible after all!' she exclaimed.

'No, Joyce. You need not come with me again, now. And as soon as you think I'm ready, you must go home to Frank. Poor man, he's put up with a lot on account of a total stranger!'

'Yer can stop that daft talk fer a start, my girl. Yer not strangers and nivver will be!'

'Oh, Mrs Hall – Joyce, I mean – you're better than any doctor, except John, of course!'

'I've left some dinner for you and Praki. I'd best get 'ome and see how that Frank's doin'. Hope 'e's not been at the beer too seriously! If yer wants me, just pick up the 'phone.'

When John got home at about six-thirty, he immediately saw the welcome new self-assurance in his wife. She told him of her solo adventure. They were both thrilled. Just as they were about to sit down to supper, there was a ring at the door. John opened it upon Inspector Miles.

'I thought I had better come and say a few words to you both, Doctor,' he said with some embarrassment.

'Come in and welcome, Inspector. My wife can keep the supper hot as it won't spoil for a few extra minutes in the oven. It's so kind of you to have called. May I get you a drink?'

'No, Sir, thank you. I'd be outlawed!'

They all went into the drawing room. The inspector began to tell why he had come. He explained that the police had not made any progress in tracing the dreadful 'intruder' (he tactfully avoided the word 'rapist'). He said that they would keep the case open but that he did not hold out much hope. He added that they would have to go on trying in the interests of the security of other possible victims, but that eventually the file would be closed, unsolved.

'We do not want to hear any more about it, Inspector. But thank you for all your kindness and gentle consideration. My wife is now well on the mend. Contact me again if you need me. I realise that you have your job to do and a very important one it is. But I somehow wish you lack of success in this one, because I do not want to have everything revived in our minds again.'

213

'I fully understand that, Sir,' replied the inspector kindly. 'Off the record and for your sakes, I hope the same as yourself. I shall probably not be bothering you again.'

'Well, always feel free to drop in and see us sometime.'

'I think I'll take you up on that, Doctor, but when I'm off duty next time!'

John and Radhika bathed and went to bed. They lay for some time in the delectable silence that warm, early September night. They held hands and snuggled close to each other. Then John put his arm across Radhika and they hugged.

'Why not tonight, Rahul?' asked his wife in a plaintive whisper. 'It's been long.'

'We cannot until three days' time, love,' said John with regret. 'The reason is that we have to hear what Dr Jenner says. He will probably say No for a little while after.'

'Is it then still possible that I may be pregnant?'

'We have to be safe, you especially. It would be frantic if you went through with it all only to discover that I was not the father.'

For some curious reason, whether out of self-deception or ignorance, the possible likelihood of conception seemed to have eluded her recently. She shivered. John held her tight. She started to sob.

'I am certain that everything will be clear for us. Just bear with the next three days. You are well now. Don't go back again, as hard as that may be, if easy for me to say it. Although I have tried not to show it, I have shared all your fears and sufferings. I know, somehow, that you will be clear. Then we will make Ashok.'

'How do know that it will be another son, Rahul?'

'I happen to know, that's all,' said John, with loving presumption. 'But I would be nearly as happy with a daughter!' he added teasingly. 'You're so clever, that I'll leave it to you in any case,' he said unmedically. They both laughed and went to sleep.

214

*

They were a long three days until the end of the first week in September. They both pretended to normality and busied themselves as much as possible in the house and with Prakash. John was to be at home now until October, when he would be taking up his post under Doctor Macrae at the hospital. He was more than excited about that. Radhika felt proudly privileged of her clever husband. They both spent a good deal of time with Prakash, who was becoming more enquiring by the day. John was glad to see that. He was grateful that he was to have a more connected childhood than he, although, God knew, he fortunately had not suffered for it. Perhaps it had even made him more compassionate in life?

Meanwhile, the holidays were postponed and neither mentioned them. As it happened, although they were to miss going to India, feeling also that they had let down the family, they were more than content in their private peace and away from the hustled urgencies of life. It would do them both good, they told themselves, to pause for breath. John was awaiting his results, but, despite all the upsets of recent days, he was confident of distinction. His confidence was not misplaced. He was to hear of his success in mid-September. Immediately afterwards he was summoned by Doctor Macrae. His future was gruffly assured. Unable to invite Radhika and John to his chaotic flat – chaotic still, despite the frenzied ministrations of a daily maid – he took the young couple out to a sumptuous dinner. Taxis were the order of the night, although neither of the doctors knew much about the return journeys.

Radhika was amused at the two foolish 'boys' and put John to bed in fits of laughter. He did not feel quite so healthy the next morning, but recovered, thanks to some salts, by lunchtime.

Between the future and now, there was Dr Jenner. He was solicitude itself. He took a urine sample, soon to return with a broad smile.

215

'All's well, my love,' he said simply. 'You have been brave, but it was worth the wait.'

Radhika burst into tears of relief.

'Now, it is really forgotten!' she cried in her release from a frantic anxiety.

'It is indeed, dear. Don't look back or think of this business again, will you? And, if you don't think it's too forward of me, I'd like to give you a piece of advice. Make another child as soon as you can, but not for a few weeks yet. You don't want too much of a gap between the first two, you know.'

'We have already decided to do just what you say, Dr Jenner.'

When she got home, John, who had thought it better that she went alone to the hospital, sealed in her private hopes, which were, of course, his as well, was standing looking vacantly at nothing in the kitchen. He was not without thought for long, his wife's delirium of joy told everything. They swung each other around in their arms until they were nearly giddy.

'I've anticipated everything,' laughed John, 'and, completely without penitence, I have disobeyed the rule. I think that we shall be forgiven and I've said my prayers already! Go into the drawing room and I will bring two things in for you.'

Radhika did as she had been bid. She could hardly wait, although she had some inkling that her generous husband would provide a touching gesture to make the day and its news perfect. She was not to be disappointed.

'Here, take this,' he said simply.

She opened a small box to discover an emerald and diamond gold ring. It must have broken the bank. She put it on and kissed it. The green suited her dark, olive skin and her black eyes. She was speechless.

'That's for being a clever girl,' he said. 'And now you are going to be cleverer still!'

He then dashed into his act of disobedience and brought in a chilled bottle of Lanson. They had two large glasses each and felt deliciously wicked.

'Look,' said John suddenly. 'We've forgotten some other people. We've forgotten the Halls. You go and make some silly pieces of nonsense on little biscuits, while I have a wash and then go and get another bottle and Frank and Joyce.'

In no time, it seemed to him, he had accomplished all these things and a silver tray was covered in attractively decorated and tasty things to eat. Their great helpers arrived in half an hour. Frank was still in his shirtsleeves and stud and Joyce had inexpertly splotched on some charmingly ill-judged make-up. It was a wonderfully impromtu early evening, after which the couple just had a modest supper at home. They both kissed their son goodnight in his sleep, silently promising him a new companion one day fairly soon.

*

To the perhaps selfish unbelief of John, Radhika changed after the wonderful all-clear. He was in the same hurry as she had been. He must have Ashok. He must make delicate, lovely love again. It was, of course, too soon. Releases from anxiety can often be almost as shocking as the original event that made the trauma. John and Radhika were both to suffer painfully in the next few weeks.

When they went to bed that night which was intended to be perfect, Radhika turned away from John and started crying. He felt her shoulders heaving silently. He tried to turn her towards him but she resisted. He only wanted a kiss he told her.

'Why not?' John asked pitifully, his voice tinged with a hint of unjust impatience.

'Because I'm simply not ready, even for a kiss, and I don't know that I ever will be for anything further. I shall never be the same again.'

'But we've just heard the most wonderful news, my love, and we are both terribly lucky,' replied John sadly.

'I don't think I want to know life as it was any longer,'

sobbed Radhika. 'It was too sweet and now it is too bitter. I don't really know what I feel now. I will look after Prakash, I promise.'

And here she started sobbing even more violently. John turned away in desperation. He felt a strange anger welling in his offended soul. It was directed against God. He felt that he was tasting the bitter herbs that should never have been given to him. The word 'why' traversed and travailed his mind until he fell into a companionless and fitful sleep.

In the succeeding days, John seemed to be a changed man, his wife a changed woman. Their very closeness made them both blind to a simple truth. It took someone else to explain to a clever doctor what he should have seen at once.

The jovial yet sympathetic Doctor Osmond showed a sullen face at the hospital and was abrupt with his assistants. He had a good word for no one and was only just polite to his patients. His zest for life seemed to have evaporated. He was depressed as well as angry. He even made a rather insulting call to Inspector Miles, who kindly disregarded it in full understanding.

Everyone noticed the change in John, including his wife. When he came home, often at difficult hours, there was always something beautifully prepared for him. For despite her depression, Radhika kept the house clean, Prakash tidy and her husband well-fed.

'What the hell do you think this is on the table?' he cruelly exclaimed one night, after a particularly trying day.

'It is your favourite chicken tikka, John,' said Radhika thinly.

'Well you can take it away then. I had something similar yesterday. I'll get myself some tinned soup and you can get off to your solitary little bed. And think of some changes to the menu.'

She burst into tears which streaked their way down her lovely soft cheeks.

'You do hurt me, John. You have been so unkind to me recently. Be patient and I will get my confidence back.'

'I wonder!' exclaimed her husband with a brutality that

218

suddenly surprised him.

He got up to put his arm round Radhika, but she pushed him away and went up to bed, still downcast and crying.

The day after this latest outburst, which had not been the only one, he entered the hospital in his now frequently sullen mood. He was angrier than ever against the criminal. He asked himself whether he had ruined their lives at home, and right at the beautiful beginning of their young married time.

He went to his consulting room, sat at his desk and opened his appointment book at the right day. Here he discovered a small envelope. He opened it.

> Dear Doctor Osmond,
>   I wonder if you would mind coming to see me in my office as soon as you can? I shall be there for the next hour.
>   Matron.

John thought that this was rather a nuisance, but that he had better go. It would be about one of his patients, most probably. He did not then know that the patient was himself.

'Good morning, Matron,' said John, rather coldly. 'What can I do for you?'

'Nothing at all, John,' she replied coolly, 'it is what I can do for you.'

There was a pause. John suddenly felt disgusted and ashamed of his behaviour the night before.

'I have noticed, we have all noticed, that you are not your usual charming self, John. Do not think that I wish to interfere or to criticise, but I think that you ought to tell somebody about what is troubling you and why you are so moody and sullen. It does not become you.'

Here John made to interrupt, but the Matron cut him short.

'You may think that I am a crabby old woman who could not advise a young man. I would not blame you for that! In fact, I was married to an army officer and we had a daughter.

219

Despite my efforts, they both died of typhus in Delhi, where I was a nurse. I think that that fate was worse than yours, don't you?'

John felt humbled. He immediately told her about life at home. He wept for his selfishness.

'What you need, my lad, is a bit of patience. Your lovely wife is having a natural reaction. She is not ready yet. But the more gentle you are, the more quickly she will be. Go home when you have finished here today and wipe the slate clean. You are such a fine doctor that we would not wish to see you spoil everything.'

John smiled.

'Thank you, Matron, you old mother; I'll go and see to my patients now – and my patience!'

'Good morning then, Doctor,' she replied, an affectionately wry, wistful smile playing upon her lips.

When he got home that evening, John entered the house smiling for the first time in days. Radhika had put Prakash to bed long ago and was sitting in the kitchen reading a magazine without interest. She looked very depressed.

'Hello, my love of loves!' he cried, as he smelt another delicious meal in the cooking.

'Hello, John,' she replied dully.

From behind his back John produced a very large bunch of flowers.

'Now, just put that silly women's magazine down and get on with getting these into some vases while I have a celebratory glass of forbidden whisky.'

'Why, Rahul, they are wonderful! Thank you.'

'They are not as lovely as you, but they can't help that!' smiled John.

'You are all different today, John.'

'And you are going to be exactly the same soon, as well, love.'

There was a pleasing and silent pause. Both felt slightly better.

'Now,' said John with authority, 'we are having Matron to dinner some time next week.'

'Whatever for? She's a battleaxe.'

'No, she isn't!'

Then John told her all about his motherly interview and her advice.

'Of course she'll have to come,' said Radhika lovingly. 'What a dear she really is!'

'We will make Ashok whenever you like,' said John tenderly.

In three weeks, and quite spontaneously, they did. It was a wonderful mending time. The gentle passion returned, the mutual fragrancies and the warmth of each other's body which was to pulsate into a second fine son.

In the languid aftermath they both laughed for joy. The bad time was over.

*

Teddy arrived in a few days, just in time for lunch. He could hardly wait for the door to be opened to him. He burst in, in his usual hearty, sincere, spontaneous way. He banged down his travelling bag, the impact of which nearly knocked over a vase of flowers on a small table in the hall, and rushed into their arms. He picked up his grandson and hugged him nearly breathless. Then he sat down in the kitchen and said, in his bald bluntness:

'Well, I'm here in one piece. Joan wanted to come but I told her that she ought to stay at home and look after Penelope. She gives you all her best love and has told me to behave myself. As you know, I have always found that difficult, but I'm here to do my best. You do now know how glad I am for you both for the happy outcome. Now, let's have a drink!'

'You can, Edward, my Father, but Radhika and I will join you only in a fresh orange juice. We have already disobeyed the rules more than once!'

The father and the son looked into the eyes of each other. They spoke years of shared experience and understanding.

Eventually, after a lapse into contented and relieved silence, John told his father all about his prospects. He said that the month of September would be spent with the family; he and Radhika both needed a break from anxieties. The relief, he told him was so enormous that it needed a period of peaceful recovery. Teddy told them not to worry and that he fully understood; both he and Joan. It would be much the best, he averred, that they stayed together instead of going on foreign forays. John's post was to be taken up in October and his mind would be filled with thought and mental preparation.

'We can go to India next year, perhaps,' ventured Teddy. 'I have now, in conjunction with Joan, come up with an idea. To disappoint the Mahendras would be unforgivable, if not unkind. They naturally want to see their own, among whom you are fortunately numbered. So am I, come to that. It is now Joan and I that are making the plans and giving the orders. Wait, I'll have lunch first.'

'No you won't, Edward, you'll just sit there and tell us what you have hatched up,' the doctor said at once.

Teddy drew his mischievous flask from his hip pocket, took a swig with a wink or two and revealed all his plan.

'You, John, will have had over two months in which to settle in with Doctor Macrae. You will have established your credentials, if they need any establishing. You will, if I know you two, have another child on the way. That is just as it should be. It will be too late to go to India for a spell. Joan and I want you to all to come to New Farm for Christmas; we want the Mahendras, very badly, to come too. You know how much at home Joan will make us all and Radhika's parents will feel entirely at ease, although they have never ventured to England before. We will make certain that dietary requirements are met in naturally accorded courtesy. You make the plans for their journey. You will all come, won't you?'

'I can't think of a better idea, Edward,' said John, without a moment's hesitation. 'And, by that time, Radhika will be bearing our next son. That should please Roshan!'

Thus was all arranged. They had a pleasant supper later, and humbly, in the kitchen. They all went to bed early. John and his wife were one again and in late October she was announced to be pregnant. John telephoned Joan and Teddy and then Roshan. The time had come, they realised, for them to tell Roshan the truth and to make the invitation for Christmas. They had delayed too long, without their having wanted to have done so.

At the same time as John wrote to India, so did Joan. Before this, John had started his new job. It was not to prove an always easy passage, working with the senior doctor, because John was incredibly popular for his easy manner, never oily but always sympathetic. More and more patients wanted to see the younger man. They did not seem to realise that the young doctor owed everything to the experience of the elder of the two and did not appear to see beyond his gruffness. John always asked him his advice and felt rather ashamed of the demands which were flatteringly made upon him.

One evening, after some tiring operations which tested the immediacy of his decision, John went into Macrae's office to say goodnight to him.

'Sit down, Son,' he said. 'You've got the image, I've got the experience and the knowledge. Never be swayed by popularity. Fashionable doctors are to be despised. I am old, ugly and unprepossessing. I am not jealous of you.'

'I have felt a little chill between us of late,' replied John uncertainly. 'Believe me, I have never tried to steal your thunder.'

'I know that, John, Laddie. That's why I respect you. Your young confidence infuriates me at times, but I admire you for it.'

The two men looked at one another for a few silent moments. Neither seemed to know where this conversation was leading. It was the elder man who broke the silence.

'I have never been a vain man, John. When the hopes of your private life have been early dashed, there is nothing to do but to get on with the job in humility and dedication. I think that I have done that. I am going to retire in about eighteen months and I want you to take my post. Do you think that you'll be up to it?'

Aghast, John said:

'I'll do my level best, Sir. I owe all that I know to you. I shall not let you down, but I shall call upon your advice whenever I need it, and I expect that that will be not infrequently.'

'That's kind of you, Laddie, and I feel honoured. Don't tell anyone other than your wife what I have said.'

John promised. There was a look of sad gladness in both pairs of eyes. John rose to go.

'There's another thing,' added Macrae standing to make the order. 'You will be making another bairn, of course, and I should think you have started! I'm bloody well going to be his godfather, or whatever they have in India! They always say that mongrels are the best! Don't take that wrong, boy,' he added.

John made another promise. He did not break it. He turned quickly on his heel and walked smartly out. He felt the tears starting to prick him behind the eyes.

*

The pressure of work made the days fly by until Christmas. Radhika was already preparing things for the new baby and Joyce Hall was excited as well. Frank took to the racing pages, but he was glad for 'his' young couple in his quiet way. In his workshop, he was already preparing a small surprise for everyone; until the event, no one was to be admitted into his woody sanctum, which smelt beckoningly of stout and oak shavings.

The letters to India received a prompt reply. Radhika's mother and father fully understood their daughter's wish to stay at home and were only too glad that it was such a happy one. Roshan was shocked but ineffably understanding about what had happened and only too glad that all had ended –

and begun again – so well. He never told his wife, not for shame but rather out of delicacy. They could hardly wait to see England, the farm, Joan, Penelope and, of course their daughter and grandson. All their friends, of which there were naturally a multitude, were enthralled and glad for them.

At New Farm, things quietened as the winter deepened. One evening, a strange recollection struck Teddy. Foley's bedroom, apart from having been tidied, had not been opened since his departure from the earth that he appeared to hate. Teddy thought to go up there one night and clear away the rest of what would have reminded anyone of his half-brother.

The room smelt mouldy and full of a lost person. He felt moved, in a rather distant way, to say a prayer for the repose of the soul of Foley. He had never wished anyone ill, but he had come quite close to unworthy sentiments with his slave-driver of a brother. Now, he had almost forgotten the dismality of his existence. He made a pile of clothes from the wardrobe and he heaped them in the middle of the floor. He emptied his chest of drawers and threw the contents upon his shabby but expensive suits. Next, he turned his attention to his bureau. He had already been through all his papers, although he remembered that he had been unable to open one of the drawers. It was locked and he had never discovered the key. He now looked behind cupboards and under tables. He had decided that he could not face looking through the pockets of suits, so he went downstairs to find a strong screwdriver. With this, and despite its valuable antiquity, he prised open the locked drawer.

He found bundles of unimportant and outdated letters, most of which he did not bother to read. The drawer was deep and he pulled it out further. At the very back there was a bundle of high denomination notes. He counted a thousand pounds.

'What did he put this here for?' he asked himself. 'What kind of emergency could Foley have been expecting? Is this why he had kept his bedroom door locked?'

225

Underneath the notes there was a stamped and sealed letter addressed to his solicitor. Edward opened it. It was dated the day before his all-debilitating stroke. The writing was scrawly and barely legible in parts. It appeared that he had wanted to make a codicil to his will, in which he designed to leave merely a respectable amount to his wife, a small amount to Penelope and the vast bulk of his considerable fortune to Fiona. He had added a postscript at the end of the letter:

> *I have good reason to believe that my rascally, wastrel of a step-brother is deceiving me. I cannot imagine why. That is the reason for these proposed new dispositions.*

Fortunately for all, the letter was never sent. Teddy showed it to Joan.

'How lucky we are.' she said without emotion. 'I don't feel in the slightest degree guilty. He gave me the hell of a life and now he's paying for it! He's paying for you and your family, which he might well have offered to have done. You slaved for him without any immediate reward, but you now have it! And you deserve that.'

Teddy put the letter in the fire.

'We can do without this as well,' he said gallantly.

The tainted thousand pounds went after it.

'Now it is finished,' he pronounced, without remorse.

'Let's talk about Christmas,' suggested Joan brightly. 'We're all going to have a wonderful, carefree, extravagant family time. I think we all deserve it!'

*

Towards the end of December, arrangements were finally made for the long-expected arrival of Varsha and Roshan. Prakash was very excited about seeing his grandparents. Although he did not know it, they were just the same way, too. Neither of them could wait until they saw their pregnant

226

daughter. Some people have said that the pregnant woman is the most beautiful sight in a man's life. It certainly was for all the men in the family. There would always be for them the inexpressible and saintly holiness of that state. And then the element of surprise was not to lack; John thought it would be disgusting to have a check on the sex of the baby; what was to be given by God would be accepted with untouchable gratitude by the recipients of his gift. Radhika thought the same; that the anticipation was part of the delight.

On a chilly December 20th, Teddy and John drove to Heathrow. They did not say much to each other on the way. They shared the driving in the rather ancient, comfortable and capacious Humber. They both had the suspicion, shortly to be confirmed, that the couple would arrive with considerably excess baggage. When they all met, they knew that their best forecasts had been confirmed. It took ages for everything to be delivered to the car and even then there was hardly room for all of them.

Before that, there they both were, standing mute and bewildered, wrapped up warmly and unnationally, awaiting their luggage, in the large foyer. Their hearts were pounding. Their gaze stretched to any distance for the home of their hearts that they so much loved. Racing up soon, came John and his father. There were just long and firm embraces which made the elder couple warm inside and gave them their much-needed confidence straight away.

'The luggage won't be a minute, I hope,' said Roshan.

'I don't care if it takes a month, Father,' said John. 'The main thing is that you are here. I have so much to tell you, but that will have to wait. I'll organise everything and get the luggage transported to the car. The journey won't be long now, and then you can both bathe and relax.'

'We're just glad to be with you, my Son.'

'No gladder than I am, Father.'

'I am so glad to be going to be a grandfather again, Rahul.'

The two men embraced once more, in a sort of loving

complicity. They evidently shared the love of engendering children, the elevation of the greatest miracle in the world. They shared too a spirituality that they recognised in one another; the holiness of a family and the thread that cannot be broken. John remembered The Thread. That was, and always would be, hallowed and kept in his life.

'Come on, you two!' said Teddy. 'The luggage has arrived and they are putting it into the car. We'll all get frozen here!'

The cramped journey back to Hampshire and New Farm took about two hours. It was now sleeting, which made driving difficult. John insisted upon taking the wheel. They arrived, tired and slightly dishevelled, at about ten o'clock at night. When they had the door opened to them, everyone was there. Penelope and little Prakash, Joan, and even Fiona. There were fires lit against the winter chill in nearly every room. The two younger men heaved in the packages, dumped them without ceremony in the hall and repaired to the drawing room.

Everyone stood mute and dazed for a moment or two. They then all burst into laughter and embraces.

'You are so very, very welcome,' said Joan. 'Don't look bewildered, we're all here for you both. You're at home now, really at home.'

Roshan and Varsha hardly heard a word that they had said. They were entirely taken with Penelope and Prakash. Pride and love welled in their eyes.

'We do not know what to say just now,' said Roshan for himself and his wife.

'The best would be to say nothing, Father,' Joan replied comfortingly. 'Just be quiet and at home. I hope that I shall be the same in yours, one day,' a secret fear touching her voice, but this was, as yet, something that no one could detect; for the moment, she was proud and gay; she would not have for all the world disparaged the joyous hopes of her family.

After the men had taken up their things to their room and showed them all that was necessary, the couple washed briefly and descended for a light supper.

'All news tomorrow,' announced Joan considerately. 'I think we all need to go to bed. Especially the children.'

Reluctantly, they all agreed, despite the ill-timed insistence of the children. Everyone slept peacefully that night, even those in a strange land.

The few days before Christmas were busy and full of mutual solicitude. In the daytimes, the guests relaxed, played with the children and took them for walks along the frosty farm lanes. In the evenings, they exchanged volumes of interesting news. Fiona read elevating books alternatively with financial bulletins, but she kept happy in her dowdy tweeds and in her thoughts of future, exciting business meetings. She did not help Joan in the vast kitchen very much, but she did make a few gestural but useless offers. Joan was amused rather than annoyed; poor Fiona, she must live out of packets and tins, she thought.

After dinner on the second night, Roshan announced that he had come to a decision. They would all come to India to stay the next Christmas or in the New Year.

'I will brook no objections,' he said with authority. 'By December or January, the baby will be weaned and you can leave him with Mr and Mrs Hall with safety for a couple of weeks. She is an experienced lady and will know all the right things to do.'

'That would be absolutely grand,' said Joan unexpectedly.

John and Radhika wondered why she had seemed to answer so suddenly and even almost out of turn. However, they both agreed provisionally, saying that final arrangements would have to wait for a few months. Teddy was eager, so were Penelope and Prakash. Fiona declined politely, as everyone knew that she would.

'I'm sorry everyone,' she moaned, 'but I have so many business interests to look after and I hate flies and that sort of thing!'

'You old stodge,' laughed Teddy, 'you're afraid of anything outside Cheltenham! You are tactless, Fiona. It is a doctor's house and there are only snakes in the bathrooms and

Bengal tigers guarding the verandahs. I'll give you a gun to keep by your bedside and you'll find the men more than appealing!'

'Edward, you're your usual frightful self, I see.' Fiona laughed good-naturedly at herself. 'How on earth you think all the children are going to grow up under your influence gives me cause to wonder with trepidation!'

Teddy had thought of a rather witty, if somewhat indecent, reply, but he did not make it. She would not have understood it anyhow. John smiled and looked away in an affected absence of concentration.

It was now the day before Christmas Eve. Joan had been very busy and looked rather tired and pale. Teddy sensed that she was over-strained. The old maid had hobbled home ages ago. He told everyone that he would do the washing-up and that they were all to have an early night; there was going to be a party the next evening when everyone would be late up. All departed with gestures of affection and Fiona said that she would put the children to bed, how incompetently they could only guess.

Just before Teddy had reached the kitchen, Joan arose from the table upon some pretext or other. The former busied himself with the plates and followed her out, just in time to find her swallowing tablets.

'What on earth are you doing, Joan? You look frightful. I thought that you did not seem too well at dinner. I just innocently concluded that you were naturally over-tired. What are these for?' he asked with great concern.

'Oh, they are just something I have to take from time to time, Teddy. I did not think that they were worth telling you about.'

'Everything that concerns us is worth telling about, Joan. This is most unlike you. What is the matter? Blast the washing-up! Come and sit and tell me. I will not go to bed until you have done.'

Joan knew that deception with Teddy would be unforgivable and impossible as well. She explained painfully that she had not been well for two or three months. Early in the days of her discomfort, she had been to her doctor who had sent her for tests at the hospital. Teddy had not suspected anything in her day's absence, because she had said, quite plausibly, that she was going to stay with an old school friend in Salisbury, as from time to time she did.

'They are pretty sure that I have cancer of the rectum, my old dear. I said that I must be at home for Christmas, for all the family. They advised me against it, but I somehow knew that my days would be numbered and wanted so badly to make it all splendid for everyone. I am going to go in on January 3rd for an exploratory operation. I know what it will be,' she continued without the pause that would have made even her heart break, 'they will cut me open, have a good look and stitch me up again. I shall make my exit from the world armed with buckets of painkillers. These are some of them, but they'll get stronger.'

Here she stopped at last. Teddy was speechless in his devastation and grief. He could not even cry. Neither of them could. They simply gazed at each other vacantly.

'God in His Heaven! What on earth can we do, my darling of life?' besought Teddy.

'Nothing at all, Teddy. I shall probably have a few months left. That is why I accepted India with such unseemly alacrity, when I knew that it was really up to you and John. I hope that there will be time. I will be able to tell you in a few days. In the meantime, you are not to tell anyone; no one, that is, except John, who will be bound to notice something.'

The two hugged for ages, wallowing helplessly in uncertainty and floundering in feet of the cold waters of fear. Not knowing what else to say, Teddy offered, with some incongruity:

'You go to bed. I'll bring you a hot drink. Then I'll do the stuff in the kitchen.'

He felt powerlessly inadequate, helpless before another disaster in his life. And the same one, unbelievably. He felt like waking John, but decided that this would have been unfair. Instead, he sat down by the kitchen table in front of

231

the dirty plates and wept his way through half a bottle of whisky. He knew that this would not improve anything and was definitely the wrong thing to do. Somehow, he tidied up and wound his way unsteadily upstairs and to bed beside Joan, now sleeping without pain. Despite the alcohol, Teddy slept but fitfully until early morning. He noticed a bottle of pills and a glass of water beside Joan's half of their bed. They had not been there when he had gone upstairs; she must have had recourse to relief sometime during the night.

On Christmas Eve, John had to visit the hospital in order to see and comfort his patients. He had an assistant, as he had been himself but a short while ago. Even when he was not strictly on duty, he most often went to see his 'people' as he called them, just before lunch. Teddy had decided that the morning would not therefore be a propitious time to tell him the grim news, this especially because he had asked his father-in-law if he would like to accompany him on his rounds. The elder man was delighted. His bedside manner, John knew, would breathe compassion and comfort.

'When are we off, John?' he asked eagerly.

'At about half-past eight, Father. Let's have breakfast first!'

They drove through the cold, snowy miles to the hospital in Oxford, where every door seemed automatically to open before them. John decided to see Matron as a matter of courtesy before he showed his father-in-law into the wards to see his patients. He knew that there would be no obstacle, for there had grown between them a sense of interreliance and trust. The stately Matron had a strong regard for the young surgeon and he often invited her advice. After all, she was old enough to have been his mother. They even teased one another a good deal; it relieved the direness of many situations. Some operations, John came painfully to know, cannot but have very sad results. When these occurred, which, fortunately, was rarely, he always felt guilty and remorseful. 'Could I have done better?' he used to ask himself.

Matron looked up when they walked in. Amongst her piles

of papers there nestled several cups of unfinished, cold coffee. Her smile was broad.

'So, you've come to visit your patients, Doctor? I told you that you needed a rest and to stay with your neglected family,' she chided. 'I know that you want to,' she added, 'but you're not coming in tomorrow. If I need you I shall call you. That's an order, my boy!'

'I know who's the boss around here, Matron. For once, I think that I may do as I have been told! But don't forget, I'm always at the ready. Now, you have not asked who my distinguished guest is.'

'My God, Doctor! she exclaimed, almost reverting to hospital formality, 'I think I know. Doctor Mahendra, you are very welcome. I have heard all about you. Go and see John's patients with him. They would like that. I expect that they may be rather curious, but, that will do them good and take their minds off it all. It's wonderful to meet you, I hope that your holiday will be happy and you must be thrilled to see your daughter and her now growing family.

Roshan hardly knew what to say. He did not realise that Matron had so much knowledge of everything. His distinguished, silver-grey moustache twisted above a frank, open smile. He stretched out his hand.

'It is a privilege to meet you, Matron. Thank you for looking after my daughter and my rascally son-in-law! I shall enjoy my visit here, I know. I'm not much better than John is, anyhow, am I Rahul?'

'You said that, Father!'

They went to two wards of John's patients, but not to those in intensive care, which John visited alone. Roshan sat on as many beds as he had time for. They were delighted, especially when he explained proudly who he was. They were comforted and intrigued all at once.

'I knew the doctor had married an Indian lady, but I didn't really believe it until I saw you!' exclaimed one sufferer bluntly. 'I wonder what it's like to be different?' he asked almost to himself.

'Well, my friend, we aren't really different and it does not

233

matter at all. This is my first time in your country and I'm enjoying it. Thank you for having me.'

There were several encounters of this kind before John returned from his patients in more dangerous circumstance. He looked rather distraught.

'I think I have lost one,' he said. 'I will find out tomorrow.'

'We have to live our lives in separate compartments, my son,' advised Roshan.

John thought that he had heard that before, but he constantly needed the hearing of it again. They went home the long distance to relax and wash before a very late lunch. To the astonishment of Fiona, the boy and the three men spoke a relaxing Hindi, sharing amusing pleasantries of life several thousand miles away. India was, as if by a miracle of mere speech, in the drawing room.

Teddy was somewhat abstracted, but pretended not to be. 'When and how shall I tell John?' he kept on asking himself. He went out to the kitchen to see how Joan was faring. There were a bottle of tablets and a glass of water on a shelf near the kitchen table. He did not allude to them.

*

The evening of Christmas Eve brought the party. After their long return journey, the two men had to make their best efforts to stay up to it. No end of friends came with presents and welcomes were exchanged. There were mince pies, pieces of cheese and a rather strong punch. Teddy and Joan made their bravest and most cheerful efforts, although privately and with a sense of a last time about it. They were far too brave to betray anything. Teddy and John sang a few idiotic songs and everyone kissed good-bye at about nine o'clock. Shortly after Teddy had taken the plates and glasses to the kitchen, they all sat down to cold pheasant, red currant jelly, bread sauce, beetroot and jacket potatoes. This was topped off with cheese, a good, ripe Stilton injected medically with port, and a fine bottle of claret. John drank most of this and the children a sip or two only, just for the festival, which only Joan celebrated with any conviction anyway. Teddy was not looking forward to imparting the obligatory information to John and Roshan.

'Girls,' he announced cheerfully, 'you all go to bed. We men will do everything else. And, Prakash, it is far too late for you, my son. Take the ladies upstairs like a gentleman.'

The three men were left together in the kitchen. John and Roshan did not know quite what to expect, but they seemed by their anxious looks to be wondering about something. There was a kind of moveable silence, during which none but Teddy knew any direction. Their eyes were lost question marks, their faces without signification, their hands dangling by their sides, devoid of the movements of expression.

'I think we had better go and sit down,' began Teddy. 'There is something that I have got to tell you both. I am about to encounter and experience my third tragedy in life. I do not require any pity, merely understanding. Just you two, help me by listening.'

The evening, charming as it had been, owing to Joan's bravery, had now fallen on its face. The pretence had now to be over. The stark facts had to be faced. Teddy wanted his son and his old friend to help him to share the burden and the pain wrought by another cruel twist in his life. He told them about Joan's condition, with frankness and no embroidery. He said that he would be able, in his now eased circumstances, to look after Penelope and the farm. They were not to worry about that. He told them that everyone would be cared for and that they need not be worried about his marrying again.

'I shall have had two wonderful wives,' he concluded, 'to neither of whom I have been married, except in my heart, and I think that that is the most important place. I do not feel ashamed or that I have shamed either of them. I could never have done without children, although they were got in a rather unconventional way. When I shall have buried Joan,' he continued with astounding collection and courage, 'we will all come to India and start life all over again. John and I

235

know about new starts, several times over, don't we, John?'

His son sat silent, in mute assent. Both he and Roshan were shocked. Their respect was boundless and their compassion without limits. The fire went cold, cold as their hearts; only their souls were warm. Teddy knew it and it mattered more than gold.

'I suppose that, now you have told us everything, I had better face the rest myself,' said John. 'In a word, you have no need to worry. It all sounds very pragmatic and cruel, but I have got to tell you what I intend to do for you.'

'You have no need to do that now, John,' countered Teddy. 'Leave it to riper consideration.'

'It does not need that, Edward,' rejoined his son. 'I will buy New Farm from Fiona, and generously, too; you and Penelope will live there for always. That is a promise. I do not break those, as you know. I had thought that I might try to buy back Hetherick as well.'

'Listen, John. That would be a foolishly sentimental thing to do. I know that you could afford it, supposing that you could persuade its present owner, but I would never want to live there again. I can still see myself standing in front of your grandfather and being belittled for your very existence, hearing your wonderful mother insulted and denigrated. I want never to see the place again. Let it be buried in the ashes of regret, but with no remorse. You never knew it, in any case.'

'That is a fact, Father, but I thought that this would have been a gesture. You would love those broad fields again.'

'My new pastures are my children and grandchildren. I shall be quite happy here, if very lonely at times. I know that you will comfort me and keep me company when I am at a low ebb.'

There was a silence. It was replete with reflection. The time grew late. Teddy wore the solemnity which comes after a hard task is done. Roshan, leaving a decent interval, left father and son together. They stood and embraced in sympathy, understanding and in the bravery which impending doom demands of a man. Neither shunned the day.

236

*

The private Christmas was brief. It was eaten and enjoyed in silent understanding. The love of eyes needed no complement. Everyone, except the children, understood how much a last time meant. Joan was magnificent. Tactfully, she had prepared an enormous leg of roast lamb, accompanied by many vegetables and red currant jelly. Summer pudding and cream followed the immense portions which Teddy had served.

On the 31st, Teddy took Varsha and Roshan to Heathrow. Their journey was silent. No one knew what to say. Roshan had by now told Varsha of the situation. She was mortified. They all travelled the journey deprived of words. When they were at the right place, Teddy said:

'Next year may be happier. You will have another grandson. Who is left of us all will come out to stay with you. There would be nothing gladder to my heart than that. I shall be in my 'prayer room' for you both tonight, and for my wife and children. Don't forget me!'

It would be in two days' time, that he would have the truth, but it did not make any difference.

They exchanged a kiss of luck and good fortune. He had no need to have added the last remark. Their prayers started from the moment of their departure, as did Teddy's. At the same time, John was at Joan's bedside. She was in a bad way. Although he should not have done so, and knew it, he gave her an injection from his bag that he had prepared beforehand. He always carried things for emergencies, about which no one would ever know, because he knew that compassion and very immediate help were better than interminable waits for relief. He put her out of her miserable pain until his father returned.

In the meantime, the young couple had got the dinner ready. It was cold roast lamb with Indian creamed mint sauces and a number of side-dishes. Teddy and John managed to eat nearly nothing. Joan did bravely. The

237

children were in bed and had eaten well previously. There was little to say and they did not try to say it. They just hugged each other to bed. They accepted the old-fashioned flock mattresses and the iron springs with gratitude and sank into the sleep of they-did-not-know-where-or-what. The morning was mercifully slow in coming to the whole family.

The next two days were a show of bravery. Everyone kept as bright as was manageable, for the sake of the children. Teddy wanted to be alone for some time, which was understandable. He walked the paths and hedgerows, thinking of the times when he and his 'anonymous' son had worked on them. One day, he had taken his gun with him and a pocketful of cartridges. John had looked at him askance when he left the house.

'You are not going to do anything to yourself, Edward?' he asked him, distress in his eyes. 'Shall I come with you?'

'Things had crossed my mind, old lad, but you may rest assured that I am far too much of a coward for that. Whenever such ideas have come to me, they have been immediately dispelled by the thoughts of my human duties. I still have no end for which to live, and I'm going to live for you all. Actually, I'm going to shoot a couple of brace of pheasant.'

'Do you want me to come with you?' asked John again.

'That is kind of you, John. You must trust me. You must also understand that I want to be alone to clear my mind. I have a good deal to face.'

'Yes, Edward, my Father, I know. I have to face danger and disappointing tragedy every day. It is part of my job. But it still affects me and rends my heart and wounds my soul.'

'That is why you are such a good man, my son.'

With that, Teddy walked into the late frosty morning, broken gun on his arm. It was one of a priceless pair of Purdy's, the only one of his father's possessions that he ever had, and that was by accident. He had given them to Foley who had never known how to fire a shot from them. The blued and filigreed barrels glinted in the bright, cold sunlight. Teddy trod heavily to make the pheasant fly up. He was a fine shot. Aiming just in front of the head, he brought down a brace in no time, then another. As he was in a large, open field he did not need one of the dogs to retrieve. He wondered whether he would get anything else, but nothing presented itself.

He walked slowly back to the house and hung the birds in a cool larder from hooks in the ceiling. One brace would stay there for fourteen days, especially in the cold weather, because he liked his game high. As he gave the second brace to Radhika, he provided instructions about how to hang them for the best flavour, when they got to Oxford, and how to pluck and clean them.

'If the weather turns suddenly mild,' he said, 'take them down a day or two early. And mind out for the shot!'

She looked slightly unconfident, but knew that her husband would see to the unpleasant parts. He smiled at the thought of the medical precision with which he would conduct operations. On January 2nd, the young couple and their son went back to Oxford. John had to be on duty the next day. He felt that he could not leave his patients or his junior any longer at the present time. He had confidence in Philip Strange, but he knew that there was no substitute for experience. Doctor Macrae had felt exactly the same when he had started under him. John had already given Philip his telephone number in case of emergency. A panic and mistakes were the last things that he would have wanted, both on account of the patients and the learning doctor. After a very early supper, Teddy and Joan bid their guests farewell. Their mutual thanks were profuse. Everyone forced eyes to remain clear and dry. It was the best and only way to make things easier. The departure was deliberately swift. As Teddy shut the doors of the car, John said very quietly:

'If you want any help, just let me know. I'll drop everything as soon as I can. If I have a very tricky case, I might be a day or two late, but don't be put off by that.'

'I shall remember,' replied Teddy. 'When we get the results from the hospital, I will telephone you late at night, after Joan has gone to bed. Then I shall have to tell Penelope. That's going to be difficult.'

'I would like to help you with that, Edward, but I think you're the only person qualified to do it. The best is to say what you will have to simply, kindly and straight out. Children hate concealment of the truth, curiously enough; I have already had to tell other people's sons and daughters of sad states of affairs. They have always taken things remarkably well. You will be surprised. Be brief and don't dwell on things.'

'Thank you, John. I think I shall know how to do it. After all, I had some practice with you!'

'So you did, Father, now I come to think of it – and you were damned good, too!'

A firm handshake saw them off into the darkness. Teddy wondered how he would see his way in the same. He told Joan to go up to bed and that he would be there after tidying a few things downstairs.

Teddy and Joan set off for the hospital on January 3rd. Joan was bright and courageous, whilst Teddy tried to be the same, without much success. His soft heart felt dented and inept. He just kept his eyes on the road. He had the shrewd suspicion that it would be almost a one-way journey. Joan knew the same, but the confidence born of the fatalities of life somehow buoyed her up.

'Come on, Teddy,' she enjoined, 'stop being mournful. Think of all the good things and of all our love. Think of what you have to live for. I shall live for you all in another realm and I know that you will never forget me. You are too good a man for that. I know about the faith that you have given the two women in your life. I am not jealous about your Mary; how could I be? I love John, his wife and son. And his son to come, for that matter. I expect it will be, you old fool!' she added harmlessly.

'You have always been far too good to me, Joan. I don't think that I have deserved anything like it. I'm just a weak old sinner. We are nearly here now. Just let's stop a moment. I will see you in and then go quickly away. I will come to see you tomorrow morning.'

'And see the surgeon', he thought. That was the part that he dreaded. He was such a gregarious man, hating to be alone and unheard. He would go and see dear Nancy at The Three Trees later. He would tell her everything, but vowed, as he had to Joan, that he would not get maudlin and drunk. Fiona would look after Penelope and had prepared him a light supper, for which he would have duty but no appetite.

He took Joan in and the clinical smell, which attends all places of medicine, assailed his nostrils unwelcomely. The hardness of reality came to him with these essential odours. He preferred those of honest farmyard dung, gunshot, mown corn and the woods. They were sweet. So was the scent of new-born children to him. All these sacred perfumes came freshly from God. All he smelt now was the stale of grimness.

He said good-bye to Joan and to the ward sister. He made it brief. They all understood why. Teddy, more than Joan, was in pieces. He just managed to park the car in front of the house, get out, thank the maid, look in at Penelope and eat a few spoonfuls of cold stew with Fiona, who was to go the next day. He went to bed, awaiting only the morning, when he would go to the hospital and hear the surgeon's verdict. He knew it already.

In the morning, he arose early, after the arrival of the maid, whom he instructed by all means to await his return, and drove to the hospital. Before he went to see Joan, he asked to meet the surgeon. He was a large benign, gangling man, but he had kind eyes.

'Sit down with me, Mr Osmond,' he said. 'I will tell you anything that you would like to know. Would you like to ask the questions or shall I paint the picture?'

'I think that you had better start, Doctor. I do not want anything, not anything whatsoever, hidden. I have lived with concealed possibilities for far too long. My own life has been as full of joy and tragedy as that of your patient.'

Here his lips trembled, but he managed to sustain himself. He thought of his brave John and Radhika. They had

241

managed in the face of incredible adversity, it would now be his duty to do the same.

'You are obviously a brave man, Mr Osmond. That is why I am emboldened to tell you the truth. It is kinder that way, if you know that the recipient of it can stand it. It is my opinion that you can. Your wife has about three months to live. I will make her as comfortable as I can and she will be able to join you at home within a week. She must heal a little first from the incisions. She will suffer no more pain I promise you. There is nothing I can do for her.'

Teddy stared at the walls and at the carpet. His hands went dry and cold. The chapter of a book, as it were, slammed dustily closed in his tortured face.

'Thank you, Doctor,' said Teddy meekly, 'then I shall do what I can. We were going to go to India, for reasons that you know, but now that would be unthinkable. What a disappointment that will be for Joan. As she is a brave woman,' he added, 'I shall take it upon myself to tell her everything without any disguises or dissimulations.'

'I somehow knew that you would think like that, Mr Osmond. If you are in trouble, contact me, or, preferably, your son. Everyone knows about him.'

Teddy left, with kindness and desolation alternately comforting and rending his heart. Once again, they were all going to make the best of what fate had bestowed upon them. He went straight to the telephone and told John everything.

'Tell me when you want me,' said his son.

11

The Waiting

It was just over a week later that Teddy went to the hospital to collect Joan. He had left Penny at school in the morning, having asked if, under the circumstances, he could leave her there for an extra term. The headmistress perfectly understood, saying that she would be happy and undisturbed in that quarter of life among her friends. She suggested that it would be better to send her away as a boarder afterwards.

'Afterwards', thought Teddy. 'What would the desolate afterwards be like?'

In the meantime, he would have to prepare his daughter for the deprivation of a mother. He shuddered at the thought and wondered how he would even begin the telling. He knew that he could call upon no one else and that not even his faithful son could help him. The father had already begun the lonely journey into desperation. He hated saying good-bye to people, even after a party, so what would the announcement and its consequences be like? Penelope was intelligent beyond her years, as some children are who are born comparatively late in a woman's child-bearing span. Uncertainty, he decided, would be worse than the bare truth, however brutal. Kind as Fiona was, he could not call much upon her, as she had no comparable experience and was delightfully tactless and impractical. He could load nothing off on John. He had never felt so alone; alone in advance of events.

He parked the car on the bleak tarmac. The wind was bitter and he wished that he had worn an overcoat. His heart was colder than the wind and his soul an aching void. It would take him all his courage and resolve to keep a cheerful, hopeful face. He had been in to see her every day, but they had only discussed banalities. Joan had talked about the family and asked for general news. What Teddy could not remember or had not heard, he invented. For much of the time, Joan was obviously drowsy and sedated. Sometimes she fell asleep while he was at her bedside.

This morning, she was wide awake and looked bright, if drawn in the face. Teddy carried her small amount of luggage and the nurse armed her to the car. She got in with laboured movements, despite the help.

'Do you want to rest a while before I drive?' asked Teddy.

'Just a couple of minutes, while I get my breath back, and then it's mercifully off home. I want a large glass of the best port when we get there! Cheer up, you old sinner!'

'Not so much of the "old",' said Teddy, suddenly realising what a stupid remark that had been.

Within minutes of their arrival, Teddy had unpacked her possessions and put them away in the bedroom. Within a few more, they were safely installed in the drawing room, where a fire had been lit. Drinks were poured. Neither knew how to start the conversation. There ensued a lengthening delay which sapped the confidence of both.

'Well, I had better begin,' said Teddy. 'You have been told the same as I have, I am informed. There is nothing that they can do for you and you will pass painlessly away in about three months.'

'I know all about it,' said Joan quietly. 'I have come to terms with it, but not with the fact that I have let you all down. It's not my fault, but I still feel disappointment and guilt, in a strange sort of way. You must all forgive me for such an unfortunate and untimely exit!'

She still preserved her brave, sardonic wit and a touch of

that essential sarcasm which can bridge the ugly swirl of troubled waters in the final realisation of stark truths.

'I shall try not to be a burden to the family, and especially to you, Teddy. Just treat me as normal. I have buckets of pills and I shall swallow them in shovelfuls, if necessary,' she continued.

'John will come down in a couple of days, I expect,' said Teddy, 'and that will be a comfort to us both. He knows everything. He always has! I will look after Penelope, as you know. As you know also, I must tell her about the situation. It would be unfair not to do so, but I cannot deny that I am nervous and that it will be a great shock to her. You must leave that to me; it is my appalling duty and I shall not shrink from it.'

'Edward,' said Joan, after a pause, 'there is a world that I want to say to you. You have been a wonderful husband to me, whatever officially may be thought; and who cares about that anyway? I have to tell you how deeply you have made me happy; I love you body and soul. You are the best of men. You are intensely human and you are still young. If you want to marry again or take a kind woman, you must feel free to do this. I would not like you to be in bondage to the memory of the dead. You have served your slavery, I know full well, and it rent my heart. There was nothing much that I could have done about it. Don't forget love, which is what I know that you will always need. Above all, don't feel shame. You will always love me, as you still love your Mary; those loves are noble and will live on in your children.'

Teddy sat silent and near to tears. He was an emotional man, which quality had earnt him the respect of women rather than their cold contempt. He did not consider it unmanly to weep. To him, those who despised the physical outpourings of the heart had no soul. He had always understood those who gave way, if that is the right expression, to the same manifestations as those he could not disguise.

Finally he composed himself and summoned up the courage to speak.

'I have been the luckiest man in the world,' he faltered, 'All that you have told me is too generous to believe, yet I must do so. I really don't think that I shall ever get married again; it would seem to me somewhat sacreligious. I shall live exclusively for my family. Everyone will look after me because, unaccountably, they love me. And at my age, I think that casual affairs are sordid and undignified. You may not believe it, but I have a certain pride. It will be a difficult path for me. I am, as you know, a very simple, immediate sort of man. I will take a profound lesson from your selfless bravery, Joan.'

'What are we having for lunch? asked Joan, deliberately bringing things down to earthiness. 'I fancy a morsel of cold pheasant.'

'What an old dear you are!' said Teddy. 'I did a brace especially for you. It's all ready in the larder. There's cold bread sauce and redcurrant jelly, too. The claret is just right and there is summer pudding and cream afterwards. How'll that do you?'

'My dear old dear, how I shall get through all that I have no idea, but I'll start life again now and have a bloody good try!'

She did and they laughed again.

*

It was a different chill from the frozen fields outside. It was that of the future. In the immediate part of this, there had to be the explanations. Teddy knew that things would have to be settled soon and that refuge in drink would only be a hindrance now; afterwards, perhaps he would allow himself a little solace. He recognised that it would be difficult not to take the resource of the bottle; it would cure nothing, for all its temporary comfort, and would make him all the more depressed in the mornings. Depression was the mood that he would have to evince least.

He collected Penelope from school. She noticed that he

246

was very quiet when he was questioned articulately about her mother. She was growing into an attractive little girl and, Teddy thought with pride, would one day be a beautiful woman. She realised that her father was preoccupied and had the tact already not to interrupt his thoughts. They descended from the car and went swiftly into the house. Joan was upstairs having a rest. The maid had already gone. Father and daughter were alone. The moment had come.

'I want to tell you two things, Penny. Come and sit down here in the drawing room – or would you prefer the kitchen?'

'Wherever you would like, Edward,' she said, with a puzzled look in her bright young eyes.

They sat down at either end of the long, comfortable sofa.

'We will have supper when Mother comes down,' announced Teddy, just to break the anticipatory silence. 'She will probably need a longish rest after her operation, so we will have to wait a little while.'

'That doesn't matter at all, Edward. What is it that you wanted to tell? I have got quite a lot of extra homework to do, so you won't be long, will you?'

'Not very,' said her father, but he knew that she would not get very much done that evening and that she would probably not find supper very easy either. She would be sitting opposite tragedy.

'The first thing is this, Penelope. I was going to delay it until you were older, but now I cannot put it off any more. It is not that I am not brave enough, but I wanted to avoid hurting or surprising you cruelly.'

The little girl made to interrupt him with, no doubt, protestations of denial, but Teddy asked her just to sit quietly and listen, then ask any questions which came to her afterwards. She did as she was bid.

Then, somehow, Teddy could not begin. His mouth moved but no words emerged. His mind went numb and all that he had rehearsed for ages seemed suddenly inadequate, if not clumsy. His hands went damp. He felt frightened and pathetic.

247

'Come on, Edward, what is it? Or have you forgotten?' asked Penelope cheerfully.

He certainly had not forgotten and that was the trouble. He almost wished he had not started what he now knew he must finish. He remembered the Sundays when they both went down through the glade to the village and to The Three Trees. He remembered how he swung her arm and scuffed the leaves and how she used to drink a glass of ginger beer as if it were champagne. Most of all he remembered how he hoped that somehow she knew that she was his daughter, although that was impossible. His eyes were already moist and he knew that he had better start as bravely as possible. And at once.

'You see, my love, you are my daughter and Foley wasn't whom you have always supposed to be your father. He is dead now, as you know, but I could never have told you this whilst he was alive. It may come as a surprise to you to know that he was not kind to your mother and very unkind to me. He never wanted to know John and Radhika. John is my son and his mother died when he was quite a little boy. Somehow I managed to bring him up properly, and look how distinguished he is today! Then I came to work for the farm, because the army in India had come to an end and the job that I had before, in a bank, was not very nice. I loved your mother and we made you together. As you have been brought up in the country, I expect that you know what I mean by that. It is why you do not look like Fiona or her father but like your mother and me instead. No one but the family knows this and there is no reason why anyone else should. Human life is never a disgrace. Now you may understand why I have always treated you with so much love, like the father that I really am to you.'

Teddy gabbled it off, not daring to stop in case of another difficult start. Looking at Penelope, he waited in a torment. He wondered whether he had hurt her. For life, perhaps. He shuddered. Penelope stared back at him in silence with her big round eyes.

Suddenly she said, 'Do you remember the woods and all

those leaves and how you used to hold my hand and how we used to pick flowers in the …'

'Of course I do, darling,' interrupted Teddy.

'Well, I shall never, never forget and I am pleased that you are really my father. You have always been to me just like the one I wanted. Anyway, I can hardly remember Foley now.'

Then she leapt into his arms and gave him the hug of a lifetime. Teddy was incredibly relieved. Then came the even tougher step. Once again, he took his courage in both his rather uncertain hands.

'The second of the two things is going to upset you, Penny. There is nothing that I can do about that. I'm going to make it very simple and short. It will hurt less then. Your beloved mother is going to die soon.' He did not know how to continue, but he rushed on. 'She went into hospital a little while ago because she had severe pains in the lower stomach. She did not tell anybody but me, and, to save me worrying, did not do that until she absolutely had to. The doctors looked inside her and have said that they cannot cure her. Sometime in April, she will probably be dead. We shall never forget her. I shall look after you, just as she looked after us both and we will have John and his family to keep us company here whenever they want to come. Obviously, we shall not be able to go to India all together, as we had planned, until a while later.'

Teddy's voice tailed into nothing. He hardly dared look at Penny. It was quite a time until the silence was broken. Quite suddenly, Penny spoke:

'Now I'm going to call you 'Edward, my Father', just like John!'

With this gesture of understanding and trust, she left the room quickly. Teddy saw her walking in the garden, quietly, slowly and alone.

Life continued quietly at New Farm. Joan became thinner and more sickly. John and his wife made visits as frequently as their busy life permitted and Fiona came to stay at several weekends. Teddy told his foreman all about the situation, asking him to relay the information to the labourers. This, he said, would obviate for him the painful enquiries, however kindly his people. They were all very understanding. As Joan became worse, presents of pies, cakes and other dishes arrived on the kitchen table whilst he was out on the farm. They were all anonymous, but he knew their provenance. John brought packets of homemade curries and The Three Trees, under Nancy's instructions, gave him frequent lunches. He was never allowed to pay for them. Even the vicar, whom Teddy had often described irreverently as an 'old fart', now, much to his shame, came round at least once a week offering comfort to both Teddy and Joan. He told them that he would make all the final arrangements, about which they would not have to bother themselves.

'I am very grateful to you,' said Teddy, one day, 'but, please not next to Foley.' The vicar looked rather puzzled, but agreed. Perhaps he only meant to be polite, in a show of curiosity. He did not ask for any explanation.

Later on, John asked about Penelope's education. He suggested that she might come to stay with them in Oxford during the terms and go to school there. Teddy was very touched by the offer, but he said that, in all obedience to duty, he must look after her on his own. She would never be left alone in the house and, anyway, he explained, she would have to learn quickly to stand on her own feet, even if they would not be set far away. Starting in the summer term, she would be a boarder at a fine school for girls in Salisbury. He would be able to visit her frequently, she would soon learn to become the accomplished mistress of the house. Fiona had made some offers, merely out of politeness but, poor dear, she would have found no difficulty in spoiling a pan of water! What they would have eaten might have given them all indigestion for life, he reflected. As John had sampled one or two of her masterpieces, he fully understood.

A month or so after he had told his daughter about the family situation, he explained about boarding school. To his amazement, because she loved the farm and home life, she showed no resistance. Some of her friends in the village were already there. This was a great relief to her father, who had enough on his mind as it was.

By early April, Joan came downstairs less and less. Teddy took her frugal meals up to her in the bedroom and she ate very little of anything, although he chose her favourite things with consummate care and consideration. She looked terribly pallid and thin. Her eyes seemed to sink deeper and deeper into their sockets, but the look of love never wavered. She constantly told Teddy not to hesitate but to be strong. He now had to bathe her, a ceremony upon which she insisted every morning. He performed it with the greatest tenderness. When John came down, next time with Radhika, they made their help available and without the slightest embarrassment. They met in the bathroom, which became a kind of temple to the cleanliness of the soul. Radhika dried her and John prepared something tasteful in the kitchen. The whole family would eat a little of it with her in the bedroom and then would disappear quietly downstairs and leave Joan and Teddy together. Thanks to her medication, it was not long before Joan would sink into a deep sleep. John noticed that his father was pitching into the whisky bottle, but said nothing. The latter could not help but notice his son's anxious glances.

'That will all stop when it's over, my son,' he said weakly. 'For now you must forgive me. You can only guess what I'm going through. I hope that you never, either of you, will have to do the same.'

'We don't reproach you, Father. No doubt we would do the same, too. Think of India. We are all going to go after the difficult time and after you and Penelope have had a quiet rest with us in Oxford. I have decided upon that. The farm will be looked after and Prakash has waited patiently, without knowing why, for a year. So have the Mahendras. You have never disappointed anyone in your life, so we are not going to disappoint you. For the moment, just think about what will have to be done. Call upon me as soon as you want me. My assistant is a talented young man and I can come down at any time, with confidence. If there is a really tricky case, I can call upon a friend of mine in London; as it is, I have already done him some favours. I trust him implicitly.'

'Thank you, John. I will not fail to ask your help. Let's have supper and listen to some Chopin followed by a little of the sitar. The last would soothe me before I go to bed.' Then he added, after a reflective minute:

'You never thought of me as much of a philosopher, but I am making a start. I realise already that another door is opening as another closes, even now, on someone's life. You and your Radhika have another life that you have made to begin. That life will be a part of me.'

*

Teddy wound his way unsteadily and with slight shame to bed. He had left his two beloveds below and another was upstairs in their little bedroom. He washed and grabbed his way into bed beside Joan. He did not know what to expect by the day, by the hour. Tonight, Joan was cold, but breathing. He nestled up close and put his arm round her unconscious body. He wondered whether it would be awake tomorrow. The torture of uncertainty was crucifying; he knew that it was only the whisky that would make him sleep at all, and that probably briefly. He tried to warm her with his arms and his hands. He felt cold and inadequate. His mind was blinded with fear. He asked himself about the summoning up of courage at desperate moments, only to realise that he had managed to do this before. He would have to do so again. The dreaded again was not long to be awaited.

A week later, he woke up, after another cheerless and frightened night. The body next to him was cold. He closed the sightless eyes of his love and buried his head in the pillows. It was finally over. He lay motionless, not knowing what exactly to do next. He had alerted John that the end was near and luckily he had arrived, alone, the evening before. Teddy staggered into his bedroom and said:

'Do everything for me. I cannot do more. She is dead.'

Father and son fell into each others' arms. They were both sobbing. John was the first of the two to pull himself together.

'You knew that it was inevitable, Edward, my Father. Just you leave everything to me, now. I will bring you a coffee and a brandy. Just wrap yourself up and leave this room. I will stoke the fire in the range and do all the rest of the things that have to be done. God, you have done enough for me; now, it's my turn.'

'What about Prakash and Radhika?' Teddy asked at once. 'What are they going to do without you?'

'Although it was not your fault, what did my mother do without you, Edward? We were both made of the same stern material, you know. You are, too, although you would be the last to believe it.'

He put his strong arms round his father, telling him that he, above all people, would never be alone in the world.

'You old lifegiver, I'll never desert you. Your new ways are about to open, although this is not exactly the time to tell you. I am about as blunt as you are. You're going to be safe forever.'

John left his father quietly for a few minutes.

The rest of what occurred need not be told, except in the briefest detail and for kindness. The whole village came to Joan's funeral. Penelope came too, hand in hand with John and Edward. The ceremony and interment were deliberately short. They all made their silent return to New Farm, walking through the autumn leaves that were still left. They noticed a few clumps of wild daffodils. Although yellow was, in earlier times, the colour of mourning, their dancing trumpets seemed to herald a bright and heavenly future for Teddy's wife. They blared her goodness gently to the breeze. Painfully, both men lifted their heart.

Teddy determined immediately to embark upon life anew. He knew that most men had not the good fortune, if varied, that he had enjoyed, so he decided that gratitude and not remorse or deprivation of the soul would be the key to a future life that would gladden both Mary and Joan, both John and Penelope. They were all astonished at his pluck and courage. This they by no means construed as callousness. He had taken his son's advice, much of which had never been spoken.

A few weeks later, when John came into his inheritance, he bought New Farm for his father. He told him that he would keep his word. He said that he could stay there, reap the benefits and have an allowance from Joan's estate for the rest of his life. This would be enough to free him from any anxieties and to educate Penelope. Teddy accepted everything in mute humility.

After he was confident that Teddy would be able to look after himself and take to life again, John left for his family. Radhika would be growing apace and he wanted to see that. He knew, at the same time, that she would have understood his painful absence. He was, he thought with justification, so lucky to have such a beautiful, understanding wife. He could not wait for the maturity of his son nor for the birth of what he hoped would be his second. He kept on telling himself that he must not be so impatient. There were only three months to go. His thoughts were split between regrets for his father and hopes for his wife. At the time of his late arrival at Oxford station, he did not know which had won.

'God!' he exclaimed to himself, 'I might never have been born at all, then neither then would my children have been!'

The human mind cannot encompass the infinite. John gave up trying to do so. Home was warm and sweet. He suddenly thought of all his patients, some of whom had neither warmth not sweetness in a home to which to look forward. Suddenly too, and not for the first time, he accounted himself incredibly fortunate. There are few of us so lucky. He had known suffering, but that is not in any way as hard as deprivation.

*

Life for the family in Oxford resumed its normal course. there were parties and friendships, difficulties that are naturally attendant upon a responsible profession and the touching, healing delight of home. Prakash was now doing well at school and all that his mother and father had taught him put him well in advance of most of the others. They did not regret having not sent him to school before the age of five. Learning for him was, and always would be, a pleasure. He was brown, strong and happy.

For Teddy, things were a little harder. A chill wind often blew over his soul. His sleeps were naturally lonely and the empty space beside him in bed made him depressed. He decided to sleep in the middle of it, with his Mary one side of him and his Joan on the other. He did not bother his family. He often examined himself and journeyed through his life again, privately and with no regret other than that of loss. Then, immediately afterwards, he was consoled by the thought of what had been so generously left to him; this was nothing to do with money or possessions; it was the people for whom he lived.

He often unquietly wondered how long John and his family would stay in England. Would they go back to India, once the boys had been educated? That would, he thought, make him feel more remote than ever. Then he told himself that no one can govern or intrude upon the life of others; after all, he had led his own and everyone else was entitled to lead theirs. Who better than he to know that? He laughed at himself, a little bitterly, perhaps. This sentiment, which often raked his heart, was always dispelled by the thought that he was his grandchildren's founder. In the morning, the concerns of the farm took his mind off spasms of despair and doubt. He and his farm manager always had a drink together at lunchtimes and now and then he went to his house nearby for a meal. His wife was a homely darling. He looked forward to that because he had not the inclination, these days, to eat more than a plain adequacy at home.

In June 1958, he had a telephone call that more than lifted his heart. It was John.

'Next week,' said an excited voice, 'Radhika will probably go into hospital for the new birth. I need someone to look after us two men. Will you come up and do that?'

'God, John, how wonderful! Of course I will. Shall I get in the car tomorrow?'

'Get into the old heap yesterday, if you like, Edward,' replied John with silly gusto. 'I can't wait to see you. You can drink your whisky in the garden, whatever the weather!'

'I take your insults as an honour, my lad!' exclaimed Teddy. 'I will be with you all by midday.'

He could not wait for the morning and arrived early, at eleven. It was a very jolly meeting. The difficulties of the past were swept away by the following winds of confident love. Prakash was a frightful nuisance and kept on asking his grandfather if he could learn to be a farmer during the holidays. Teddy was delighted, but told him that it might take a little longer than that.

'Then I'll come for as long as it takes,' he said, innocently.

'Before you reply,' said John, 'that would be a grand idea. You take him for a week or two and then we may all have a bit of peace!'

And so it was arranged. Prakash joined his grandfather, learnt to call him 'Edward' and started to learn about farming at the end of July. In the meantime, Ashok was born. Unfortunately, it was a breach birth and not easy, but he was withdrawn without damage by forceps and the lengthy and uncomfortable procedure ended successfully. The infant emerged into the world in perfection. John watched the skillful and trusted Jenner throughout, in agonies of sympathetic fright.

'I couldn't have done that,' said John afterwards.

'I was shitting bricks, as the elegant saying goes,' replied Jenner humourously and with relief, 'but thank the Lord that I did not bugger it up!'

'Thank you, too, my friend. And I must say that I do admire your wonderful medical language. It is worthy of a saint.'

'I know,' replied the genial man. 'Now,' he added, 'go and see your wife, give her and your new son a kiss and take me home. I had to get a bloody taxi to do this because I had already had a couple too many before I was called!'

'God!' exclaimed John, 'but I'm glad it was you all the same, you dreadful man!'

They drove home and John put him up for the night. He certainly deserved that and a halo to go with it. Teddy was in fine form, full of enquiries, among other substances! No one was in a position to ask any questions and they all sat down to a convivially euphoric curry.

'This will take my arse off in the morning,' said Jenner in fun, as he wound his jolly way up to bed.

The other two men went their separate ways shortly afterwards and John kissed Prakash, congratulating him on having a brother.

Radhika came home from hospital very shortly. Both John and Prakash loved the sight of her feeding Ashok at her breasts in the kitchen. They sat enraptured at the miracle of naturality and amid the sweet scent of a baby and his mother's milk. They all enjoyed these times.

'Did I do that?' asked Prakash, one day.

'You certainly did,' replied his mother, 'otherwise you would not be the strong young man you are today. Now, go away with you! I have got to take Ashok upstairs. There are various things to do, at which you men do not have to be present. Just get on with your work.'

They obeyed. Then John took Prakash for a walk. The wonder of new life seemed to have taken the boy by surprise. He thought how amazing it all was.

'It won't be long before I have to tell him about it', thought John to himself. He knew that neither of them would shrink from anything; it was part of their tradition. That it always would be. God was never ashamed of creation, so how could anyone be?

It was then that John told Prakash that he would not be

disappointed about India next year. They were all going to go. The lad wondered about Ashok. His father told him that his little brother would be weaned by the end of the year; he said that he would not be able to go as well, but that the Halls would look after him and feed him.

'I shall feel lonely without Ashok,' he said quietly.

'I am glad that you feel like that, my son, but your father and mother need a little time with your grandparents, and so do you. You do want to go, don't you?'

'I can't wait, father, for us all,' said Prakash honestly. 'But what does "weaned" mean?'

John told him kindly and cleanly and he understood at once.

'I am longing to be a father like you, John,' he said, 'it must be wonderful.'

'It certainly is,' replied his father, suddenly realising that the family tradition had unconsciously been preserved. His son had called him by his first name, without any invitation but that of sincerity. He was delighted. He at once knew that his son would be just the father that he would have wanted him to be. His thoughts grew slightly impatient with time as they walked home. Once he had been told everything about his family and background, which chapter had to wait for a little, Prakash would become equally eager. His mind was filled with unidentified thoughts already.

12

The Brooch

The whole family went to India. The holiday was a wonderful success. It was not to be for more than a month, because Radhika could not leave Ashok for long. She already, almost as soon as she arrived, felt the grip of the gnawing claws of guilt, but she released them temporarily in the knowledge that she owed an allegiance to her mother and father also. She owed that to Prakash, too. She owed everything to everybody. Debts, she thought, as her husband did, can never fully be repaid. It was at once delightful and dreadful that the strings of her generous heart should be stretched in two ways.

'Do you want to go home tomorrow?' her father asked her when she was on her own in the garden one evening.

'No, not yet Father; and still, I do. I expect that you know what I mean.'

'That is true and natural, my daughter. You tell me when you want to go. You are welcome to stay as long as you like, but I understand that the ties of your family matter beyond anything. Do not think by any means that our love is the less for you. The greater is the understanding. You must be with my grandson as soon as you can. Go away and come back again. We will come to you whenever you invite us.'

'You have no need to be invited, Father. Just tell us when you are coming. You, as a doctor know the call upon a medical man's time. You know that Rahul will be delighted at your arrival at any time of the day or night. He seems to be inexhaustible in his energy.'

'I was, at his age,' replied her father, with a certain regretful wisdom.

The family departed after three weeks, or slightly less. They were, as usual, laden with presents. John laid the rugs and went immediately to his prayer room, barefoot, in humility and gratitude. He then went to collect Ashok from Frank and Joyce. It was late and the boy did not even wake up in his arms. John gave them a rug which he had bought specially.

'Take your shoes off when you stand on that one, Frank,' he said with humour.

'I'm not sure that that is wise,' replied Joyce, in the same mood, 'but I'll make sure it becomes a tradition. What a lovely thing for you to have done!'

'Joyce,' replied John, 'we are both so grateful to you both. I think that I may be able to make you honorary Indians!'

'We're quite all right as we are,' said Frank, 'but thank you all the same. I couldn't be bloody black if I tried!'

'Frank!' exclaimed Joyce, 'I'm darned if yer not the most tactless man I knows! You'll have ter forgive 'im, John, he's just the bloody end sometimes!'

'I've done that long ago, Joyce, and I know that no harm was ever meant.'

Meanwhile, Frank had got up from his chair, switched off the racing results and disappeared.

'Wait on, John, where's our Frank? The good Lord only knows. He'll be back in two shakes.'

In two shakes, he was. He was carrying the new cot-bed in his broad arms.

' 'Ere it is, then' he said plainly. 'Tek it 'ome for the little'un. 'E's been sleepin' in it sound this past three weeks. It's teken a fair few stouts ter build this bugger!'

His face was broad with pride. Joyce tried to look shocked by his blunt language. She did not succeed. The piece of furniture was beautifully made and finely polished. Joyce had made the mattress and the bedclothes. They all stood in quiet admiration. No one knew exactly what to say in the cosy, old kitchen. As it happened, Frank was the first to speak, for a change.

'You'd better make 'aste and get another, you and yer missus. That's what I made it for. Now, off with yer both and with all our love!'

John left the house with his son, the bed and a glowing heart. Radhika could not believe Frank's work and kindness. She put him to bed at once in all three things.

The couple went to their own bed. It was a soft, kind time.

*

In the absence of a wife, Teddy thought one day that he ought to tidy out his drawers. He was the cleanest man alive, but he tended to leave his clothes, not unfolded, but in some disorder. The day was rainy and he felt disinclined to go out on the farm. He began with his country suits, one of which was certainly destined for gardening attire, and then threw out a few old shirts and some handkerchiefs at which the dogs had had a go. There were not any letters, because he always dealt promptly with those. He discarded a few buttons that had escaped. Finally, he found a little box in red Morocco leather, which he had not seen for years. He opened it. It must have been at the back of that particular drawer for an unaccounted time. His own curiosity was aroused because he could not remember what it could possibly have contained.

There was only one thing inside; a silver Victorian shilling, mounted and on a silver bar, with a long pin at the back of it. It was the only thing that he had taken from his Mary's house, all those years ago. He sank to his bed and looked at it. It was now black with tarnish, although never with shame. He went downstairs, found the silver polish and brightened it to how he had given it to Mary, that summer morning. The times of his life came flowing back; it was then that he finally realised that he did not regret a minute of them. He squeezed the brooch in his hand, which bled as it had done when he was eighteen.

'That's John's blood,' he said to himself. 'And that of his children.'

The rest of his thoughts were beyond expression. He kissed the brooch and took it downstairs again. He had determined already what he would do with it. He booked a train to Oxford the next day. There was a small, Morocco leather box in his pocket.

'I have just arrived,' he announced unnecessarily.

Radhika had just opened the door, to which he had the key anyway.

'What on earth has brought you here, Edward?' she asked, more in delight than surprise. 'It is absolutely wonderful to see you. Have a snack with me while I feed Ashok, then have a peaceful afternoon while I do the washing and then, when the children are in bed, we'll all have a jolly time. Rahul will be home at any hour. He told me that today would be frantically busy. Sit down, Edward, and stop jumping first on one foot then on the other!'

Teddy liked being teased, but his hand was still on the little red box in his overcoat pocket.

'It's wonderful to be here, my girl, but I have come on a special mission. Do not be afraid. It's nothing terrible. I've just got a little thing for you both that I found by accident the other day. I'm a bit tired now, so could you get me a cup of tea?'

Radhika knew Teddy inside-out. She gave him an enormous glass of port and a great slice of ripe stilton.

'Don't let's pretend,' she said laughingly.

'Thank you, Love,' he replied, 'I think it's better that way! God, isn't John a lucky lad!'

'I'm a lucky girl, Edward! Your son is the best man in the world, except when he's worried about a patient; then he's dreadful!'

'Concern takes its toll,' said Teddy. 'I know a bit about

262

that.'

Radhika assented with humility. She loved her father-in-law, particularly for his faults. They were many and glaring, but he never tried to hide them. His soul was as bare as the green grass in the fields.

*

Teddy kept his secret under his pillow until the next morning, which was Sunday. The whole family arose late. Everyone sat in the kitchen whilst Radhika fed Ashok, although she need not have done by then. It was a wonderful, moving time, which none of the men would have missed for a moment if they could possibly have been there. The ripe breasts and the suckling baby meant the start of another life for them all. It was with the starting that Teddy was concerned.

'Rahul, my son, walk with me in the garden for a few minutes. There is something that I have to give you. It is not advice, I promise you. You would be better at giving that to me than I would be in dispensing it to you!'

They walked, in silence, for a few minutes. The sun was shining into their faces and upon a small lawn. Both men waited for the other to speak, although they were quite happy in their own, trusting silence. Eventually, Teddy said:

'Here, Rahul, take this. It is what I gave your lovely mother when I was a boy and when she conceived you. I want you to keep it in her memory, because you belong to her. If you wish to give it to your wife, you may do, but don't ever lose it, will you?'

John was mute. He held the wonderful little brooch in his hands and realised finally what a kind man his father was. He had never doubted that, but now he understood that he had released to him his most treasured possession.

Turning away, John said: 'Radhika will wear this and, if we have a daughter, so shall she. If not, Prakash's eldest daughter. It will go right down the family. Just as your love was not, so shall our love never be lost.'

Teddy felt strangely relieved, as if no more bonds were left to be forged. Now, apart from the rest of his stay, which he always made tactfully brief, he looked forward to the next time. He had already decided upon something which he had not exactly formulated yet.

EPILOGUE
FULL CIRCLE

A new year had begun. Teddy worked steadily at the farm, but his heart felt at once full and empty. Full for the love that he had had and empty for the void that its absence now left. All that he lived for was too far away for him, but he realised that he could not be selfish. He often wondered about the future of his family, and about his own for that matter. He was long times reflective in the quiet evenings at the farm; he lacked what he always wanted, which was the sense of closer belonging. He knew that he did belong to people, but he also wished that they were present. If wishes were horses, beggars would ride. He felt a beggar for affection. He knew that it was always available, but he did not want to trouble the people who gave it to him. He could hardly understand that he was nearly fifty. It was not ever always long before he thought of his children and grandchildren and then he was young again. It was at those times that he thought how lucky he was. 'Life is incredible', he said to himself.

In September, John, Radhika, Prakash and Ashok came to stay. Teddy's life sprang into fullness. He had a secret plan. He had thought about a little ceremony which he alone could perform. In his lonely nights, he could see the execution of it and where it would take place. He had even staked out the hallowed ground. He had stood there, under the moon, holding invisible hands. He had touched those hands, even though they were not there.

'God', he said, 'thank you for my family! What on earth would I do without them?'

In early October, John said to Radhika, one evening:

'Go to bed, my love. We men have something to do. We are going for a special walk. Three generations mean something which is untellable.'

John carried Ashok and Prakash walked hand in hand with his grandfather. None of them, except Teddy, knew what to expect. They just walked into the cold, frosty night. They walked into a field. Behind them was a river and in front the trees. Above in a mauve heaven, was the moon.

'Stand just here,' said Teddy quietly. 'There is no more fear, now. You are all my sons. Stand with me a while and look upon what should have been mine so very many years ago. Now, it is yours. Although I shall live upon it, loving the furrows that I have ploughed for you all. You have started the giving and I have ended the slavery. We are all free. I have loved the giving and, unbelievably, some of the slavery. It was to a good end.'

In the silver quietness, they all blessed one another in the peace of understanding. Edward prayed that God would guide all their footsteps. And He did.